Eliza Tabor

**Annette**

Eliza Tabor

**Annette**

ISBN/EAN: 9783337044381

Printed in Europe, USA, Canada, Australia, Japan

Cover: Foto ©Andreas Hilbeck / pixelio.de

More available books at **www.hansebooks.com**

# ANNETTE

# ANNETTE

# A Novel

BY THE AUTHOR OF

"ST. OLAVE'S," "JANITA'S CROSS,"

"THE BLUE RIBBON," "LITTLE MISS PRIMROSE,"

ETC., ETC.

"What a man thinketh in his heart, that is he, and no more."

LONDON

SPENCER BLACKETT

35, ST. BRIDE STREET, LUDGATE CIRCUS, E.C.

# ANNETTE.

## CHAPTER I.

"S.S. *Nawab*," *April 7th,*
*Homeward-bound.*

THANK God that, after fifteen years of hard work amongst those Hindoo women, work in which I have had help neither of father nor mother, sister nor brother, to cheer me on, I am able at last to write concerning myself, the good words, "Homeward-bound."

And yet, if I had been so minded, I might have placed these good words at the beginning, instead of the end, of those fifteen years. Indeed that was where some very excellent and well-meaning people thought I ought to have placed them when my brother Mark's death left me alone in a strange land. For, as they represented to me, I was too far advanced in life, being then on the shady side of thirty, to strike out for myself an independent career; and I had no relative out there to make a home for me, if I wished to take employment as mission or zenana teacher; and in a country like India, where everything goes by position

and good looks, I, who was possessed of neither, might
reasonably expect to find myself very much at a dis-
count ; and therefore, as the most straightforward thing
for myself, and possibly also the most convenient for
them, they recommended me to return home at once,
take lodgings in some tidy, respectable little town, and
live on my means, which amounted then to the modest
sum of a hundred and twenty pounds a year.

But I really did enjoy the work which, during poor
Mark's life, I had tried to do, of visiting the native
women in their homes, and dropping into their often
ready minds a few words of thought, not always strictly
religious, as the phrase goes, but such as I hoped might
spring up and clothe the bare ground of their lives with
something like beauty and freshness.  Then, too, I had
got through the most vexing difficulties of the language.
The women were beginning to feel that I was their
friend, and it did seem a pity to throw away that five
years of foundation work, and start again as an idle
woman in my own country.

For, though I was far on to thirty when Mark was
gazetted chaplain, and I had decided to come out with
him, I had as yet found nothing to do in our quiet little
town of Abbotsby.  The place was already swamped
with well-disposed women of leisure, who did everything
that could be done in the way of Sunday-school teaching, tract distribution, committees, and all that sort of
thing.  And I had no special talent of any kind, no
artistic faculty, which, well cultivated, might have
brought me either pleasure or profit.  I had been educated up to the average standard of those days.  I knew

enough of music to lift up my voice in church, or sing an old-fashioned ballad to my father when he was weary with his day's work of clerkship ; enough of French to guide me successfully through a quotation, if I stumbled upon it ; and enough of drawing to sketch a cottage or a tree, a tumble-down windmill or an ivy-covered willow-stump. But I knew not enough of anything to earn a living by it. My vocation was housekeeping ; my chief resource solid reading, especially of subjects connected with social economy, and from these I learned to mistrust the ordinary efforts of so-called charity, so that almost the only outlet for a woman's energies was shut out from me, common sense showing me that it was often more a luxury than a useful means to a profitable end.

So when my father and mother died, and my Aunt Miriam, who had always been accustomed to live by herself, proposed to occupy the house which my means would not allow me to keep up, what was there for me but to come out with my brother Mark ? And when he died, what was there for me but to remain in the station of which he had been chaplain, and go on with the work which was beginning to gather round me there ? More especially as one of the wealthiest residents, who took great interest in the native women, had offered me a sufficient salary for a certain number of hours spent daily in zenana teaching ; and the wife of Mr. Leslie, the Presbyterian chaplain, offered me a home in her house so long as they remained in the station, which fortunately has been to the end of my own stay. And then the kind of work which the wealthy civilian wanted me to do, was

exactly that which I had most capacity for, being not
direct religious teaching, that is, doctrinal, but social
and moral education, gradually preparing the way for it.
He did not wish me to pull down the house of these
poor women's faith upon them, and drive them rudely
forth into entirely strange conditions of life.    Rather he
wished that I should try to place some little shoot of
divine truth within the crevices of the house, and  leave
it there until, like the sacred peepul planted by the
porch of the Hindoo temple, it should silently grow,
strengthen, and at last, by the unconscious force of its
own life, undermine and drag down, stone by stone, the
worn-out and useless fabric.

To do this seemed to me better, despite the
recommendations mentioned before, than going home
and adding one more to the army of unemployed women
already there.    So I have stayed on and on through all
these fifteen years, discouraged sometimes in my work,
but much oftener cheered in it by the growing confidence
and expanded intelligence of those I was trying to teach,
until, six months ago, the death of Aunt Miriam brought
another change into my life.    Her little property, which
she held apart from her annuity, has fallen to me, and I
must go home to attend to it, as I have no other relative
in England, except my Cheltenham cousin Delia, who is
almost a stranger to me.    It seems to me, also, that
twenty years of such work as I have had here, with only
a yearly sea-voyage or trip to the hills, by way of holiday,
is enough to give me a right to rest the remainder of my
days, even if the addition to my income had not made it
comparatively easy for me to do so.    I say comparatively,

for even a hundred and eighty pounds, with a house rent free, is not a magnificent income, and I daresay people would smile at me for proposing to live upon it ; but I mean to try, and perhaps do a little good, too, in my own quiet way, for I could not very well settle down to idleness all at once.

So in a month from this time I shall be at home again, and not only at home in the old country, but at home in the very house where all the sweetest years of my life were passed.

Sometimes I think that is the pleasantest part of all, for Aunt Miriam was very good. She would never have any change made in the place, not a window put out, nor a door blocked up, nor a piece of furniture sold, nor a tree cut down, nor a flower-bed altered. She knew how I loved everything belonging to my home life, and so she kept that home for me, that I might one day, without any pang of strangeness, return to finish my appointed time in it. Please God I shall do so now, and He only knows how sweet the rest will be, after these years of toil.

But, dear me ! I never meant to write all this, when, a couple of hours ago, I brought my things on deck and settled myself down on the shady side of the skylight, as far as possible from that dreadful scramble of quoit-playing, which is always going on amongst the gentlemen.

How naturally one takes to journalising on board ship. Though for that matter I have taken to it ever since I was a small child of seven, stitching blank halves of letter paper into little books, wherein to chronicle the

most important events of life, what flowers came up in
my garden, how many fish Mark and Gregory and I
caught in the running stream at the bottom of the grass-
plot, the exact dates at which our silkworms began to
spin their cocoons, or our white mice to make their
nests, and the things mother gave us to make feasts of
on our birthdays.  As these interests died out, others
arose which seemed to me worthy of being recorded in a
properly bound sixpenny book, bought out of careful
weekly savings.  And when childhood had passed, and
the period of girlish aspiration and romance set in, my
journal, advanced then to a piece of morocco-covered
extravagance with silver clasp, became a sort of soliloquy,
in which I talked my views and opinions over to myself,
having no one else to talk them over to.

So that the habit of writing about what interests me
has grown with my growth and strengthened with my
strength.  And then, of course, all through my Indian
life I have been obliged to keep a daily record of visits
paid, in order that Mr. Grant might see to what purpose
his money was being employed.  And a fifteen years'
course of this has made journal-writing such a necessity
to me that now I scarcely feel I have behaved properly
to the day, unless I have done something towards
shaping out its little story in pen and ink.

Then on board ship—at least, on board this ship—
talking to oneself is almost the only resource left.  Truth
to tell, we seem at present, and I do not except myself,
a very uninteresting set of passengers.  I don't think
five-and-twenty people could be picked out anywhere
more heterogeneous, unsympathetic, commonplace than

ourselves. Perhaps we have capabilities which have not yet been brought out. We may be a set of wind instruments, waiting for the breath to blow into us ; or we may be like the keys of a piano before the wires are got ready for them to strike upon ; or a box of marionettes, motionless until the big hand appears which shall jerk us into activity, and evolve a brisk little play from our dreary inaction ; but I am sure now no one would think we had any interests in common, except when the bell sounds for meals. That is the only force which, so far, has awakened a chord of united action amongst us.

Talk of angels, and you hear their wings. That bell has sounded just now for luncheon. I must put my things away.

# CHAPTER II.

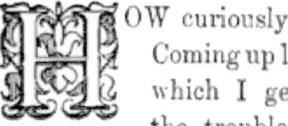OW curiously the law of association works.
Coming up here, with the bag of miscellanies
which I generally carry about, to avoid
the trouble of frequent journeys to our
cabin, and establishing myself, as before, on the quiet
side of the skylight, there comes back to me exactly
the same picture which was arranging itself before
my mind's eye when the luncheon bell shivered it into
fragments an hour ago.

I had said that we were all very uninteresting, and I
was going to make a list of the passengers, and write
down from day to day particulars of our voyage, because,
in years to come, when I am sitting quietly by my own
fireside, it will be pleasant to look back upon this curious
little slice of my life.

We have only been at sea two days, therefore some
of our company are still invisible, only manifesting
themselves by groans and other sounds issuing from the
closed doors of their cabins. For myself, I have never,
since my first voyage, suffered for more than a few hours
from sea-sickness, but my recollection of its horrors is
vivid enough to give me deep sympathy with the

utterers of those groans. I should like to be a sister of mercy, and go amongst them with cups of tea and doses of lemon-juice, only the stewardess would suspect me of an unworthy longing after her prospective half-sovereigns. And the victims themselves, who appeared at our first meal on board with smiling faces and well-arranged hair and toilettes, might reasonably object to being seen by a stranger in their present condition. So I refrain. But the will to help is present with me.

My cabin companion is a Miss Lislethorpe. I have scarcely seen anything of her yet, as she spends nearly all her time in the next cabin, which is occupied exclusively by Mrs. Marsham, the very rich wife of a very rich Colonel in the Punjaub. Mrs. Marsham is going home for "change," and I fancy, from the way in which she keeps sending Miss Lislethorpe about on one errand or other, that the poor girl is acting as a sort of paid companion to her.

Strangely different companionship that from what Miss Lislethorpe must have expected a year ago, when I saw her for the first time at Moorkee, where I had gone for my three months' holiday.

Indian society is like a coursed hare. It is continually turning and doubling upon its own path, so that wherever you go in the same coursing neighbourhood—that is, the same Presidency—you are sure to meet some one you have known or heard of somewhere else. No woman could lead a quieter life than I have been leading for the last fifteen years, yet at different hill stations which I have visited during my holiday times, I have come across five or six out of the eleven ladies on board. Miss Lislethorpe's father was chaplain of Moorkee. When I was there, she had but lately come out from England, with all the latest fashions in her outfit—bonnets and dresses which were the envy of the women and the wonder of the men, whilst the grace with which she wore them was the admiration of both.

She was then the pet of the station—one of those bright, pretty creatures who seem made to live on love and caresses, and of whom one cannot think in connection with anything uncomfortable. We never knew each other personally, for she was out when I made my duty-call at the parsonage, and I was out when she made hers. We never met, either, in society, for the balls and Badmintons at which she was so popular were quite out of my way. But I have sat in church many a time and watched her face through the firstly, secondly, and thirdly of her father's somewhat tedious sermons. It was a sweet face, with just a touch of sadness in its expression when quite at rest. Evidently balls and Badmintons could not fill up all her life, even supplemented by social success, and the distinction of an outfit good enough for a Lieutenant-Governor's lady, as every one said hers was.

But once I saw Annette Lislethorpe with no touch of sadness in her face. I was out collecting ferns and grasses on one of the little hillside paths of Moorkee, when she suddenly appeared round a bend in the road, on horseback, accompanied by Captain Asperton, a young officer whom I knew by sight. They were going leisurely along, absorbed in a conversation which gave them no leisure to espy the stout, middle-aged lady, with her basket of specimens, half hidden amongst the luxuriant foliage of the rising ground ; but I shall never forget the happy light in her eyes, and the rosy glow upon her cheeks, and the sweetness of her laugh as it rang out upon the stillness. I kept out of sight. They wanted no companionship of mine. I wonder if I felt a little touch of envy, to look upon a joy which, for me, was past and done with well on for thirty years before. Perhaps I did.

I went back to my work amongst the zenanas, and the next thing I heard was that Mr. Lislethorpe had died suddenly, leaving no provision whatever for his only child. Ill-natured people said that he had invested his capital in her education at a fashionable West-end school, and in the outfit which was so far beyond his means, hoping to realise a profitable return in her speedy and brilliant settlement. In that case Captain Asperton would scarcely have suited, having nothing beyond his pay ; but it could only have been a passing fancy—at least, I think so, or he would surely have claimed her when her father's death left her so desolate.

And the end of it is that she is the sharer of my cabin in the ship *Nawab*, working her passage home as companion to a selfish rich woman. Literally working it, for the demands Mrs. Marsham is constantly making leave scarcely time for rest or sleep. And only a year ago she was so happy that I, seeing her happiness afar off, felt the pang of being left out in the cold. Now for me there waits, close at hand, the warmth and sweetness of home ; and for her—what ? So the world goes.

I don't suppose she remembers me. There are too

many Miss Browns in the world for the name, painted ever so neatly, in the whitest of letters, on my cabin luggage, to attract her notice. And as for my face, nobody has ever looked at *that* in church, or indeed anywhere else, for long and long enough. She shows no wish either for better acquaintance, though she has heard me talking to Mrs. Truro, one of the chaplains' wives on board, about Moorkee and the people I knew there. As her circumstances are so different now, I feel it would be a sort of impertinence on my part to refer to the days of her prosperity, unless she made some opening for it. As yet she is entirely reserved to me. We have advanced no further than the merest civilities necessary between people who are brought so closely into contact as we are.

But I feel sometimes a great longing to comfort her. I want to put my arms round her, and draw down to mine the thin cheek which was once so bright and rosy. I am sure I could make life a little pleasanter to her during this voyage, if she would only let me. Perhaps the way may open out by-and-by. I will wait my time.

But about the other passengers. Ladies are in the minority. Besides these two, Annette Lislethorpe and Mrs. Marsham, we have a Mrs. Aberall, also very rich and very important, between whom and Mrs. Marsham there exists a deadly feud on the subject of precedence. Then come three officers' wives, each taking home a pretty, pale-faced little girl ; then a Mrs. Flexon, who lost her husband a year and a half ago, and seems not inconsolable—I met her, too, at Moorkee last hot weather—then a civilian's widow, a quiet, ladylike woman ; and lastly, two chaplains' wives, with their husbands, going home on furlough. Though the chaplains, owing to my awkwardness in composition, make their appearance on the list of lady passengers, I do not therefore imply the slightest disrespect to them, because, so far as I am able to judge, they are both clever men, and with a good share of that common sense which is never so valuable as when one finds it in a clergyman.

Indeed, if they had not a great deal of good sense, and good temper too, they would be sorely tried by the onslaughts of Dr. Byte, our medical officer, who is continually endeavouring to draw them into religious discussions, apparently to air a certain flippant scepticism upon which he plumes himself. Another of the passengers is a Mr. Justin, a shrewd, clever, and, I should think, rather sarcastic sort of man. He listens to the discussions that go on, though he seldom takes any part in them, except when he finds that the brilliant sword-play of the doctor is becoming too much for the steadier but less adroit fencing of the chaplains. Once or twice he has swooped down upon them in the midst of a tough combat, and set the whole matter straight by sweeping away the arguments on both sides, and so making the disputants look rather foolish. On that account neither the chaplains nor the sceptics appear to like him very much, though his weight is always put into the scale for truth. I don't know who he is, though there is something in his face that seems curiously familiar to me. It was a little Gregory Justin who used to fish with us, when we were

children, in the stream at the bottom of the garden.
How strange if this should be the same ! I should like
to ask him, but he seems to prefer keeping himself apart
from the other people, especially the ladies.   And when
I come to ask myself what is that familiar something
in his face, it fades away.  I cannot get hold of it.
Gregory was a very small child when we all used to
play together, and Mark and I, who were three or four
years older, used to patronise him, though often enough
he showed himself cleverer than the two of us put
together.  It must be the remembrance of how our juvenile arguments used to be " squashed " by his sharper
intellect, that makes me fancy he has some connection
with this sceptic-and-chaplain-conquering Mr. Justin.

Then we have three young men, who came out
expecting, as they told the captain last night, to " hit
upon something," and not having hit upon it, are now
going home again.  What a comical way of seeking that
life work which is a man's glory !  Well, I hope their
next aim will reach the mark.  Judging by the way
those three young men go through the most impossible
gymnastics on the lower deck, there must be any amount
of physical toughness and endurance in them, and so
they ought, by-and-by, to be of some use in the world—
the sort of young men that, having " hit " upon the
right thing, might make Balaclava heroes, and here
they are playing quoits, and tying themselves into knots
round a pole, for want of anything better to do.

There are several other gentlemen passengers, but I
have not so much as learned their names yet.  I hope
before long I shall find out about Mr. Justin,

# CHAPTER III.

ANNETTE LISLETHORPE and I are very good friends now, and this is how it has come about.

Soon after I finished my writing the other day, the dressing-bell rang, and I had to go down to our cabin to divest myself of the plain white linen cuffs and collar which are never allowed to make their appearance at the dinner-table. Annette was lying in her berth, looking the very picture of despair and misery. I have noticed ever since we sailed that the poor girl has been struggling with sickness. She eats nothing, takes interest in nothing, and drags herself about in a dreary sort of way, which is pitiful to behold. Mrs. Marsham does not appear to be conscious of this, or she would surely give the girl a little more rest. I don't think I have ever sat here on deck for an hour together without hearing that woman call out, in such sharp ringing tones :

" Miss Lislethorpe !  Miss Lislethorpe ! "

And when the poor girl has made her appearance, pale with that incessant nausea which is so much worse than a downright attack of sickness, she has been sent

B 2

down again for a skein of wool, a reel of cotton, a
missing handkerchief, or some other trifle, which the
rubicund matron could much more easily have fetched
for herself. But Mrs. Marsham belongs to the upper
ten, who wish all the world to know that they are born
to be waited upon.

Annette turned her face away as I went into the
cabin. Evidently she did not wish me to speak or take
any notice of her ill-health. Her tenacity of reserve
shut me up. I went on with my dressing in silence,
and had just finished when Mrs. Marsham's call was
heard from the next cabin.

"Miss Lislethorpe! Miss Lislethorpe!"

Oh! the utterly spent and hopeless look which
came over the girl's face as she tried to raise herself to
obey the summons.

"Lie still," I said, in a very quiet, matter-of-fact
way. "I will go and see what Mrs. Marsham wants."

She let me go, for she was in that condition which
cannot have respect any longer to reserves or scruples.
When I went into Mrs. Marsham's cabin, first meekly
knocking at the door, and receiving a somewhat tart
summons to enter, that lady was standing in front of
the looking-glass, with her back to me, vainly endeavouring to make a yard of belt ribbon meet round her
capacious waist.

"Miss Lislethorpe," she said to me, in by no means
the mildest of tones, "I *do* wish, when the dressing-bell
sounds, you would make a point of coming to my cabin.
Really, if I am to wait upon myself in this way, I might
as well——"

Here Mrs. Marsham turned and found me, Miss Hester Brown, a comfortable, jolly little woman, standing in the open doorway.

"I beg your pardon, Miss Brown."

"I beg your pardon, Mrs. Marsham."

Well, it *was* an uncomfortable situation—I mean for Mrs. Marsham. When a lady appears in public all smiles, amiability, and condescension, the acknowledged *burra mem Sahib* of the vessel, it is, to say the least of it, awkward to be surprised in her cabin, quite destitute either of smiles or amiability—destitute, too, of the Honiton lace and pink bows which supply its sole grace to her matronly head, and of the white teeth which produce such a charming effect when displayed in a good-tempered laugh. If Mrs. Marsham only ignored me before, I think from that time she must have begun to dislike me, though I am sure I knocked at the door, and coughed, and did everything that was necessary to make her aware of my presence.

"Can I assist you?" I asked politely, and, I hope, without the faintest touch of amusement in my face.

"Not in the least," Mrs. Marsham replied, with great dignity. "Pray do not let me detain you a moment longer. Will you be kind enough to send Miss Lislethorpe to me at once?"

"Miss Lislethorpe is very ill, and not able to move from her berth," I said; "and I came to see if I could do anything for you."

"I am excessively obliged, but I will not trouble you."

And Mrs. Marsham resumed her efforts to clasp the belt, looking redder and more ill-tempered than ever, whilst I returned to Annette, to find her half fainting from hunger and sickness. The girl had eaten scarcely anything since we came on board.

Without speaking to her, I got my little Etna stove, heated some water, made a cup of good strong tea, and insisted upon her drinking it. When she had finished it, I smoothed her pillows for her. As I was doing so, I could not help laying my hand with a sort of caressing touch upon her forehead. It is not my way to "fuss" over people, but she did look so wretched. I thought, if I had been in her case, I should have been glad for any one to do the same for me. And I began to feel, too, how much she must have gone through with that dreadful Mrs. Marsham.

I don't think I meant it; but that little caress was the one thing which broke down the barrier of reserve between us. She threw her arms round my neck, and burst into such a passion of tears as I have never seen before; and when I once took hold of her hand, she clutched mine deliberately, with a force I could scarcely have thought those little fingers had in them. Then I laid her quietly down and kissed her, and slipped into my place at the end of the dinner-table, in time for the third course.

Miss Lislethorpe and I, having no position on the Civil List, are relegated to the bottom of the first dinner-table. Our tea and toast, or beef and pudding, are often rather cold in consequence; but we find the advantage of an end seat in being able to slip in and out whenever we like, a convenience, I think, the upper people must sorely envy us, who are obliged to sit through a long stately dinner and dessert, when they would thankfully exchange both for a mouthful of fresh air on deck, or a quiet little snooze in their respective berths.

Since then Annette and I have found our way into each other's heart. She knows that I would like to be kind to her, without in any way intruding upon her great sorrow, or prying into her prospects, whatever they may be. I cannot tell how pleasant it is to me, the feeling of watching over her and taking care of her. I never had it before with any one, for all through my Indian life, though I had to work hard enough, and manage my own affairs, and look after my own business matters, still I had no one dependent on me, no one who would greatly miss love and care that I could give. Next to the sweetness of being cared for oneself by some one wiser, stronger, better, is that of having some one to whom you can give such care. It is like a new sense in my life. Only it will last such a little while.

We have now been at sea nearly a week. It seems to me more like a month. Not that I am unhappy or discontented; how could that be when I am going home to rest and peace after long years of toil? But there is so much to see, there are so many fresh faces to study. And then, on board ship, the very fact that your field of view is so limited, makes you look with microscopic carefulness upon everything that comes within it. You cannot afford to let anything slip, because there is so little to take hold of

But then, looking off this little patch of human life into the great wide life of nature which stretches round us, how much there is to wonder over and enjoy! The manifold soft tints of the ocean, the sunrises and sunsets, the black storm-clouds sweeping round the horizon, the rosy glow of the west, reflected at evening time upon the breaking waves, the clear calm of moonlight nights, when I watch from my cabin window the long silver streaks upon the water, and the stars sparkling up one by one above the wide sea line, how beautiful it all is! And day by day I look westward to the purple and gold, and remember that there is my home; and though none wait for me there now but the spirits of those I love, still they are very real to me. I have not lost them at all. So remembering and hoping, the days seem long, though long with a most quiet content.

We have now fallen into the groove which I suppose we shall remain in to the end of the voyage; I mean the groove of association and companionship. Mrs. Marsham and Mrs. Aberall, in virtue of their rank as colonels' wives, are a little too grand to mix with the rest of us, and would naturally, therefore, be thrown upon each other's society were it not that there has been a settled enmity between them ever since the captain ruled that Mrs. Marsham should sit at his right. Thus, being shut out by pique from each other, and by position from every one else, the two ladies remain apart, each a solitary island in the ocean of her own dignity.

The two chaplains and their wives have, of course, interests in common, and with Mrs. Barret, the civilian's widow, have formed a little clerical settlement at the poop end of the deck.

The officers' wives naturally gather together, with their pretty little children, who are quite the playthings of the ship. Mrs. Flexon, the not-inconsolable widow, has taken kindly both to the doctor and to the three young men who are waiting for something to hit. At first it was a general friendly intimacy amongst them all. Now two, one of them the doctor, appear to be singled out as special objects of regard, the others having gradually drifted away as they found themselves *de trop.* If things pursue their natural course, I think one of the remaining two—but not the doctor—will also find himself *de trop,* and have to retire.

The two chaplains' wives look severe, and say that Mrs. Flexon ought to know better. I think she ought, looking at the matter from my old-fashioned point of view. But then people of much higher rank do exactly the same thing, and are received all the time in the very best society. I suppose it is carrying on the flirtation within the very limited area of a steamer's poop deck which makes it objectionable. However, as Mrs. Flexon has never taken any notice of me, even by the slightest of passing bows, I need not trouble myself as to the line that I should pursue, in case her conduct becomes reprehensible. Annette and I, when she can come on deck at all, sit here under the skylight, and no one takes any notice of us.

I have not yet summoned up courage to ask Mr. Justin if he has any connection with the little Gregory of our juvenile fishing expeditions. He is not an easy man to approach. He talks very little, but looks at us all as if he were inwardly making fun of us. I dare· say he is a man who does see the ludicrous side of everything, and ship society certainly has its ludicrous side. I believe he is very clever. I see him occasionally engaged in conversation with the captain—whose duty it is, of course, to be polite to everybody—or the first officer, or the chief engineer; and from the way they listen to him, I am sure what he says must be interesting; but he does not seem to take kindly to the rest of us.

I had my first talk with him yesterday. I had come on deck very early to watch the sunrise, and found he was there for the same purpose. Under the circumstances, we were obliged to be polite. He brought my deck-chair, placed it conveniently for me out of the way of the sailors' hose, a civility which compelled some little attempt at conversation on my part; and from a remark on the beauty of the weather, other subjects arose, and others and others, until, after at least an hour and a half, we were disturbed by the sound of the first breakfast bell. I say disturbed, because I think we were both of us sorry to hear it.

If I am ever again tempted to say that we are uninteresting company, I will certainly except Mr. Justin from the indictment. I wonder what there was he did not talk about with intelligence and ability during that long time. We dipped into art, poetry, literature, and even Indian politics, about which last subject I know next to nothing myself; but I do know when I hear a man talk well about it. He has made himself acquainted with the results of zenana work, so that we had interests in common there, and we ventured a little way within extreme high-water mark of religious thought.

With what curious humility and self-distrust Mr. Justin, whose opinions seem generally decided, if not dogmatic, expresses himself upon that subject. If I never felt humble before, I certainly did whilst listening to him then. He spoke hesitatingly, and with a sense of reverent reserve, on matters which I have been accustomed to talk about with the utmost fluency, as though I had completely mastered them. Shame on me! But I will never do it again. I would fain hope I did not betray any of this detestable self-sufficiency to him, for, as the bell startled us both from a discussion on certain texts, he said, very cordially :

" We must finish this another time."

And I hope we shall. But I *must* ask him, when the other time comes, whether he knows anything about the little town of Abbotsby, in the north of England.

# CHAPTER IV.

T Aden, which we passed last evening, a strong wind sprang up, the ship began to roll, and poor Annette is worse than ever. This is very disappointing, for she was just beginning to get a little colour into her face, which made her look more like the Annette I remember last year at this time.

Hers is clearly one of those cases in which a sea voyage does not do good. She is slowly starving herself to death on a square inch of ship biscuit, and half a teacupful of soup daily. By the time she reaches England, if she ever reaches it at all, she will be little better than a skeleton. And then the poor child vexes herself so because she is not able to perform her duties properly towards this Mrs. Marsham, who is always wanting something to be fetched, or carried, or done for her.

Last night, when she began to be so ill again, she asked me if I would have an interview with Mrs. Marsham, and prevail upon her to cancel the arrangement about the companionship affair. I thought the woman was paying part of her passage-money, for the

sake of her services during the voyage ; but instead of
that, Annette pays her own expenses, and Mrs. Marsham
is giving her twenty pounds for her attendance as companion for a whole year, from the time we left Bombay,
only providing her with board and lodging from our
landing in England.  Heavens ! what are some people
made of?  And not content with this one-sided bargain,
Mrs. Marsham was complaining to Annette last night
that she does not sufficiently fulfil her share of the
contract.  She told her, so poor Annette says, that in
England girls of her position and education, when left
unprovided for, are thankful enough to give their
services in return for a comfortable home ; and even in
many cases to offer themselves a small sum in acknowledgment of the privilege of being treated as ladies.

Under these circumstances, I took it upon me to
visit Mrs. Marsham on deck this morning—she has
never looked at me since that unlucky affair of the
belt ribbon—and suggest that, as Miss Lislethorpe,
in consequence of her very feeble health, was not likely
to be of much further use as companion—I might more
truly have said maid-of-all-work—it might be advan-
tageous to both sides to have the engagement cancelled.

After a due show of dignity, the colonel's wife
consented, but not without impressing upon me that
she was making a great sacrifice, and considered herself
decidedly an ill-used woman.  Which perhaps she is,
as I don't think she will get any one else to do so
much for the money.  A couple of hours later, I heard
her talking to one of the officers' wives, whom she
has graciously condescended to notice since the feud

with Mrs. Aberall, and congratulating herself upon
being rid of such a burden.

"Not of the slightest use to me in any one thing,
Mrs. Mateby—never at hand when I want her, and so
full of airs and nonsense that really one would think
the favour was quite on her part. I have had to speak
very plainly to her, and say that, when people are left
penniless in that way, they must be content to accept
their position, and not look for all the privileges of
gentlewomen. But it is that disagreeable Miss Brown
who encourages her, making her fancy she is weak and
ill—such rubbish! When I go to my own place at
the seaside, I shall advertise for a lady without salary.
They are always the most accommodating in their
manners. The more you give, the less people will
do for you."

Mrs. Mateby assented. Indeed, she is so glad to
be confided in by a colonel's wife that I think she
would assent to anything.

So now it is all settled, and I feel as glad as if I
had won the release for myself. Annette and I will
be left to ourselves. We can make up a bed of shawls
for her on the shady side of the skylight, and I can
write or knit, or amuse myself with what goes on round
me, whilst she just dozes the time away in that half-
sleeping, half-waking state which is the only one possible
to sufferers from sea-sickness. How delightful to be
able to do just as we like, without ever being disturbed
by that terrible " Miss Lislethorpe ! Miss Lislethorpe ! "
which has been poor Annette's nightmare since she
first came on board. I am sure that call was as

dreadful to me as though I had been obliged to get up and attend to it myself.

Last night I dreamed about going home. Waking, what a joy to know that it was not all a dream. I suppose things are sweet or bitter by contrast. If I had been for the last twenty years living peacefully with my father and mother in the old house which is preparing for me now, and had then lost them both, and been left to myself, people would have said, "How sad!" as they found me sitting by my solitary fireside. But compared with long years of work in a foreign land, with no links, except of memory, to bind me to my home, this loneliness to which I am coming seems so sweet.

I wonder if I shall find many of my old friends. Aunt Miriam was not much of a correspondent, and when she did enter into details, they were chiefly about household and domestic matters. Not belonging to Abbotsby herself, she did not favour the dust thereof, as I have done all the days of my life. By the newspapers which she sent me regularly once a month, I know that some are married, some are dead, but I have not had a newspaper now since she began to be ill, nearly a year ago.

The first person I shall go to see will be Mrs. Carbery, my mother's friend, if she is living still. How well I remember her brisk, bright, practical ways, her kindness to us children, the intense delight we used to have in going to her house to tea, playing in the lumber-room amongst piles of old pictures and newspapers, and creeping out of its window into the branches of an apple-tree, which stretched right across the bottom row

of panes. Mrs. Carbery was living last time my Aunt
Miriam wrote to me, but she was beginning even then,
and that is a year ago, to fail very much. It would be
pleasant to talk with her about my father and mother,
and the old times, and the friends who are dead and gone.
I want little from any one, so long as I may live my life
with the old memories, and be faithful to the old friends.

Hilary Bennet, too. Is she above ground, or are her
troubles ended? She lived as cook with my father and
mother when they were first married, and then she went
to live with her mother, and kept the little goodstuff
shop in the lane at the bottom of our road. Many a
penny Mark and I have spent there over gingerbread
horses with gilt bridles, and biscuits with the alphabet
stamped all round them in caraway seeds, our nurse
never letting us bite a letter off until we could tell its
name. Hilary was a rosy-cheeked young woman then,
looking bonnie enough in her Sunday pink ribbons
and clean pink gown; but when her mother died
she married a man who turned out badly, the little
goodstuff shop came to grief, and when I went away
to India, poor Hilary, at fifty, was a bent, worn-out
woman, earning her living by taking in washing.
Every now and then her drunken husband, who left
her soon after they were married, used to swoop
down upon her, carry off her little savings, pawn
everything in the house, and then leave her, coming
back when he thought she had had time to scrape a little
money together again.

Poor Hilary! Yet there was the making of a true
lady in her. No born gentlewoman could have had

finer ideas of honour, or turned more proudly away from the taking of dishonest gain. How many a cake has she given me from her little shop, in the good old times, and how many a tin of soup has she thankfully carried away from our house, when for her, poor thing, the good old days were over, and that drunken sot of a husband had taken the light from her eyes and the colour from her cheeks. I could scarcely wish to find her alive if the last twenty years have brought her as much sorrow as she had known when I looked my last upon her.

I have never summoned up courage yet to ask Mr. Justin if he knows Abbotsby. Once or twice he has had pleasant little talks with us, when I have been sitting with Annette on deck, but we always seemed to stop short of the point at which I could venture to ask him any questions about himself. Because he never talks about his own affairs. He has said nothing yet which gives me the least idea what his profession is. Whatever subject he takes up is handled so well that one might almost fancy it had been the study of his life. He seems to have read as much theology as either of the chaplains, and to know quite as much about practical religion. His scientific knowledge seems to me far beyond that of our sceptical doctor, and he has read all sorts of books on social subjects. These are the things to talk about, and not his own experiences or sayings or doings; so that whether he is a clergyman in plain clothes, or a doctor, or a lawyer, or a professor of some sort, I don't know, and I don't believe anybody else on board knows. All that we have

c

yet found out about him is, that he is returning from a
six months' tour in India, from which I infer that he is
a man of means.

Well, supposing that he turned out to be my little
friend Gregory, the only child of Mr. Justin, who used
to be the Recorder of Abbotsby, he might by this time
be a man of means. For Mr. Justin was considered
one of the great people of the town, and used to mix in
the best society, and I remember looking with a sort of
awe upon Mrs. Justin's velvets and furs when she came
to see my mother. Mr. Justin died when Gregory was
about eight years old, and then she went away to live
with her own friends in the south, taking the little boy
with her, and we heard no more about them. I believe
she rather looked down upon us because we lived so
quietly; but still she was always ready to let Gregory
come and play with us. I could fancy sometimes that
Mr. Justin has a little touch of the same "stand-off"
manner. It is very difficult to become at home with him.

But oh! if he really is little Gregory, how pleasant
it will be to talk of the old days with him. For fifteen
years now I have clasped hands with no one who had
ever seen my father and mother, no one who knows my
home, no one to whom I can speak of anything but the
outside life. The past is gone out of sight, like a tree
whose branches have been forced underground. My
life is that of an orchid, with no roots at all, nothing
but leaves and flowers, living on the air of the present.
No wonder I am obliged to talk to myself so much of
what is gone, for in no other way can I keep it with me
at all.

# CHAPTER V.

 SAID last time I wrote here, "It would be very pleasant." Now I say, "It *is* very pleasant."

Yesterday morning I was on deck very early, whilst the eastern sky was yet one mass of rose and purple, with dashes and flecks of gold where the yet unrisen sun caught the edges of the clouds. As the little ripples curled and broke, their foam reflected the rosy light for an instant, making it seem like sprays of amethyst and ruby. The air had that cool, sweet freshness which none but those who have wearied through the heat of Indian summers know how to prize ; and breathing it in alone there in the early April morning I felt young in heart again, with almost the youth of the old days at home.

I was stretched out in my comfortable deck-chair, enjoying the luxury of the stillness, for it is so delightful not to hear the cackling and babbling of voices all around, when Mr. Justin sauntered up and wished me good morning.

I suppose we found each other ready for conversation, for soon we drifted into a pleasant talk about things in general. I listened, as I always do, to his

o 2

clear, large, liberal thoughts—whether addressed to myself or not—with an internal sense of freshness as welcome as that which the early morning air was giving to the outward part of me.  For the first time he began to tell me something about his own wishes and purposes in life.  He said that, having travelled for some time in the East, he was now going to be settled down in the quiet little English town where his childhood had been spent.  And as he should have abundant time for thought and study there, he meant to give his attention to writing, taking for his department the science of social well-being, health, education, ventilation, all these being subjects on which even a little knowledge gained might have great results.

I agreed with him ; such thought as I had been able to give to anything in my reading days having been spent in much the same direction, though, as yet, with no great practical result.  I asked him, however, to add to these subjects almsgiving and profitable employment for women, these two things, or rather the understanding of them, being exceedingly necessary to the increasing number of benevolent and inexperienced women who were unable to direct their energies in any useful direction.

The interest he took in this suggestion, and the kindly manner in which he listened to my lame remarks, encouraged me to ask the question which I must confess had been bubbling up in my thoughts all the time.  I said, with as much self-possession as I could muster—for Mr. Justin is not a man who tolerates anything like inquisitiveness in a woman :

"You spoke just now of being settled down in a quiet little English town I wonder if it is Abbotsby, up in the north. I used to live there myself once. We knew a family named Justin. My name is Hester Brown."

Mr. Justin bent his keen, clever eyes down upon me, as if he would look me through and through, but I could not find any dawn of recognition in his face. Instead, I fancied I found a sort of annoyance, as if he were vexed with me for trying to ferret out what was no business of mine. And I began to be conscious that I had put the question in a very awkward way. just the way to irritate a rather proud man. However, having begun, I was determined to flounder through, feeling certain that I should never have courage to enter upon the subject again.

"I daresay you have met a good many Miss Browns before now," I said.

"Well, yes," he replied, with a comical look, "I must confess I have."

And there he stopped again, making me feel more uncomfortable than ever. He certainly has the coolest way of putting any one down.

"But," I persisted, "I have not met so many Mr. Justins, and I very much want to know if you are the same. A little boy named Gregory Justin used to come and play with us. We lived out of the town, at the Northgate end, in a house off the road, and there was a stream at the bottom of the garden where we used to fish. I was not called Hester then, but Fudge, because I was so short and stout."

"Yes, and good, too—the best little woman in the

world," said Mr. Justin, facing round upon me so
suddenly that I dropped a whole row of stitches in the
stocking I was knitting. "Why, you don't mean to
say you are the dear old Fudge who used to sew bags for
our marbles, and make fishing-rods for us out of pins
and bits of string. Why, of course, it all comes back on
me as clear as daylight. And you made me a book-
mark, too, when we went away. It was only the other
day I turned it out amongst a lot of things, when I was
starting for India. I wonder it never got lost, for I'm
sure I did not take particular care of it."

That was very like Gregory, too. No, he was not a
specially affectionate little boy, nor much given to
keepsakes and sentimentalities. He was always more
for finding out and reasoning about things, trying
experiments, spoiling his shoes and socks by wading
into the stream to investigate spiders and water-beetles.
How often have I, the motherly Fudge of ten years,
washed those socks for him, and spread them out to dry on
the currant-bush in my own garden, that he might not run
the risk of a scolding from his nurse when he got home.
But he used to take it very quietly, as if he had a right
to be ministered to. Not that Gregory was selfish, not a
bit of it. He would spend any amount of time finding
out what was the matter with our toys when they got
broken, or collecting butterflies and things for us ; but
he never cared for being made a fuss over, or petted, or
that sort of thing.

After facing round upon me in that sudden way, he
faced back as suddenly, and leaned over the bulwarks
for a long time ; at least it seemed to me a long time,
because I did not know whether he was pleased or

vexed at what had happened. Perhaps he did not care
to have the old times brought back, and, in that case,
what a fool I had made of myself, and what a complete
extinguisher I had put on any pleasant conversation!
So far the whole interview had been rather a disappoint-
ing one. However, he presently set my mind at rest by
turning round and giving my hand such a hearty grip
as I have not felt for many and many a year. There
were even tears in his eyes, and, I expect, in mine too.

"Come along," he said, abruptly, "let us talk about
it all."

And then we went back and back over the pleasant old
days. I told him about my brother Mark, how he had
gone into the Church, and afterwards had been appointed chaplain in India ; how, my father and mother
being both dead then, I had come out with him ; and
how, after my brother's death, I had kept on working
amongst the Indian women, until now I was returning
to rest in the old home. Then he told me his own
story. After they had been a little while in London, his
mother took him to Germany, to be educated there.
Afterwards he took to his father's profession, that of the
law, and settled in Abbotsby. After being there some
years, a considerable property came into his possession,
and he determined to travel for a while, leaving a
partner to attend to his practice. When he returned,
he found that the Recorder of Abbotsby was resigning
his office at the end of the twelvemonth, and the vacant
appointment was offered to himself. So now, after
spending the intervening time in making a tour in
India, he is on his way to our quiet old town, to be
installed in his office.

A good, prosperous, honourable career, just such as I could imagine our practical little Gregory Justin to make. And I have no doubt by-and-by he will make himself a name in literature, too. I am glad to think he is going to live at Abbotsby, for we shall be friends still, though of course he will move in a very different circle from mine, if mine can be considered a circle at all. If I judge Gregory aright, he will not be ashamed, great man though he may be in his native town, to keep up the acquaintance of the quiet, old-fashioned maiden lady who was good to him when he was a little boy.

Oh ! it was pleasant to remember those days again. Little by little we excavated a whole Herculaneum of memories from beneath the lava and ashes of these more than thirty years past. He hit upon one thing, I upon another, of the dear old child life, until it all looked fresh and clear, as though we had left it but yesterday.

What wonder, sitting there, recalling our buried treasures, we neither of us saw how the passengers had come up one by one on deck, and were watching our eager, animated conversation ? What wonder, too, that neither of us heard the first breakfast bell, or had a thought of anything in the present, until Mrs. Flexon, passing us with an envious gleam in her pretty gray-green eyes, remarked :

" What a wonderfully interesting conversation you appear to be having."

For, during the last few days, Mrs. Flexon has been trying, without success, to draw Mr. Justin into the circle of her admirers.

# CHAPTER VI.

POOR body! she need not have troubled herself. Her arrow flew wide enough of the mark. I daresay Mr. Justin knows he may talk with tolerable safety to a woman who played the mother to him when he was a little boy. And as for me, I can look up to all I love in Heaven, and say truly that my treasure is garnered there. Most quiet and peaceful is the life I look forward to on earth, nothing more than that.

But Mrs. Flexon has looked dissatisfied ever since Annette and I took to the shady side of that skylight, and Mr. Justin established himself in our neighbourhood.

I must just stop a little while to laugh at the idea of a stout, comfortable, practical Miss Brown like myself being even suspected of anything like flirtation with a man of Mr. Justin's stamp, a man with so much knowledge of the world about him, and a proper amount of self-esteem. If it was Annette—but Annette takes no interest in anything or anybody now. She just lies back with her cheek against my shoulder, and gazes out over the sea with melancholy eyes, that seem to behold nothing. Mrs. Flexon need not distress herself about any of us.

It is strange how two unkindly disposed women can
direct the helm of feeling in a little society like this of
ours on board ship. We have been at sea little more
than a week, and already the passengers are divided
into two distinct parties, in consequence of the feud
between Mrs. Marsham and Mrs. Aberall, arising out
of that question of precedence. Mrs. Aberall thinks
she ought to sit at the captain's right—Mrs. Marsham
sits there. In consequence the two ladies do not speak
to each other. For some time, being higher in position
than the rest of us, they did not speak to any one else
either; but that state of things could not be expected
to last. Women must have sympathy, and they must
have some one to talk to. Half the delight of a
grievance lies in being able to air it freely. Therefore
Mrs. Aberall, the vanquished, has succeeded in convincing three or four of the ladies on board, to whom,
under other circumstances, she would scarcely have
spoken at all, that she is an injured woman, and these
ladies, proud of being noticed by her, uphold her cause
with all the eloquence of which they are capable, and
still further to show their sympathy, refuse friendly
intercourse with those who have sided with the conquering party.

Mrs. Marsham, the triumphant, draws after her an
equal number, to whom she explains how it is that,
although she does not really care a straw for her
position as wife of a colonel in command, and though
no one looks upon petty distinctions of rank with more
indifference than herself, still the question of precedence
is one which must be considered, or the whole fabric

of society would fall to pieces ; and therefore she puts
aside her own feelings, and as a matter of principle
asserts her right to the place of honour. But she
would not on any account have Mrs. Aberall and the
rest of the passengers think, etc., etc.

Annette and myself, not being of sufficient account
to belong to either of the parties, hear a little of what
goes on on both sides, the ladies not considering it
necessary to drop their voices if we make an appearance whilst they are discussing the subject. Moreover,
as no one enters into conversation with us, except
Mr. Justin, and he cannot gossip, we are in no danger
of repeating what we hear.

I have quite given over now trying to get out of the
way of remarks which are not intended for my hearing.
At first I made it a point of conscience to move my
chair away whenever, in the heat of discussion, the
ladies raised their voices beyond that sweet, low, and
gentle key which is such an excellent thing in woman.
But I soon found that, if I allowed conscience to rule
over me in that manner, I should become more of a
peripatetic than any of the old Greek philosophers,
besides getting myself laughed at for my pains, and
running the risk of many a tumble, if the vessel
happened to be rolling at the time. So now I do
as others do—keep my seat, and either hear or not,
as it happens.

The other day, Mrs. Truro, the senior chaplain's
wife, and Mrs. Beverley, the exceedingly bright and
merry little military woman, who is taking her youngest
child home, were having a chat about things in general.

Fortunately, I was alone, Annette writing letters in her cabin ready to post at Suez; by-and-by the conversation turned upon Mrs. Flexon, who, like a wise woman, has cast in her lot with the government side. Mrs. Truro and Mrs. Beverley belong to the opposition.

"So rudely as she behaves to that poor inoffensive Miss Lislethorpe, too," said the captain's wife, after several of the shortcomings of our coquettish widow had been discussed. "She should really remember that all the first-class passengers on board a vessel like this are supposed to be ladies, whether they happen to be rich or poor."

"Of course," said Mrs. Truro decidedly. "Though poor Miss Lislethorpe hasn't a penny of her own, and will most probably have to earn her own bread as long as she needs any, yet I dare say, in point of position, she is quite equal to Mrs. Flexon. I believe he was very low down in the service."

"Quite, and a competition wallah, too, not at all one of the old Indian families. But I fancy she has a very different reason for being so disagreeable to Miss Lislethorpe. It is nothing connected with position."

"Indeed!" said Mrs. Truro, looking mildly curious. "I was not aware of anything."

"Why, Mrs. Truro, you don't mean to say you were up at Moorkee all last hot weather without hearing anything about it?"

Mrs. Truro admitted the fact, but justified herself by saying that, as a chaplain's wife, she made it her business to avoid personal gossip. Still in the present instance, she intimated her willingness to be enlightened.

"Oh! for that matter," said merry little Mrs. Beverley, "I like to hear about everything that is going on. Why, what else have you to do in a hill station but pay attention to your neighbours' affairs? And, after all, it is only tit for tat. You may be quite sure they know everything about you, and I don't see why you should not live up to your privileges, and be as wise as they are. Are you *sure* you never heard about Miss Lislethorpe and Captain Asperton?"

Mrs. Truro admitted that she had heard something, but could not exactly remember what. Would Mrs. Beverley kindly recall it to her memory?

"Why, every one knew that they were as good as engaged to each other, and a very nice match for her, too, though his pay was not remarkably good. But he had splendid interest, and was a thorough gentleman. You could see as plainly as possible that he worshipped the very ground she walked upon. And I don't wonder, for she was exceeding pretty then."

"Yes, said Mrs. Truro, tentatively. "I believe, though," she added, beginning to betray a little more knowledge of Moorkee gossip than was quite consistent with the rôle she had adopted, "Miss Lislethorpe had several other admirers. Young Dennison was always at her side when he could get a chance. And then there was that old Mr. Moberley, that rich old indigo planter, you remember, with scarcely a tooth in his head."

"Yes, but with so many shares in the Agra and

Delhi Bank," put in Mrs. Beverley; "and every one knows that shares are worth a great deal more than teeth. I have no doubt Mr. Lislethorpe would have liked *that* match very much. But it was an unfortunate thing for the poor girl that it got talked about, for it was the beginning of all the mischief. If you remember, Mrs. Flexon came to Moorkee just at the time. Her husband had only been dead eight months, but she made it very plain that she was ready for another, and the first person she resolved to elect into the vacant place was Captain Asperton."

"You don't say so!" exclaimed Mrs. Truro, holding up her hands. "Is it possible?"

"Oh, yes, quite possible, especially in India. Captain Asperton did not see it, you know, because he had eyes for no one but Miss Lislethorpe. And the report is——"

Here Mrs. Beverley lowered her voice a little.

"The report is that she put it about all over the station that Miss Lislethorpe was engaged to old Mr. Moberley. It was easy enough to do that, for the old man was always up at the Parsonage, and Mr. Lislethorpe was so evidently encouraging him. So poor young Asperton was taken in, and no one saw him after that paying the least attention to her. I believe it cut him up dreadfully. He never looked the same again, poor fellow!"

"Dreadful!" said Mrs. Truro. "I do hope the woman will some day get punished for her wickedness. But, at any rate, if she spoiled poor Miss Lislethorpe's prospects, she has not bettered her own, so far. She

did not manage to get engaged to him herself, I
suppose?"

"No, thank goodness! I expect she thought he
would be able to transfer his affections as easily as
she transfers her own; but he took it so to heart that
he left the station almost immediately, and soon after
went on furlough to England. I suppose he is there
now. It must have been a great blow to Miss Lislethorpe, although there was no regular understanding
between them. But, you know, almost immediately on
Captain Asperton's leaving the station, Mr. Lislethorpe
died, leaving the poor girl without a penny, and, of
course, that was quite enough to account for her
dejection. She did not have to go through the
humiliation of being pitied all over the place."

"I am very sorry," said Mrs. Truro, with that
air of compassionate complacency which a woman who
is comfortably established with a good income sometimes puts on, when glancing for a time upon the great
and terrible wilderness across which one and another
of her less favoured sisters have to travel. "It is a
most painful story. I shall never speak to Mrs. Flexon
again. All the ship ought to know what a wicked
woman she is."

"Oh! it would not make very much difference if
they did. You see, as it is, none of the ladies care
for her, and as for the gentlemen, why, so long as
a woman has those lovely gray-green eyes and exquisite
braids of golden hair, and pretty appealing ways like
Mrs. Flexon's, she may have done what she likes in
the past. They don't care. You see she is beginning

just the same game again here. From the first day we came on board she had a knot of young men about her, and it was just a question which of them she should draw the farthest. Then she saw that the chief engineer was paying rather more than usual attention to that nice quiet Mrs. Barret, the civilian's widow, really a modest, lady-like woman, and immediately she began to use her arts upon him. She cannot bear any one to be admired more than herself. She is experimenting now upon Mr. Justin, but he is too clever for her. He does look so quizzical when she comes up to him with her pretty airs and graces."

Here the first dinner bell sounded, and Mrs. Beverley hurried away. That soft brown hair of hers must take so much "doing."

"What a lovely sunset we are going to have!" she remarked, pleasantly enough, as she put away her embroidery. And then they both tripped past me, and I daresay their soup and sparkling hocks would taste none the worse for the story which they had been talking over.

# CHAPTER VII.

E are going up the Red Sea now. It is "tolerably warm," as the captain says, but not too much so, after the fierce summer heat I have been accustomed to for so many years.

How lovely these Arabian mountains are, with the tints of sunrise or sunset reflected upon them, the softest shades of pink, violet, and orange, with the intense blue of the sea beneath, and the quivering golden green of the sky beyond. I have dreamed of such colouring before, but never seen it.

And yet it is all outside beauty. They are in reality so bleak and barren. Not a blade of grass, not a tree, not a flower upon them. When the sunrise glow has faded they just show like huge gray masses of rock, with no form nor softness about them. They are like some people I have seen, only beautiful in a reflected light. Mrs. Marsham, for instance, who smiles so rosily from the captain's right upon the ladies who support her side of the question, and looks so complacent when reflecting the sunlight of compliment and flattery; but oh! so *very* bleak and craggy when

D

turning to rebuke the supposed "companion" for not coming quickly enough to clasp that belt ribbon of hers.

Yet why should I talk? To this same Mrs. Marsham, nay, doubtless to most of all the people on board, I myself am an Arabian mountain, without even the power of reflecting any pink and violet tints; a mere mass of crag, forbidding alike under all conditions. Let such thoughts teach me humility. And let me remember that if some people, like Arabian mountains, can only shine in a reflected beauty, others, like those great Bombay headlands which show so black and frowning in the distance, have yet many a sweet and flowery dell nestling beneath the shelter of their sternness.

I suppose it is quite right for me to have had such a bitter burning sense of injustice ever since I heard Mrs. Beverley's story. I could almost put my hands round Mrs. Flexon's pretty little white throat, and lift her up and drop her, crape frilling, golden braids, and everything, into the deep sea. Are human lives to be spoiled as Annette's has been, and is no one to be punished for the spoiling of them? There she is, on the other side of the deck now, chatting away so confidingly with the doctor and the chief engineer, lifting her round eyelids and casting a half-appealing, half-coquettish glance, first at one, then at another, the very picture of innocence and simplicity, as though no Annette Lislethorpe, with heart bruised and suffering, were wearying through the long days with none to comfort her.

This morning I was walking up and down the deck before breakfast. The chaplains, who both know Moorkee, were talking about some of the people there. Mrs. Flexon, within hearing of them, was flirting with the doctor. Captain Asperton's name was mentioned. I turned round and looked Mrs. Flexon full in the face, a long, quiet, steady look.

She returned it for a moment with wonderful self-possession. Then that curious glimmer came into her eyes, and she moved away to make some careless remark to Dr. Byte about the loveliness of the tints upon the water. She deserves a nearer acquaintance both with the tints and the water. I believe she thought I was very rude. I wonder if she thought anything else.

Well, never mind. As Lancelot says, Alas! who may trust this world?

But these things seem to have brought me nearer to Annette. I want more than ever to be a friend to her. If I could only be sure that it was all true, and if I dare tell her that I knew anything about it! She has never mentioned Captain Asperton's name to me, and there is a gentle reserve of pride about Annette which keeps even those she loves out of her inner life.

It does vex me so when I think how men are deceived. How *could* he believe that about a girl? They talk about men's powerful reasoning. Where is it in such cases as these? Mrs. Flexon could not have deceived a woman in that way. But I suppose she wound herself little by little into his confidence, and

then, under pretence of being his friend, contrived to
drop the seeds of suspicion which sprang up and
flourished so well. Probably a man would believe
anything that was accompanied by such sweetly appealing looks, and now and then the gentle pressure of
a little white hand upon his arm. Away! it makes me
feel wicked even to think about it. But Mrs. Flexon
does look so resigned and good when the prayers are
read on Sundays.

Last night, after dinner, when nearly every one
was down in the saloon, the ladies playing and singing,
the gentlemen listening to them, I came up here on
deck, and Annette came and lay down beside me,
leaning her head on my shoulder, as she often does
now. Oh! the long sigh she gave as she stretched out
her hand to feel for mine! I seem to hear it now.
Poor child! so young, and yet knowing so much
sorrow! I did wish that I could have told her even
a little, but I could only be silent. If anything else
is to come, it will come in its own way.

Sitting there in the darkness of that summer night,
over us the great bright stars, all round and about us
the deep sea, which was bearing me on to home and
rest, I thanked God as I had never thanked Him before
that in the years of my own girlhood death, and not
deceit, had parted my beloved from me. And as I
thought of the happy six months through whose golden
gate I had passed into the gray years of my woman-
hood, I felt how good my lot had been, to have loved
and lost, with faith still firm in the lost one. Better
far this than to go forth into the lonely future, as

Annette was going, with a wrong of human working shut down in her heart, and no trust left.

For she must think that Captain Asperton had only been playing with her, when she gave and he took so much. If only I could tell her! But I must be quiet.

This morning, when we were sitting together under our skylight, we had a long talk about ways and means. She has an aunt in Cheltenham, of whom she does not know very much. Before she engaged herself as companion to Mrs. Marsham, it was arranged that she should go to this aunt until she could meet with a suitable situation, and the poor child evidently does not relish the prospect. To be an unwelcome burden on family charity is only a shade better—scarcely that —than to be slaving for a selfish rich woman; and from what Annette tells me, this Mrs. Vermont, at Cheltenham, looks forward to the visit of her orphan niece as rather a burden than anything else. She showed me one or two of her aunt's letters, written since the intelligence of Mr. Lislethorpe's death, and I know that I would live on dry bread rather than be dependent on the household mercies of a woman who had addressed such words to me. These letters were the cause of Annette engaging herself to Mrs. Marsham; but that having fallen through on account of her weak health, she has to turn to her aunt again. An unpleasant prospect. No wonder that the poor child looks pale and wretched, even if she had no other cause for pain.

I have a pleasanter plan in my mind, though I have not said anything to her yet. When we land, she

shall come straight on with me to Abbotsby, and share
my lodgings in the Northgate, where I mean to stay
for a day or two before I go to my own house.   I have
a curious fancy for going to the house alone very early
in the morning, after I arrive at Abbotsby, and wander-
ing about in the garden before Keren knows that I
am there.   I must be by myself when I see my home
for the first time after twenty years.

Then, when I really take possession, Annette shall
go with me, and stay until she can decide what to
do for herself.   Indeed, I could be well content to have
her always with me, a sort of link between myself and
the life that I have left; and I have no doubt in
Abbotsby, where girls' schools are not plentiful, she
could easily meet with a daily engagement which would
bring in enough for clothes and pocket-money.   I said
to myself some time ago that I wanted some way of
doing good when I was settled down in my quiet life,
and here it is ready for me—to give a home, with
love in it, to this homeless girl.

If she stays with me long enough I will make a
clever little housewife of her.   She was telling me
the other day that she knows positively nothing of
domestic management, and how should she, brought
up since she was eleven years old with fashionable
London people, and then sent to a fashionable London
school to be finished?   The wonder is that there is so
much reality about her as I have found out since we
became intimate.

What a good creature that old godmother must
have been who brought her up until she was eleven!

Her character was formed even then in a way which the fashionmongers have not been able quite to destroy, though they have managed to plaster a considerable amount of useless material upon it. Annette is like a marble column in a cathedral, which stupid people have covered with paint and whitewash, until all the fair veinings are lost. Her troubles during the last few months have worn a little of this away, and by-and-by the marble will show out again pure as ever.

There is a wonderful sweetness and grace about her—not much strength. She will always want somebody to lean up against. Hers is not an original mind. She has very few views or opinions about anything, but a sort of subtle perception in choosing the good and refusing the evil. I should think, in a great struggle, she would fail entirely for want of what is called backbone. But in ordinary life, with some practical person—shall I say like myself?—to act as a substantial wirework of common-sense, upon which the leaves and flowers of her graceful nature may entwine themselves, she will be an object of beauty, and will give back in colour and perfume what she takes in strength.

Oh, dear, what castles in the air I do keep building about this going home to Abbotsby!

# CHAPTER VIII.

 FEAR I am making for myself enemies. Yesterday, Mr. Truro asked if he could have a little quiet conversation with me, and when the favour was granted, I found that it had been asked in order to set before me the impropriety of which I had been guilty in separating myself from the bulk of the passengers, and confining myself almost exclusively to the companionship of Miss Lislethorpe and Mr. Justin.

Such conduct, Mr. Truro ventured to hint, was neither lady-like nor Christian. It argued either a spirit of Pharisaism or selfishness, and one or two of the ladies, his wife included, had asked him to speak to me about it, though he said he did it with diffidence, knowing that my work in India had been such as to secure for me the respect of every one with whom I came in contact, and that probably my practice of self-isolation at present arose more from natural temperament than from any personal feeling against the rest of the passengers, yet, etc.

How kind of Mr. Truro. How more than kind of the ladies, considering that during the first few days of the voyage I had done my poor little best to be pleasant and agreeable to every one on board, with the result of being systematically ignored by them all, Mr. Justin and Miss Lislethorpe excepted! To those who were well did I not speak cheerily of the prospects of the voyage? To those who were ill did I not offer smelling salts and pyretic saline, to say nothing of conducting them to the places where they would least feel the motion of the vessel, or the horrible jarring of the screw? Was it not in my heart to be as friendly to every one of them at first as I have been since with Annette and Mr. Justin? My conscience returns a most vigorous and decided Yes.

But being a somewhat shabbily dressed and exceedingly unstylish woman, with nothing to set me forth but my name, printed, with that of my companion, over our cabin door, I was left to myself; the best intentions, unaccompanied by stylish manners and plenty of lace, being utterly futile.

Therefore, being thrust into my present position, I choose to keep it. And if I said the same with a little asperity to Mr. Truro, whose wife ignored me as much as anybody, I do not in the least repent it.

I think if Annette and I had kept entirely to ourselves we should not have been interfered with. The companionship of Mr. Justin is the real indictment against us. People are beginning to find out that he is a gentleman, and a man of means, and very clever, too, invaluable at the readings which we have two or three times a week, and able to hold his own with any one on board the ship. Under these circumstances, it is inexcusable that he should be so often found at our side of the skylight, instead of conferring the lustre of his companionship on those who are so much more worthy of it. What *can* he find, I heard Mrs. Marsham say the other day, in a washed-out girl and stupid old woman, to make him be continually paying attention to them?

Paying attention. Ah! that is the sore point. And his being unmarried, too, adds bitterness to the insult.

I wonder how it is that women who are, as the phrase goes, settled in life, have such an uncontrollable jealousy of any attention bestowed upon those who are not. Mrs. Flexon has been particularly spiteful since Mr. Justin and I have had so many pleasant talks together; Annette, who has brightened up a little since the companionship was dissolved, sometimes taking her part in the talk. I am sure Mrs. Flexon gets plenty of admiration. She has only to make her appearance on deck, looking furtively out from under her long light lashes, and all the unappropriated gentlemen rush forward to fetch her chair, or spread her rug, or put up her umbrella, or point out interesting objects in the distance. And if she will but condescend to play at quoits, what a queen she is! A separate gentleman is in attendance upon her for each quoit. One presents it to her for action, another picks it up when it is done with, another scores her numbers, a fourth hovers about with a camp-stool. Could a living woman desire more? And with such a following, can she not look on mildly whilst Mr. Justin has a little chat with us two unprotected females? Apparently not.

She has been coquetting with him very prettily lately, but I don't think he appreciates his good fortune. I never saw him look so bored as when she asked him to hold her quoits for her this morning. How pleasantly she did it, too, with such a sidelong look, as he was on his way to take possession of a chair by Annette's side; and how she kept turning and watching, to see if any pang of disappointment was on the girl's face.

Oh, Mr. Truro, I think you ought to go and speak to Mrs. Flexon, if you *must* have something to say against selfishness. Why pick me out, who never, so far as I know, broke a heart, or spoiled a human life, and whose only crime is that I like to be quiet? Has not your wife told you the story of Moorkee, and must this destroying angel fly amongst us with her wings all unclipped, whilst an ordinary mortal like myself is hunted down, and preached to, and told to behave herself? It is a very curious world.

We are in the Canal now. Was ever anything so beautiful as the colouring on land and sea, as we passed Suez yesterday afternoon? I had seen paintings of it which seemed to me extravagant caricatures, but now I know that no brush can do more than give a very feeble idea of the deep amethyst purple of the hills, and the dazzling blue of the waves that sweep at their feet. Then the perfect stillness of last night, when we were moored to the bank of the Canal. There was no sound but the plash of the water, and the sough of the wind through the whispering reed-beds. All this morning, as we quietly glided along, I have been watching these beautiful reed-beds, broken here and there by patches of bright green moss, or the lovely little gardens planted around the stations. Each hour, as we go along, is a wonder and a delight. Sometimes we see a caravan of merchants with their camels resting in the desert, the huge ungainly beasts stretched upon the sand, the piles of merchandise scattered around, the Arabs crouching under their skin-covered tents, the little, naked, brown children running into the water for coppers, which the passengers throw to them.

Sometimes we have to draw on one side, to let a magnificent steamer, outward bound, pass us. Ah! how I pity that steamer, even with her flags flying and her gilded prow glittering in the sun, as she careers so proudly on. Outward bound, with men and women destined to who knows what of toil and trouble in the far-off land, while I am going home to be at rest in my own country! Oh! the good words : at rest in my own country! One must buy the key to all their meaning by long years of exile such as I have spent.

So far as the future of any human life can be seen, mine lies clearly enough for me now, and most sweet and pleasant it is. I hope it will not be a useless one. I have got so into the habit of regular work that I do not think I could be happy without plenty to do. Only it must be something that I can do by myself, without any one interfering with me. I am tired of reports and committees, and secretaryships and patrons, some pulling one way, some the other ; great noise, but in the end very little done to make the world either better or wiser.

When I was talking to Mr. Justin the other morning,

about employment for women of leisure, something suggested itself to me that would, I think, be very useful. I used to be considered a good little house-keeper in my young days, quite in my element amongst cooking and domestic management. I will try the experiment of taking a young girl from the Abbotsby workhouse, and training her myself, under old Keren, to be a useful servant. Suppose I take her at eleven or twelve, and keep her for three or four years. She will then, if she has any sort of ability, be ready for employ-ment in some respectable family, and I shall feel that I have done good, both to the girl and to the public. This is a thing in which no one can interfere with me, and, if I fail, I shall only hurt myself. And I think Keren, who, of course, will stay with me until her death, will get on better with a young girl of this sort, over whom she would have unquestioned authority, than with a full-blown servant of the modern times, which, I understand now, are very unsatisfactory times.

Then I should try to train her in character, too, give her good sorts of notions about her duty to God and her neighbour, teach her plain sewing, reading, writing, and arithmetic, and bring her up, so far as I could, in the honest ways of my youth. I don't know if it will come to anything, but it shapes itself pleasantly enough as I think about it. And Mr. Justin, to whom I mentioned the subject, thinks it a very good idea.

Annette was so delighted when I proposed that she should come on to Abbotsby and stay awhile with me.

It is all settled now, unless, when we reach Port Said, there should be letters from her aunt which interfere with our plans.     The letter which Annette expects to receive there will be an answer to the one in which she sent the news of her engaging herself as companion to Mrs. Marsham for a year.     If Mrs. Vermont should object to this, and wish her instead to go to Cheltenham, Annette must do so—at least, for a time; but I do not think there is much danger.     I fancy Mrs. Vermont will be only too glad for her penniless niece to be comfortably disposed of anywhere.

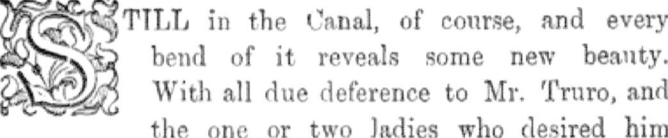

# CHAPTER IX

TILL in the Canal, of course, and every bend of it reveals some new beauty. With all due deference to Mr. Truro, and the one or two ladies who desired him to speak to me, I think it is just as profitable an employment of time to sit alone here, watching the exquisite reflections of the clouds, purple, amber, crimson, in the pools that lie scattered in the vast stretches of sand on each side of us, as to speculate with Mrs. Aberall's party as to how long Mrs. Flexon and the doctor will be in making up matters ; or with Mrs. Marsham's, on the exceeding bad taste which Mrs. Aberall displays in coming to dinner every evening in satins and jewels, which are only fit for a drawing-room.   As if every one did not know that her husband was already over head and ears in debt, and in consequence of gambling, too, people said.   Dreadful.   But it would come to an end before long, and perhaps that was why she was going home in such a hurry.

Sometimes we see a flock of flamingoes with the sunlight on their wings, showing like a rosy cloud upon the dim gray distance.  The white ones wade about by hundreds in these little sand pools.  At nightfall the jackals prowl stealthily along the level of the banks. Sometimes we get a curious mirage, the semblance of hills, water, and trees, where we know there can be nothing but a burning waste of sand. Then the beauty of daybreak over the low purple hills on our right, what a splendour of colour slowly chasing away the twilight, and turning every little shallow pool into a jewel of ruby, or amethyst, or sapphire! "Awfully pretty, isn't it?" said one of these young men to me this morning, as the first golden streaks quivered up behind the palm-trees of Ismailia.

Yes, indeed; awfully so, in a sense he never meant.

A strange thing happened yesterday afternoon.

Mrs. Flexon and Mrs. Mateby were chatting over their fancy work on the shady side of the deck. I don't mean that that was the strange thing, though Mrs. Flexon does not often waste her time over ladies. The reason of her doing so this afternoon was that all the gentlemen were on the lower deck, practising gymnastics, and ladies are not allowed on the lower deck, at least, they are considered out of place there.

We certainly do miss the gentlemen very much on these gymnastic afternoons. The conversation diminishes to a fine treble, or vanishes altogether. Often we go to sleep. I generally take to my writing. One hears the sound of yawning in all directions. Scarcely a laugh breaks in upon the dull monotony of the ship noises. We say to ourselves that afternoon is always "such a stupid time," though we know, as well as can be, we are not speaking the truth. Women, as a general rule, are not made to live exclusively with each other, however much I look forward to that condition for myself; and there is a wonderful brightening up amongst us when the tramp of feet and the faint odour of cigars announce that the gentlemen are coming.

Mrs. Flexon looks very pretty in mourning. It suits her blond hair and new-milky complexion. And that little blue and gold work-bag, which has not gone into mourning with the rest of her, sets off the black crape so effectively. So does the tobacco-pouch of cream-coloured kid, upon which she is embroidering such a dainty design in crimson floss. Why *is* Mrs. Flexon always at work upon masculine things? First it was a cigar-case, now it is a tobacco-pouch, and I have seen the materials for a gorgeous smoking-cap in her work-case. Sometimes I fancy the chief engineer will carry off that pouch. Then again the doctor seems more likely to secure the prize. The other day she was asking Mr. Justin's opinion of it. But we shall see.

I am not alone in my speculations. Two of the officers' wives were discussing the same subject yesterday. One of them laid a wager of a pair of white kid gloves that the doctor would have it before we land. The other backed the chief engineer. I fancy, if Mrs. Flexon's hand could accompany the gift, she would like to bestow it upon Mr. Justin, who treats her with such provoking coolness. But upon such a subject no decisive opinion can be pronounced, the points of the compass veering so from day to day.

They were sitting towards the fore part of the deck,

E

which commanded a prospect of the gymnastic operations
below. Now and then Mrs. Flexon would clasp her
hands with pretty eagerness as one or another of her
favourites tied himself into an exceptionally clever
knot, or succeeded in hanging by one foot to the
bar. Then she would bend over the tobacco-pouch
again, and pretend to take no notice of anything,
though both the doctor and the chief engineer, she
knew well enough, were casting longing glances for her
approval.

"*What* a plague!" she exclaimed, as she unwound
the last needleful of crimson silk, and then pettishly
threw away the empty paper, "that tiresome shop-
woman at Bombay told me that this skein would just
finish the wreath, and so I put the rest away in one of
my boxes down in the hold. I must get the doctor to
go down for it. I dare say he won't mind, poor fellow;
he is very good-natured."

"That depends," said Mrs. Mateby.

Mrs. Flexon tossed her well-set little head, and
looked pleased.

"You know, I think men are so stupid."

But just then the chief engineer turned himself
round and round the bar in such an astonishingly
clever manner that the conversation was suspended.
The two ladies rushed to the deck railing to obtain a
nearer view, Mrs. Flexon waved her handkerchief, Mrs.
Mateby cried bravo, and the fancy work was forgotten.

A gust of wind had blown the little empty paper ball
upon the folds of my dress. In an idle mood I picked it
up and began to untwist it, thinking of how I had done

the same, a few months after I reached India, with a
scrap of paper upon which, years before, my mother and
I had wound some of that fine, soft linen thread which
used to be the fashion for embroidery. Unfolding the
paper there in our thatched bungalow among the palm-
trees, I found it contained some notes, written by my
father for one of his lectures at the Abbotsby Museum.
How valueless it had been once, when he tossed it into
the waste-paper basket, and I twisted it up as a
foundation for the balls which used to take so much
winding, and over which my mother and I have had
many a pleasant chat as we sat in the firelight of winter
evenings. But how precious, coming upon it again,
when the hands that had traced the words had been so
long folded under the churchyard sod. How it recalled
to me quiet evenings at home in the little parlour where
he wrote out his lectures, and drew plans and diagrams
for their illustrations, I sometimes searching out references for him, or copying extracts, or stitching and
paging the sheets as he finished them. And other
evenings when he was gone from us, and Mark was at
college, and my mother and I were left alone in the old
home, but peaceful and contented still, for we had each
other, and I had not yet begun to think of the days
when I should be quite alone.

Very carefully I had treasured up that scrap of
paper amongst things which could never now be replaced, and since then I have had a strange sort of feeling about these little worthless ball foundations, which,
when unfolded, may reveal such an unexpected past.

This one, pettishly flung away by Mrs. Flexon, and

accidentally blown upon my dress, proved to be an envelope with the seal broken. It had been sent by hand, apparently, for there was neither stamp nor postmark on it. The address was written in a square, solid sort of hand—"*Miss Lislethorpe, The Parsonage*,"—and I think the writer must have been a methodical sort of man, for the date was put in the corner, August the fourteenth, August of last year. A little bit of Mrs. Flexon's red floss silk was still sticking to the gummed edge of the envelope.

I wondered how she could have come by it. The address was not in her own handwriting. I have seen that on the cards attached to her things here, a pretty school-room hand, with no curves in it, and long spidery tails to the y's and g's. And I know, too, for Annette has told me so, that she and Mrs. Flexon never visited each other at Moorkee, because, from the beginning, there was a sort of coolness between them; so that the envelope could not have been dropped or picked up by accident in that way.

How, then, did she come into possession of it? for Annette, whatever other faults she may have, is singularly neat and orderly in her habits, never leaving things lying about, or carelessly flinging them away. Indeed, particular though I am, she sometimes tries me by the length of time she spends in folding up her things, and sorting them, and putting them away with such entirely out-of-date precision, when all the while I am waiting to get her up on deck to see the beautiful clouds, and breathe what fresh air there is to be had now. Annette is the last person in the world to drop envelopes about in other people's houses. But as she was not there to give me any explanation of the matter, I put the bit of paper into my pocket, not thinking it necessary to return it to Mrs. Flexon, and went on with my knitting, always a favourite occupation with me, when I have anything curious to speculate about.

# CHAPTER X.

QUITE early last evening we were moored to the edge of the Canal for a troop-ship to pass us. The captain, who was dreadfully disappointed about it, said we should be fast there until daybreak, because, by the time the outward-bound vessel had got fairly away, it would be too late for us to steer farther on, navigation not being allowed in that part of the Canal after nightfall.

For awhile everybody looked sulky, for there was nothing to be seen all around us but an endless reach of sand, with stumpy tufts of heath here and there. If that stupid troop-ship would only have stopped us a day or two before, in front of the Sultan's palace at Ismailia, we should have enjoyed the delay ; but to be hurried past that little earthly Paradise of marble columns, palm-trees, oleanders, and cactuses, and stopped here in the centre of an infinite circumference of brownish-yellow ochre, was rather too provoking. I could only console myself by remembering that the ship *was* outward bound. If its passengers did not know what that meant, I did. Poor soldiers' wives, looking over the bulwarks, their honest faces rosy now with the sweet breezes of England and the Mediterranean—what

will they think, I wonder, of the alternate baking and
boiling, parching, frying, and steaming, to which they
will be subjected in that country whose "coral strand"
they have sung about in Sunday-school hymns? And
when, years hence, they can say of themselves "home-
ward bound," will any roses be left, and will the honest
eyes carry any brightness back to England? I am
afraid not. Indian life, even with all the surroundings
of wealth, position, and luxury, is not exactly a satis-
fying portion. What it must be shorn of these things,
and probably shorn, too, of the educated taste which
can watch with interest a new country and new customs,
I scarcely like to think.

Our captain, who always knows how to make the
best of a bad bargain, proposed that two of the ship's
boats should be let down, and that we should all take
a trip into the Arabian desert, by way of a change.
There was light enough yet for an hour or so, and
after that the young moon, which was peering out
now amongst a lot of fleecy clouds, would help us a
little. So, just as we were, we set off.

It was not so bad as might have been expected.
The mere sensation of being on *terra firma*—if sand
may be called that—was very refreshing. Those little
stumpy tufts of heath were beautiful when we bent
closely over them, and we found some lovely grasses
and red plants on the edges of the pools, to say nothing
of the delight of climbing to the top of the sand-banks,
and letting ourselves slip quietly down, after the fashion
of the childish sport which Mark and I used to enjoy
many a year ago at the seaside.

And when, by-and-by, we had worked off this small exuberance of activity, and set ourselves seriously to think where we were, there was a strange sort of awe in the feeling that the weary feet of those Israelitish exiles, whose laws we live by, and whose poems are our inspirations unto this day, had trodden the great wastes over which we looked. Where we stood now, those poor wanderers, waiters for a day that never came, had bided their time, and passed one by one into, let us hope, the other land of promise, whose rest would be sweeter to them than even that of Canaan. Perhaps, on some such quiet evening as this, whilst the young moon brightened upon the deepening blue of the west, as it was brightening upon us last night, the man Moses, worn out with the great burden of the people, cast himself down upon these sands, and called for help to his God. And here he must many a time have walked to and fro, thinking thoughts which shaped themselves into actions in that wondrous life, resolving plans and purposes whose results we know well enough ; perhaps remembering, as those in the storm and stress of life do remember, happier days, life in the Egyptian desert, with his wife and little ones, when no undisciplined people vexed him with its murmurings, and no voice of God had called him to those mountain heights, which are grand but so lonely.

Annette and I could not go far. She was soon tired, and as for myself, I dislike going to see things in troops, and being obliged to hear what every one says about them. If one must have Mrs. Flexon's flirtations, it was easier to tolerate them on board ship,

with surroundings of modern life to match, than there
in the Arabian desert, where one wanted to be alone
with one's own thoughts. To hear sometimes a little
bit about Moses from one of the chaplains, then a bit
about Colonel Aberall's gambling debts from Mrs.
Marsham; now a parallel between Israelitish human
nature and ours of the nineteenth century, and, abruptly
dashing into it, a disquisition from one of the young
men on the best way of swinging round a leaping bar,
crossed, perhaps, with a flippant remark or two from
the sceptical doctor, who, with a wave of his mighty
hand, dismissed the whole Hebrew history, laws, poetry,
morals, and inspirations, into the realms of fiction—this
was more trying to me than I can describe. Mr. Justin
was far ahead with the principal engineer, bent upon
reaching the nearest station, and having some talk with
the people there about the making of the Canal. I was
very glad when the captain, who wished to get back
to his ship, proposed to us, seeing Annette's tiredness,
that we should return with him ; so we delved our way
back through the ankle-deep sand, got into the boat,
and were soon comfortably established again in our own
special corner of the *Nawab*.

By ourselves, too, which was such a luxury. I think
we felt as pleased as children when their elders have gone
out, and they can do just as they like, only, instead of
improving the opportunity, as children generally do, by
extra noise, we enjoyed ourselves by listening to the stillness which could now almost be felt. Only, afar off, we
heard the laughter and chatter of our pilgrims in the
Arabian desert, and at the other end of the vessel some

of the sailors were singing, as it seemed to me, deftly and musically enough. I don't think I was so sorry, after all, that the troop-ship *had* stopped us just there.

Suddenly I remembered the little scrap of paper in my pocket. The excitement of seeing our vessel moored, and the big ship passing, and then being rowed across to the opposite bank for our trip into Arabia, had driven it quite out of my mind. I took it now, gave it to Annette, and said :

" Do you know that writing ? "

What a sudden flash of eagerness came over her usually quiet, uninterested face ! She seized the paper, and looked at me almost angrily.

" Yes, I do. It is Captain Asperton's. Where did you get that ? "

" Mrs. Flexon threw it away this afternoon, when she had unwound the last needleful of floss silk from it. The wind happened to blow it into my lap, and I opened it, scarcely thinking what I was doing. I thought I might as well show it to you."

" Yes, indeed." But Annette was almost as quiet as ever again now. " Thank you very much."

She bent down over the envelope, as though she would study every letter of the handwriting there. For myself I had never thought of its being Captain Asperton's, and even when I did know, I scarcely thought of what Mrs. Flexon's possession of it might mean. But whilst she held it so tightly in her thin little fingers, turning it to the lamplight, and examining it so carefully, ideas began to shape themselves in my mind more clearly. I recalled that conversation between Mrs. Truro and the officer's wife.

"Did Mrs. Flexon know Captain Asperton?" I asked.

"Yes, I believe so. She knew all the gentlemen in Moorkee. She was staying there during the whole of the hot weather before papa died. She used to have afternoon teas and Badmintons, you know, and every one went."

"What! when she was so lately a widow?"

"Yes. I don't think that made any difference. People used to say she had not cared for him very much."

"And did this Captain Asperton go too?"

"I don't know, I'm sure," said Annette, with a little touch of irritation in her manner. "It was not my business to know where Captain Asperton went. Everybody goes everywhere in a place like Moorkee."

Annette thinks I know nothing. And it is clear that she does not wish to tell me anything. But how tightly she held the envelope, and how her face kept changing as she examined it.

"Yes," I replied, "I suppose so. And perhaps some time, when he was at her house, he might have wanted to send a note to you about something, and so wrote it there, and then he might think of something else, and open it, and then have to use a fresh envelope. That would account, you know, for her having this one."

"Yes, but," said Annette, with still that little touch

of irritation and reserve strangely mingling with restlessness in her manner, " I never had a note from
Captain Asperton. I only know the handwriting, because papa heard from him several times about a man
in the regiment."

That rather altered the aspect of matters. And did
not alter them, either, in Mrs. Flexon's favour. As
poor old Hilary Bennet used to say, " It lies very strong
upon my mind " that our fascinating fellow-passenger
had taken out the contents of that envelope, whatever
they may be, and then had forgotten to dispose of it
safely, thrown it carelessly aside, and used it next time
she wanted to twist up a ball for the skeins of silk which
gentlemen are always so ready to wind for her. A
stupid trick, but still I can imagine such a woman doing
it.

Annette did not seem disposed to talk, and I said
no more. It was an uncomfortable ending to the quiet
hour which might have been so pleasant.

But I am tired now, and yet I want to write it all
down. I shall come up again after dinner to finish. I
shall not rest until the history of this envelope is
found out.

# CHAPTER XI

OST of the night I lay awake, partly because it was so wonderfully still, and partly because I could not get Annette's affairs out of my mind. When things get into a tangle, I am never comfortable until I see my way through, in some way or other ; and last night I was wondering how Mrs. Flexon could be made to clear up the mystery of that envelope coming into her possession.

I could hear Annette turning over and over. Poor child ! it was a restless time for her. This morning her eyes looked heavy with watching, and, I think, weeping too ; but she said nothing.

I knew she would not have courage to enter upon the subject herself with Mrs. Flexon, shielded as that excellent woman always is by the most bewitching effrontery, to say nothing of a more or less numerous phalanx of admirers, each of whom is ready to fight her battles and slay her enemies. So I asked, trying not to make the matter appear of very much importance, if she would give me the envelope, and let me ask for an explanation.

"You know," I said, "you have a right to that, at

any rate.   No one can deny that the letter, whatever it
may have been, was intended for you ; but you need
not make any disagreeableness with Mrs. Flexon about
that.    Only let us find out, if we can, how she got hold
of the envelope."

"Very well," said Annette, quietly, taking out of a
little pocket-book, which was carefully locked up in her
writing-desk, the now historical bit of paper.    "But
don't let Mrs. Flexon keep it.    Be sure that you bring
it back to me."

As if I should fail to do that.   But I promised ;
and first thing after breakfast sallied forth on my
expedition, with, I am afraid, a little touch of satisfaction in the prospect of being able to make Mrs. Flexon
uncomfortable.

She was looking perfectly ladylike in black cambric,
with any quantity of diaphanous muslin frilling about
her throat and wrists.   Her luxurious deck-chair was
drawn up in one of the cosiest spots under the awning,
somewhat screened from public observation, and the
doctor was stretched at her feet, holding a skein of floss
silk for her to wind.   I suppose it was the skein she
referred to yesterday, and he has been down into the
hold to fetch it for her, or guard her whilst she fetched
it for herself.

Without preface of polite observation about the
weather, or anything else, for, as Mrs. Flexon never
volunteers to speak to me, our communications are
necessarily of a business character, I went up to her
and said :

" Miss Lislethorpe thinks I had better ask you for an explanation about this envelope. You threw it away yesterday, when you had taken the last needleful of silk from it, and the wind tossed it into my lap."

"Oh ! and you opened it, I suppose," she said, languidly, not yet troubling herself to look at the writing, but just stretching her white hand in the direction of the envelope. "One moment, please, doctor. I should have thought you would have brought it back to me, Miss Brown."

" I am very glad I did not," I replied, tartly, "as it does not seem to belong to you. It is addressed to Miss Lislethorpe. If any apologies are necessary for opening it, I must offer them to her."

Mrs. Flexon *did* look at the writing now, and she did more than stretch her white hand in the direction of the envelope. She seized upon it, expecting, of course, to get it into her possession ; but I was holding it in a tight, vice-like grip of my own, and, fortunately, Captain Asperton uses good paper, stout and strong, that will stand a pull.

Mrs. Flexon never turns red, never looks confused, never loses that elegant self-possession which sits so charmingly upon her. She only put on an appearance of surprise when I refused to let her have the envelope.

" The address is in Captain Asperton's writing," I said, "and Miss Lislethorpe would like to know where the envelope came from."

A very malignant expression broke over Mrs.

Flexon's face, but she was herself in a moment again, and replied as pleasantly as if we had been the best friends in the world :

"Really it is very kind of you to take so much trouble on Miss Lislethorpe's behalf. She is exceedingly fortunate to have met with some one who takes so much interest in her correspondence."

What delicious effrontery ! As if Mrs. Flexon herself was not the " some one " who had taken so much interest in *that* matter. But I did not say anything, and she went on :

"You know I should be delighted to give you any information ; but positively I cannot take upon myself to relate the pedigree of every scrap of paper which comes into my possession, and I do not remember that ever I saw this particular piece before. I am not the only lady on board who is using balls of silk or cotton, or even Scotch fingering."

This was added with a dainty little sneer, in allusion to the stout, comfortable pair of stockings which I had been knitting since we came on board. But Mrs. Flexon had better not have said it, and in the presence of the doctor, too, for it only put a little more determination into my own manner as I replied :

"Perhaps not ; but I believe you are the only one who is using silk of this particular colour."

And, still keeping a judiciously tight hold of the envelope, I held it so that the little bit of silk, which was yet clinging to it, touched and matched that of the latest worked rosebud on Mrs. Flexon's tobacco-pouch.

And then I matched it with the skein which the doctor
was holding.

"Oh! never mind," he said, with a bored expression.
" What is the use of making such a fuss over it ?   It is
most likely an envelope which Miss Lislethorpe herself
has dropped since we came on board, and some one has
picked it up and used it to wind cotton upon.   What
were you saying, Mrs. Flexon, about that French vessel
just in advance of us ?"

Mrs. Flexon began to tell him, evidently expecting
that thus she should get rid of me.   But I am not the
woman to be treated rudely in that way, and their
discourtesy made me stick to my purpose more resolutely
than ever.   I waited until she had repeated her remark
about the French vessel, and then I returned to the
charge.

"It is not an envelope which Miss Lislethorpe has
dropped, Dr. Byte, for she knows the handwriting to be
Captain Asperton's, and she says she has never received
a letter from him."

" Then most likely it belonged to some other lady
on board," said the doctor, rather illogically, " and she
has dropped it.   Shall I take it round for you and
ask ?"

" No, thank you, there is no need for you to take
that trouble.   I saw Mrs. Flexon throw it away when
she had finished the silk, and a gust of wind blew it to
me.   If you remember, Mrs. Flexon, I was sitting close
to you at the time."

" You don't say so," Mrs. Flexon replied, mildly.

F

"I was really quite unconscious that we were such near neighbours. We are generally so far apart."

This was a vicious little thrust at me, sitting, as I do, at the end of that long table, whilst Mrs. Flexon dispenses her smiles several meridians nearer the equator of the captain's presence. But I ignored that, too, and stood my ground like a woman who has fought her own way for twenty years in India. Nothing but facts should crush me, I was determined, and no facts had been brought to bear upon me yet.

"Perhaps it would have been more convenient," I said, "if we had been farther apart yesterday; but, I assure you, the ball of paper came to me just as it left your own hand, after you had taken it from your own work-case. Its pedigree so far, at any rate, is very clearly ascertained. All that I want now is to trace it a step farther."

Mrs. Flexon now assumed the rôle of hauteur, combined with feminine incapacity. She fixed me with a well-bred stare, then turned to her companion, and said :

"Dr. Byte, *do* come to my assistance. I am being positively broken to pieces upon the wheel of Miss Brown's masculine intellect. I had no idea that a woman could be so inexorable. I really begin to feel as if I were going through an examination for the Civil Service. Miss Brown, are you sure you were never at the London University ?"

"No, Mrs. Flexon," I replied, watching her as she lay back at full length in her chair, and studying the

curious changes which passed over her face, as she
turned it, first with disguised but not entirely un-
embarrassed dislike upon myself, and then, with sudden
sweetness of womanly appeal, upon the doctor, who
still lay at her feet, holding the skein of silk. "I
was never at any university but my mother's, and
she tried to teach me to help those who could not
help themselves. Shall I say to Miss Lislethorpe,
then, that you have no explanation to offer about this
envelope ?"

"Certainly you may, Miss Brown ; and at the same
time you may congratulate her, from me, on having
secured the services of such an able champion as yourself. Oh ! Dr. Byte, you *naughty* man, you have let
a link of the silk slip off your hand, and now it is all
in confusion. Thank you very much, Miss Brown. I
am so sorry to have given you any trouble."

With that she resumed her conversation with the
doctor, and I returned to tell Annette the result of my
interview. I felt more sure than ever that my thoughts
about the matter were the right thoughts, though they
left a very troublesome stain upon Mrs. Flexon's
straightforwardness.

We agreed that it would be better to say nothing
more about it at present, not mention the matter to
any one else ; but I said that, as we were going to remain together for some time, we should most likely
think of some way of clearing up the mystery.

Annette looks restless and ill at ease. I do not
wonder. But she says nothing, and when the subject

comes up between us, I only talk of it as a judge might talk of some curiously interesting case which he was trying to get to the bottom of, not at all as if I knew that it touched and stirred her very life.

# CHAPTER XII.

ESTERDAY we passed Port Saïd, and the grand event of the voyage happened, namely, getting letters and papers from home. How eagerly we all awaited the arrival of the little steam-tug which brought them and the ship's agent on board. How we all crowded to the bulwarks as boat after boat came alongside, thinking that each might be bringing the wished-for news from a far country. And how we buzzed round the captain when he appeared at last on the poop deck holding aloft the big bundle which was to be divided amongst us; getting letters on board ship is the best part of the voyage.

Annette had the one she expected from Mrs. Vermont. It was just the letter which a woman such as I imagine Mrs. Vermont is, would write. She congratulates her niece upon the energy and promptitude she has displayed in making the engagement with Mrs. Marsham, and thinks the companionship is a most admirable opening for her, combining, as it does, almost nominal duties with the position of a lady. She says that she should have been very glad to have received Annette at Cheltenham, if nothing else had turned up

for her ; but, at the same time, she thinks it is much
better for her to be independent. She speaks of their
house being rather small, with only one spare room for
visitors, so that it would be slightly inconvenient to
have any one staying with them for an indefinite time.
But if ever Annette should be out of health, or wanting
a holiday, or anything of that sort, she must remember
that her aunt will be very glad to see her for a week or
two.

Then she adds that Mr. Vermont would certainly
have come to meet the *Nawab*, but, unfortunately, he
is so much out of health just now, owing to the severe
east winds, that it is quite impossible for him to take
such a journey. And as for herself, she is quite a
novice in such matters, and would not know either
where to look for the ship, or what to do when she had
found it. So she hopes dear Annette will excuse her
coming up to town, but she will give directions to some
responsible person to see after the luggage and do
everything that is necessary. She concludes by committing her niece to the kind care of all-merciful
Providence which watches over the sparrows and feeds
the young ravens when they cry, from which slightly
misapplied quotation I infer that Mrs. Vermont herself
does not intend to supplement that Providence by any
exertions of her own. Perhaps she does not think it
would be correct to do so. It might be taking Annette
too much out of the hands of the Supreme One who has
promised to care for her.

So now there is nothing to prevent her from coming
with me to Abbotsby and staying as long as we both

find it pleasant. She is very glad about this ; it makes
a sort of rest for her where so much else is unrestful.

I had a letter from my solicitor, with some information about Aunt Miriam's affairs. Also another, whose
external appearance, I think, would not commend me to
the rest of the passengers, for it was from Keren, and
the address was a marvel of the most irregular text-
hand, very explicit, and completely covering the back
of the large envelope. She says that Mrs. Proud's
rooms will be quite ready for me. She is having the
old house completely cleaned from top to bottom, and
everything arranged just as it used to be in the " dear
master's time," and she hopes I shall live to have my
health and happiness there for many a year to come.
She also says she has made up her mind to stop with me
to her dying day, and serve me as she did the master and
mistress and Miss Miriam before me ; for, thank God,
she is as hale and strong as ever she used to be in the
best of times, let alone a touch of rheumatics when the
wind is contrary, and wishes nothing better for herself
than to stop in the family where she entered five-and-
forty years ago, a slip of a girl not worth her meat and
lodging.

And a great deal more to the same effect, for Keren
was never one who could epitomise.

Thank you, you good old soul ! That is better than
committing me, along with the sparrows and ravens, to
the indefiniteness of an all-merciful Providence, and
then looking out for a comfortable almshouse for
yourself, which I dare say you might have got long ago,
for there are plenty of them in Abbotsby. I think,

after all, spite of a few faults of spelling and grammar, that letter of yours will make a better show in the courts above than the other which, with such unexceptionable crest and caligraphy, travelled beside it to poor little orphan Annette.

What a business it was, reaching Port Saïd ! We stayed from four in the afternoon to daybreak of next morning, and I don't think the whole time anybody slept a wink, so that we are feeling rather subdued to-day. First of all, police officers had to come on board, before any one could land ; curious bearded fellows, with big burnous cloaks and very fierce eyes, and belts stuck full of murderous-looking weapons. When they came trooping up the ladder by the vessel's side, Mrs. Flexon rushed into the arms of the first gentleman she could see, who turned out to be Mr. Justin, thinking no other than that pirates were boarding the ship. And really I did not blame her. One could have given those fierce black eyes credit for anything

After we had shown a clear bill of health the pirates departed, and the tug of war began. We were literally besieged by swarms of boats whose owners, swarthy Moors, Egyptians, Arabs, Copts, Armenians, or Maltese, wanted to take us ashore, and would not, by any quantity of ,English or Hindustani, be persuaded that any of us preferred staying quietly where we were. Other boats were laden with oranges and vegetables for the provisioning of the ship, others with fresh fruits, others with cakes, sweets, and toys. Most of the passengers did finally go on shore, returning at all hours of the night and morning,

so that to go to sleep was simply impossible. After dark,
the coaling of the ship began, and continued until about
an hour before we started, the rattling and dragging of
the bags forming a sort of bassoon *obbligato* to all the
rest of the noises that were going on.

The three young men who have nothing to do, employed their spare time in going backwards and forwards
between the ship and the town, buying all varieties of
possible and impossible things. I believe it was partly
owing to them that we were so beset with boats, for the
Port Said people soon find out if a man cannot say no,
especially when that weakness is accompanied by a few
pounds in his pocket. For days after we left the place,
those young men came out every morning with something new in the shape of hats, scarves, ties, gloves,
walking-sticks, or slippers; and as for the boxes of
Turkish delight which they demolished, who shall count
them?

One sees all sorts of people at Port Saïd : Hindoo,
Mohamedan, Egyptian, Arab, curiously mingled with
the piquant Frenchman, the grave Italian, the polite
Spaniard, the handsome Maltese. The mighty rivers of
Eastern and Western life meet here. Leaving it, we said
good-bye to the morning-land where I have spent nearly
half my life. Port Saïd has opened to us the gate of
Europe. Whilst yet we lingered between the sand-banks
of the Canal, we came upon scattered remnants of Eastern
habit and custom which will meet us again no more.
At Malta, where we touch next, there will be nothing to
remind us of the palm-trees and plantains of India. I
am so glad to be near home, and yet I know that often

and often I shall shut my eyes to see in imagination those mild-eyed, white-robed Hindoos and leisurely-stepping, peaceful women, whom in the flesh I shall never behold again.

With my letter yesterday came a copy of *The Standard*, kindly sent to me by my solicitor, I suppose, because it contained a review of an Indian book whose writer I know. In the bustle of passing the port and getting through into the Mediterranean, to say nothing of the interest of reading the home letters, I thought no more about it ; but this afternoon I took it up and spent an hour or two over it. Strangely enough, I found in its columns of military intelligence the announcement that the regiment which Mrs. Truro says Captain Asperton changed into, is ordered to Canada immediately.

How curious that I should just have alighted upon that piece of information. How many and many a time have I read *The Standard* without ever giving a moment's notice to the military column ; and this afternoon, because I was in an idle mood, and cared neither to write nor work, I found out something which may touch Annette's whole life.

I do not know whether I am glad or sorry. It seems to put a definite stop to finding out anything more about Mrs. Flexon's deceit, if deceit it is. And it puts a definite stop, too, to any little castles in the air which I might have built about a possible meeting between Captain Asperton and Annette. Since I heard that conversation between Mrs. Truro and Mrs. Beverley, I have often fancied how delightful it would be if by any chance Captain Asperton came to Abbotsby whilst

Annette was with me. I have turned over and over in my own mind how it could be arranged, and what a delightful clearing up and mutual understanding there would be. I have seen those two in my little parlour at home, or sauntering up and down under the lime-trees that border the garden, as happy as ever they were in the old days at Moorkee ; nay, happier, for the thought of separation past, gives joy its finest touch of complete-ness. And all the brightness would come back to Annette's eyes, and the colour to her face, and we could afford to be magnanimous even to Mrs. Flexon.

Now, of course, that can never be. At least, it seems to have gone too far out of the range of probability. But then there is a feeling of relief in knowing that it has so gone. I need not build castles in the air any more. That little announcement in *The Standard* has dropped a portcullis between Annette and any hope she might have been cherishing about things coming right again. I think there is certainty for her now, though only the certainty of separation. Perhaps that is better than the dreadful uncertainty of waiting, and wondering, and hoping. I showed her the paragraph this afternoon. She said nothing. I could not tell from her face whether she was glad or sorry. I have a sort of feeling that she thinks it is better so. Thinking what she must think, that Captain Asperton is fickle and unfaithful, it must be a relief to her to know that there is no possibility of their meeting again in England. I sometimes wish I dare tell her what I have heard. I sometimes even think I ought to tell her. But then it was only the gossip of two women, and I have no right even to pre-

sume that she would wish to be informed of it.  With
all her gentleness and sweetness, one must not go a step
too far with Annette Lislethorpe.  I have no right to
repeat to her what may vex her whole life with un-
resolved doubt, when I have not perfect certainty that
what I say is the truth.  I will hold my peace, only
being to her such a friend as I can.

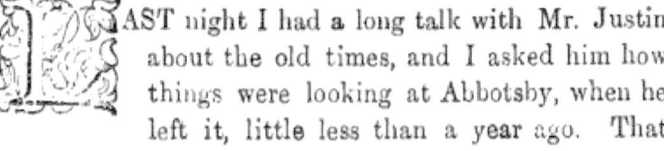AST night I had a long talk with Mr. Justin about the old times, and I asked him how things were looking at Abbotsby, when he left it, little less than a year ago. That is very recent information to one who has never seen it, nor any one who came from it, for nearly twenty years.

He says I shall see very little change in the place. Since the passing through it of the new line from London to the north-west of England, there has been an increase of business, but that has chiefly concentrated itself in the streets round about the station, and in Westgate, the street which leads almost direct from there to the Abbey church and castle. Our dear old Northgate, being snugly out of the way of most objects of interest, has been let alone. So has the whole of that end of the town, in consequence of which rents have fallen very much. But that will not affect me, as I am going to live in my own house. Most of the fashionable people have left Northgate now, and are settled at the station end of the town, where an entirely new neighbourhood has sprung up.

Mrs. Carbery is living in the same house, at the north end of the Abbey church. Of course she is very infirm now, and never goes out; but Mr. Justin says her intellect is as bright as ever. She takes quite a lively interest in the history of her own times, has the paper read to her every day, knows what new books are coming out, what topics of social interest are being talked about, and lives almost as much abreast of the age as any one in the House of Commons. Mrs. Carbery is a standing proof of the advantage of a well-used brain. She has always given hers plenty of work, but not too much; and so it is serving her faithfully, even to the end. How I do long to hear her talk of the days when my father and mother were bride and bridegroom in the little house which is to be my home.

I asked Mr. Justin about that house, too; but his recollections of it do not seem to be very definite. He says he thinks everything looks pretty much the same— at least, no change has struck him when he has happened to go past the place; but I can see he takes no special interest in it, beyond liking to be able to answer my questions. When I ask him about the very trees which I remember so well, the trees which my father planted, and beneath which I have watched him walking many and many a time, with head bent and hands loosely folded behind him, or the little garden paths where, as a child, I played, and the old sun-dial and the summer-house, he only says he cannot exactly say. He has a general idea that things are much as they used to be.

Mr. Justin has no great love for the past. There is something in his nature which rather spreads out than casts its roots deeply down. I suppose it is the develop-ment of the same disposition which, when he was a little

boy, made him not care much for keepsakes and things
of that sort.   He likes to look around, not behind him ;
to find out fresh things, rather than to cherish the
memory of those which have long since passed away.   I
suppose that is the right sort of disposition for making
a useful man ; but I begin to see that we shall not often
talk of the old times together.

Then I asked about the Northgate house, in which
he still lives.   He says he has not had it altered at all
since his father's time.   It is church property, belonging
to the feoffees of the Abbey, and it came to him with
about half of the ninety-nine years' lease unexpired ; so
that he may look upon it as his home for the remainder
of his life, if he chooses to stay in Abbotsby.   I think
he is more proud of it as a fine specimen of seventeenth-
century architecture, than attached to it because of any
memories which it recalls.   He was quite amused with
me for remembering so well everything about it, from the
carving on the oaken balustrades to the pattern of the
grape and vine-leaf cornice in the drawing-room, and the
number of the gilded nobs on the old-fashioned mirror
which was set in a panel over the fire-place.   But, indeed,
I have counted them many a time when Mark and I went
to have tea with little Gregory, and I sat in a high-
backed chair, with my feet dangling down, gravely eating the piece of cake which was always given to me
before we went away.   Mr. Justin remembers nothing of
all this ; but he says he has had every bit of paint
scraped off the fine old black oak mouldings, and the
floors polished, and everything restored as nearly as
possible to the style in which the house was first built,

two hundred years ago. He intends to have it completely refurnished when he settles at Abbotsby, and then it will be one of the prettiest houses in the place.

I felt sufficiently at my ease to say what a pity it seemed that he had not a wife to share it with him. One cannot always venture on any sort of familiar remarks to Mr. Justin, because of that stand-off manner which he has sometimes; but he did not seem at all offended with me. A pleasant, almost tender expression came into his face, as if he had some sweet secret known to himself alone. And his eyes, as they turned quickly away from mine, were full of thoughts with which I could not intermeddle. Perhaps he has found some one already. I hope I shall be able to like her, or I shall be shut out from him, and that would make me sad.

Here I paused for a long time, thinking about many things. I wonder what sort of a girl Gregory Justin would choose for his wife. Of course, she must be young and very pretty. A man in his position, marrying for the first time, can command those qualifications. And I suppose he would like her to be of very good family, a step or two higher in that respect than himself, perhaps, though the Recorder of Abbotsby was always a man of position in the place. I am not quite sure whether she must be of a mild, yielding temper, a modest little violet, to unfold its perfume only in the shelter of her own home; or whether she must be brilliant and society-loving, a woman for him to be proud of when he takes her out into public, or gathers together his friends and neighbours in the drawing-room of which she is to be queen. The violet would, I think, make a better man of him, would foster a certain something wanting just now in his character; but the rose would make him lift his head more proudly among his fellows, and do and dare more greatly, perhaps, for the sake of being praised by her. So I think it will be the rose, though I wish it might be the violet.

But what a waste of time for me either to think or wish anything about it. Gregory Justin will make his choice with respect only to himself and the woman he loves. He will not go up and down, asking the opinion of his friends. Only I hope she will like me and let me be kind to her, whether she be rose or violet.

Annette sits beside me now, watching a great, white-sailed vessel which is ploughing its way onward. How pretty the delicate, finely-cut little profile looks, as she leans her head against the dark plaid shawl which I have spread over the skylight. Something is coming back into Annette's face. Not the brightness which I remember at Moorkee, never that again, I think, but rather the wistful quietness and dawning peace of the face I used to study in church, whilst Mr. Lislethorpe preached those very long sermons.

It is three days now since we saw in *The Standard* that account of Captain Asperton's regiment being ordered to Canada. I thought it would make a difference to her, and it has done so. Though she says nothing to me about it, and I say nothing to her, I know that she is much more at rest. Instead of taking everything now in that listless, resigned way which used to be so pitiful, she begins to talk almost brightly about what we will do when we are settled down in the old house ; how she will help me to teach the little girl I mean to train for service, and how she will learn to be a clever housekeeper herself. That will soon come to her ; she has neat, dainty, orderly ways, and that carefulness about small things which is the essence of good management. And we talk about the books we will read, and the long walks we will take as she gets stronger, and how I am to show her all the places I remembered when I was a little girl—for Annette has a love for the past, a clinging to it almost equal to my own. God grant it may never embitter her life, but from this time forward be only a source of peace to her, as it is to me.

This may partly be because it is settled now that she need not go to her aunt at Cheltenham. I know the poor girl dreaded that very much ; but I think it is more because of the uncertainty which has been taken out of her life. She knows now how the days lie before her, quiet days, uneventful days, which will be filled with little pleasures and little duties, and whose happiness must be chiefly that of a contented spirit. I wish no other happiness for myself now ; but I must remember that Annette is a girl, with a girl's heart, and a girl's longing. And I must not be surprised if sometimes the old restlessness comes back upon her. She cannot begin at once and go right on with never a pause.

Looking up from this page half an hour ago, I found Mr. Justin studying us both as if we had been vessels

in the distance that had to be accounted for.   When our
eyes met, he turned away and began to walk up and down
the deck.   I wonder what he was thinking about—was
it the rose or the violet?   He seemed to have gone
completely out of himself, almost as Annette used to
go, when first we left Bombay, and I used to bring her
up here and wrap her up in shawls, and make her lean
her head against my shoulder.   Only I think she had
gone out after a happy past, and he was going out after
a happy future, which makes all the difference.

# CHAPTER XIV.

HIS morning Mr. Justin brought me a photograph of the old Northgate house to look at. There are very few of its date left in Abbotsby now. All those that belong to the Mayor and Corporation are being pulled down, as the leases expire, to make room for modern buildings, which will fetch a better rent. Only those in the possession of the Abbey feoffees are carefully preserved. They know well enough how little interest there would be in Abbotsby if these old relics of the past were swept away.

I am glad the Northgate house is in such good hands. Mr. Justin wanted me to notice in this photograph how beautifully the carved cornices above and below the tier of windows on the second floor have been brought out. I don't know if cornices is the proper word. It is rather a little belt or frieze ornament which runs along the base of each projecting storey. There are three of these projecting storeys, with two gables at the top of all, and another beautiful frieze under the gables.

In bygone times, when poor little Abbotsby had a season of its own, Northgate was the fashionable quarter

of the town, the resort of the county people, who came
for the balls, and routs, and assemblies which were
plentiful enough then. But even in my childish days,
the spirit of commercial enterprise, consequent upon the
completion of the first railroad, had begun to invade the
place. The county families, being brought by that
same railroad within easy reach of London, ceased to
come to Abbotsby any more for the winter season.
Their mansions, after standing unoccupied for years,
were pulled down, and magnificent shops, with no end
of plate-glass and decorative art about them, replaced
the beautiful old-timbered houses, whose high-pitched
gables and projecting stones and carven brackets had
once been the pride and glory of the place.

Still, even when I left Abbotsby twenty years ago,
a few of these were left in the Northgate, with their old-
fashioned gardens behind, reaching down to the river,
gardens rich with elm-trees and colonies of rooks, and
musical in April mornings with the pipe of blackbird and
thrush. Old Mr. Justin's was the best of them. It was
opposite the judge's residence, a tall, forbidding-looking
mansion of Queen Anne's time, and opposite the "Star
and Garter," too, the chief inn of Abbotsby in those
days. Its owner, when I first remember it, was a staunch
Tory, and to his hostelry, therefore, at election times the
blue candidate, when he chanced to be successful, was
triumphantly "chaired," myself and my brother Mark
always going to see the procession from old Mr. Justin's
drawing-room windows.

How vividly I remember, even yet, our delight in
those processions, which now I suppose would appear to

us, were they still in existence, the veriest tinsel and gilt-paper buffooneries. What a joy it was to have our best of possible things put on, always with plentiful dashes of blue about them, for both my father and the Recorder were Tories, and to sit at the middle window of the Northgate drawing-room, Mark, little Gregory, and myself, with some responsible person behind to take care that we did not lean too far out, and with refreshing relays of biscuits and ginger-wine given us from time to time, to make the long hours of waiting pass more pleasantly.

How picturesque the narrow old street looked! Most of the people were Conservative in those days, and so nearly every window had its cluster of ladies dressed in the favourite colour, and banners of blue and silver fluttering in the wind, and festoons of blue rosettes were wreathed across the street, and venetian masts reared from the gables, and the ribbon upon the "Star and Garter" signboard was newly painted for the occasion, and every little boy had a card, with the name of the successful candidate on it, in his cap; and even the dirty little urchins, selling sweets and gingerbread on the pavement below, would wrap their good stuffs up, for that day only, in papers of the favourite colour.

The sole break in the general cerulean aspect of things was made by the magnificent new Italian warehouse, or, as we Tories called it, grocer's shop, which had lately been erected a few doors below the "Star and Garter." It alone blossomed out in a splendour of gold, which served to make the surrounding blue bluer still. At election times it used to be wreathed with oranges. A huge rosette of that desirable fruit was placed over the door, the outline of every window was filled in with the same, curved lines of them hung across the resplendent white front of the shop, and, after dark, a lighted dip candle stuck into an orange, was placed in each pane, producing, what we then thought, a most dazzling illumination. Next day the fruit was sold for half price, the Abbotsby little boys not being averse to the taste of tallow. I believe the festoons and other decorations went back again into the shop, re-appearing probably from time to time upon our dinner-tables.

Oh, the intense excitement felt by us children as the first burst of hurrahs, from the farther end of the winding street, announced that the procession was at hand! What awe as an advanced guard of special constables, with their staves, formed into line in front of the "Star and Garter," looking as fierce as though they meant to kill us all there and then! What shouts of delight—the previous awe having abated—as the first banner, perilously supported by two very much overweighted men, reeled and tumbled into sight round the nearest turn, followed by a band playing : "See the conquering hero comes !" And then the long file, four deep, of voters, each with a blue rosette in his coat, and a card in his hat, and more banners and more flags, and more bands of music, and finally the conquering hero himself—the successful candidate—carried in his chair on the shoulders of ten or a dozen men. How he bowed and smiled to us all, looking as happy as possible, though I have thought since what an uncomfortable

seat it must have been for him, almost as risky as that
which it represented in Parliament, and which he was
pretty sure to lose at the next election, there being
such numbers of Conservative candidates for Abbotsby,
and the borough having no special hereditary pre-
ferences.

After having seen him safely deposited in the courtyard of the " Star and Garter," we were bundled into
a cab, under charge of our old nurse, and, disgraceful
little turncoats that we were, hurried off to the
business end of the town to see the whole thing
done over again in orange, if, as was often the case,
a member was returned on each side.

The assizes, too, twice a year. Why do I never
see anything now — I mean in the way of public
spectacles — which impresses me with the awe I felt
in seeing the judges go in solemn procession from
their residence at the top of the Northgate to the
Abbey church for morning service on Assize Sunday,
preceded by the mayor, the corporation, the town-
officers, mace-bearers, sheriffs, clerks, and Gregory's
papa in his recorder's gown of black velvet? Good
old Mr. Justin, always ready with a smile for the
three eager little faces poking out of his drawing-room
window.

How we held our breath—at least, Mark and I
did, not being intimate with such magnificence—when,
through the gateway of the closely-walled residence
garden, the High Sheriff's state carriage appeared,
with its embroidered hammer-cloth edged with waving
golden fringe, its velvet-coated, white-wigged, red-faced

coachman, its majestic footmen behind, looking down
upon the gaping multitude with calm superiority from
the vantage ground of the dicky, the crimson-liveried
trumpeters with their bannerets, the retainers with
their glittering halberds, ranged in close rank on each
side of the carriage, to protect the sacred object of all
this splendour from injury and insult. How fierce
those retainers looked—at least, how fierce we *thought*
they looked. Of course, men with tall battle-axes, like
those in the pictures in our great History of England,
*must* be fierce, there was no help for it. I almost think
we looked for the stain of blood upon those battle-axes ;
but, if so, we never saw any. Sure I am of this, though,
that we, one and all, even Gregory himself, felt that
if we were naughty just then, there would be no chance
for us, with the guardians, supporters, and represen-
tatives of justice so close upon us.

Then the Abbey bells began to ring. All the parish
churches in Abbotsby joined in ; the trumpeters blew a
mighty blast, and the carriage, with its massy glories
of coachman, hammer-cloth, gold fringe, coats of arms,
majestic footmen, and sacred occupant, moved slowly
forward with a dignity that became the occasion, we
three little people gazing in a silent wonder which would
not let us clap our hands, or laugh, or indulge in the
shouts which came so naturally to us at election
times.

For what words could describe the feelings with
which we peered into the mysterious depths of the
carriage, and dimly discerned the central object himself, a mass of fur and scarlet cloth, surmounted by

a wig which was calculated to strike terror into the breast of the beholder? We knew that that man, if we might be impertinent enough to call him anything so common, let me rather say the object clothed in scarlet and fur, was a *judge ;* that a single word of his could not only punish little boys and girls who disobeyed their nurses, but could send grown-up men and women away beyond the seas, or shut them fast in stone cells, or hang them by the neck until they were dead. And here we were, within reach of him. How I used to shudder at the thought ! How conscience awoke within me, and reminded me of all the buttons I had pulled off my frocks, all the elastic I had iniquitously drawn from the wrists of my Lisle thread gloves whilst listening to the sermon in church, all the blots I had made in my copy-book, all the rips and rents in my garden pinafore. Oh ! how earnestly sometimes, when a child of seven, looking at that judicial pageant from the windows of the old Northgate house, have I put my little hands together under my tippet, and asked God to forgive me for being naughty, these afore-mentioned sins pressing altogether too painfully upon me. So that the law may be said to have gained its ends, so far as I was concerned.

But that mysterious object in scarlet and fur ! He was a judge, we knew ; but was he anything else ? Did he always wear that wig ? Did it grow upon him ? How did he lie down at nights ? Did he lie down at all, or was he put into a box, fur, scarlet cloth, wig, and everything, until it was time to judge the wicked people again ? Did he ever want anything to eat ?

Had he any little boys of his own, and did he kiss them and play with them, or only *judge* them ?   Was he ever a little boy himself?   No, of course not.   He never could have been that, any more than the King George IV. we had seen in the wax-work exhibition, in crimson velvet and ermine, could have been a little boy.   He must have come  straight down  out  of somewhere, just as he was.

As I thought these thoughts, the carriage slowly rumbled out of sight behind a bend in the road.   The last gleaming battle-axe disappeared ; the pomp of gold and crimson was no more.   Only the ringing of the Abbey bells continued, as the chimes of Faith keep ringing on for us when the shows of the present have departed.

But, oh ! the mingling of contempt and relief which came upon me when, at the age of eight years, I learned that those battle-axes were *only tin !*

How the whole pageant collapsed for me then into a mere child's play of wooden swords and paper helmets ! How I scorned myself for even saying my prayers under the pressure of such utterly needless fear !   With what openly-expressed scepticism I ever afterwards regarded the nurse-girl who had dared to suggest that my head could be cut off by those make-believe things !   And with what dignity I declined next year to go and see the show at all !   I knew too much about it now. The battle-axes would not cut.   The men who held them up were worn-out shoemakers or hotel waiters, who earned a shilling a day by trying to look fierce on each side of the judge's carriage.   The judge himself was only a *person*. He sat down to dinner every day, and ate meat and drank wine like other people. He took off the scarlet robe, and there was a coat under just like my own father's. The wig came off, too ; so did the fur. What was he worth?—what was it all worth ?

Ah me ! the burst of dignity soon passed away. I learned to accept meekly the unsatisfactory nature of the show, knowing it was not what it seemed, and for years afterwards I amused myself, as well as might be, with the other things—the velvet and the gold fringe, and the powder and the bannerets, and the crimson liveries which really *were* very grand.

Later still I became acquainted with the central object himself. I learned to look up to a judge's wisdom, knowledge, patience, intellect, industry ; to the noble functions which he discharges, and the important part which he takes in the conduct of life, with far more real awe and reverence than ever in my childish days I had paid to the mere outside—the scarlet, and velvet, and fur, and tin battle-axes of his accompaniments.

So on through life. Of far other things than those old retainers' weapons, have I found out that they are "only tin " ; and with like revulsion of feeling have I learned, first to scorn what was not what it seemed, and then to take it contentedly, knowing it *was* a sham. Afterwards came the larger knowledge of the truth which underlies the shows, an ever deepening and widening aspect of the reality, around which man has gathered these little accidents of pomp and circumstance, and growing patience with those who accept them still

as part of the interior thought. The judge's Sunday
has become a type for me of the progress of life within
us. We first learn to believe implicitly, then to scorn,
then to tolerate the thing we scorn, then to see through
what we scorned to the beautiful and ever true thought
within, which afterwards we love and worship, and this
is our religion.

# CHAPTER XV.

 MIGHT have gone moralising on for ever so long about the judge's Sunday, if a sound of voices had not begun to disturb me. Looking up, I saw that Mr. Justin had joined Annette who was sitting close to me, and the two were having quite an animated conversation.

Annette said they had been talking nearly three hours, and I had been scratching away all that time. I said I had not, I had been taking notice of what was going on in the ship. As a proof of the correctness of this statement, I described the positions of all the people—how Mrs. Flexon was chatting confidentially with the doctor, whilst the chief engineer had betaken himself in despair to the civilian's widow ; how Mrs. Beverley and Mrs. Truro had been deep in a discussion about little boys' dress for the last hour, and how Mrs. Marsham and Mrs. Mateby were settling the question of Colonel Aberall and his gambling debts.

Mr. Justin thinks I must be writing a book, the history of my experience during twenty years' work amongst the Zenanas of the Punjaub. Well, let him think so. I know I do spend a great deal of time in writing, but it is because I have nothing else to do. And I told him I could still keep my eyes wide enough open for anything that might be going on around me.

"Can you?" he said, looking at me with such a comical smile.

If I really was writing for three hours yesterday, which I don't believe, I did not finish what I was thinking about. There was still another sight which Mark and I and this quizzical Mr. Justin, who was only "little Gregory" then, used to see from the windows of the old drawing-room in the Northgate.

That was the annual procession of the yeomanry troops to their review on Abbotsby Heath. Mark and I always went and had tea with Mrs. Justin on that afternoon, and also on the afternoon of the chairing procession. Gregory, in return, used to visit us when the gooseberries were ripe, and when the apples were gathered, and when the haymakers were at work in the fields behind our house. At least, those were the regular times, though he came often enough between.

These three sights: the chairing, the judge's Sunday, and the Yeomanry Review, gave me entirely distinct feelings of pleasure. The chairing was a pure, childish delight of sight-seeing, striking no deeper chords than could be worked in any little mind by flags, banners, music, rosettes, and flying blue ribbons, mingled with the accessories of ginger-wine and sponge biscuits when we had to wait very long for the procession. With the pageant of the judge's Sunday there was connected, until we found out about the tin battle-axes, a certain awe inseparable from the near and perfectly realised presence of a justice which could immediately visit upon us any little misdeeds, or, indeed, as the nurse suggested to us, pointing to the retainers, cut off our heads if we were very naughty. I had always a sense of relief, and so, I believe, had Mark and Gregory, when the High Sheriff's carriage was fairly out of sight.

But no such vague uncomfortableness visited us as that fine regiment of yeomanry, preceded by the mounted detachment of Dragoon Guards which usually kept the ground, filed down narrow little Northgate, the white plumes of the officers floating in the breeze, the horses' hoofs clattering on the stone pavement, the men's accoutrements flashing back the sunshine, those loose, white-braided, blue jackets hanging from their left shoulders giving them a jaunty, rollicking air which rather took away from their otherwise warlike appearance. Sometimes one or another of them would look up to us little folk in the window, and give us a smile which made us feel as proud as if we had been noticed by the King himself.

I believe that sight awoke in us the first dawn of patriotic feeling, of pride in our country's greatness. That Yeomanry Review was always associated in our minds with the stories my father told us about the French wars, the stir of English fleets and armies in his young days, the news of victories blazed from end to end of the country, mail coaches decorated with laurels, bonfires lighted, bells ringing in every little village church. In place of the unspoken fear which possessed us when watching the judicial pageant, there was now a splendid assurance of security; for with such an

apparently innumerable host of armed men, ready to
draw swords in our defence, what foe, either at home or
abroad, could do us any harm ?   I believe at that time
the Abbotsby yeomanry numbered about five hundred,
rather a feeble force to contend with the thousands of
our neighbours across the Channel ; but seeing them
career proudly past us, in the almost interminable file of
four deep, which was all the narrow street allowed up
and down as far as we could see, from the judge's
residence, which formed the vanishing point at one end,
to Booth and Marby's toy shop, which was the limit of
our prospect at the other, forming just one glittering
ribbon of steel and silver, dashed with the darker tints
of the men's blue and red hussar caps—on and on with
seemingly no end to their numbers, for five hundred
men four deep took a long time to pass, how could we
children but think them a force which would vanquish
the world ?

And then that assuring smile now and again from
some good-natured young fellow, who, chancing to look
up to Mr. Justin's window, saw our wonder and delight
at the great show—how it seemed to steep us in infinite
waves of safety !—how it seemed to say, "All right,
little ones, never fear ; I will take care of *you*, whatever
comes !"

Once my father took us in an open carriage to see
the review itself ; but we did not enjoy that very much.
It was too much like being in the actual danger and
turmoil of battle.  The heavily-armed dragoons, on their
prancing steeds, keeping the grounds for the troops,
*would* keep coming so alarmingly near us, and sometimes

backed almost into our carriage, filling us with dismay;
for how could we tell that they would know exactly
where to stop? And when one of the horses did really
switch his tail right in my face, and I gave a little
scream, the dragoon on his back turned and scowled at
me as if I had been a Frenchman, instead of a harm-
less, frightened little girl. To my dying day I shall
never forget how those eyes looked under that brass
helmet.

And then the noise, and the trampling, and the flash
of drawn swords, and the rapid galloping to and fro of
companies of horse, and the clang of weapons as opposing
sides met in what seemed to me deadly combat  It was
too real. I was perfectly sure they wanted to kill each
other. It could not be only practice. But to watch
them from the drawing-room window in the Northgate,
with a responsible person behind to see that we did not
lean too far out, and with an occasional largess of
biscuits and ginger-wine from Gregory's mother—*that*
was simply delightful. That was such a comfortable
way of becoming acquainted with the glory of one's
country.

And now, after—for him—years of good, successful
work, leading him to honour and position and success in
his own town; and after—for me—much loss and death,
and half a lifetime of exile in a foreign land, Gregory
Justin and I, middle-aged people, with gray hair and
large experience of the world, have met on the deck of
the *Nawab*, and talk with each other of all these things.
What wonder that I know not how the time goes as I

write down the story here! What wonder that Mr. Justin, who can never care for the past as I do, laughs at me, and says that one day I shall wake up and find how much has been going on whilst I was dreaming of what is gone!

But how quizzically he looked at me when he said that!

# CHAPTER XVI.

T is really little more than a week, but it seems like months since that affair of the envelope. Mrs. Flexon completely ignores Annette and myself now. Is she offended, or is she afraid? I think she is afraid. Her eyes have a curious, dart-like motion when they meet mine, which I take care shall be pretty often. She does not turn them—she literally flings them away from me.

If her conscience is clear, why cannot she meet my steady gaze with one as steady? Why does she always take care now to have her chair placed so far away from the skylight where Annette and I generally sit, as though she were afraid that we should want to engage her in further unpleasant inquiries? But she need not trouble herself. I know already all that I wish to know from her.

She has not quite dismissed the subject, it appears, from her thoughts. For last night Dr. Byte, who, I really think, must be engaged to her now, for they are constantly together, came to me as I was sitting here writing, and said, with a little of the manner of a man who is asking a favour, instead of putting that stupid old Miss Brown in her place:

" Excuse me for interrupting you, but Mrs. Flexon wished me to ask if you have that envelope in your possession yet. Most probably you have destroyed it ; but if not, and you will kindly give it to her, she will try if any light can be thrown upon the subject, as both you and Miss Lislethorpe appeared to be so anxious about it."

" Thank you very much," I replied, " but please tell Mrs. Flexon that Miss Lislethorpe and I have nothing more to say on the subject at present."

I emphasized that last word, for I wished Dr. Byte distinctly to understand that the whole thing was not going to drop through.

" Very well," he said, carelessly ; " I think that is much the wisest plan. It is almost a pity any inquiry was ever set on foot ; because, you see, it was the merest surmise on your part that the envelope had been in Mrs. Flexon's possession originally. In fact, now she has an almost distinct remembrance of picking it up on deck soon after we came on board. If you will kindly let her have it again, she would, perhaps, be able to decide."

" Oh, thank you !" said I, feeling tolerably sure that, if the precious scrap of paper once came into Mrs. Flexon's possession, it would soon make acquaintance with the blue waters of the Mediterranean. " I am so sorry she has troubled herself about it again. Pray tell her, too, will you, that we will let the matter rest as it is. Miss Lislethorpe has no wish to produce further unpleasantness."

" No ; and Mrs. Flexon has behaved in a most

ladylike way about it.   Of course, you know, it must
have been exceedingly annoying to her at the time,
but she wishes me to assure you that she does not
feel in the least offended."

How pretty of her !  Kisses and forgives us all
round in the sweetest manner possible, and then says :
"Look how good I am !"  Dr. Byte must think her
angelic.   Well, so she may be, only some of the angels
kept not their first estate.

"Please thank Mrs. Flexon very much," I replied,
"and tell her I have nothing more to say now.  If I find
that I am wrong, I assure you I will not rest until
the most ample apologies have been made."

And then, by way of intimating to Dr. Byte
that the interview was at an end, I dipped my pen
into the ink and prepared to go on with my writing.

Nothing more to say.   Certainly not ; but a great
deal more to do.   I am determined not to rest until
I have brought up the truth which lies at the bottom of
that well.   Sometimes I think I will find out where a
letter would find Captain Asperton, and then write
to him and tell him the story, and let him know that
Annette has never had a letter from him.   But then
again, I think it might only bring up the unhappy past,
without making any decisive ending of it.   Annette
seems passing now into a certain quiet peacefulness.
I might do her a wrong to ruffle it.   Why cannot I
leave things to a wisdom wiser than my own, and wait
until the way is so plain that I cannot mistake it ?

She and Mr. Justin are walking up and down the
deck now.   He says she wants exercise, and he means

to make her take it morning and afternoon. It brings a colour into her cheeks that makes her look quite pretty. Dear me, how often I have tried to make her walk up and down in that way, telling her it would give her an appetite and improve her digestion, and all sorts of things, but it was never any use! Now Mr. Justin gives his order, and the thing is done. Annette has the sort of nature that wants a man's influence upon it. She has not much power of resistance when a strong will is brought to bear upon her.

How I find in him now traits of character which I remember so well when he was a boy! Though he was younger than either Mark or myself, he generally managed to convince us that his way was the right way of thinking about anything. It was Gregory who decided the road we should walk, the games we should play at, the places where our bridges and summer-houses should be built. He used to be architect for them, too, whilst Mark and I took our lower stand of hewers of wood and drawers of water, meekly feeling that it was quite right for us to do so. It never vexed us that he should assume this superiority. We were wise enough to own that he was the master-spirit.

I have just the same feeling now. I should never think of contradicting Mr. Justin, scarcely of suggesting to him. He has just assumed the same quiet authority over Annette, since she became well enough to become an appreciable unit in the ship's company. He tells her that she ought to do a thing; she does it. He insists upon her putting aside her book and walking up and down. She walks up and down, without apparently any feeling of rebellion. He says she is to give over reading that very subjective book of poems which she has been studying for the last few days. It has never appeared again, and instead she is now deep in "Social Science for Beginners." An excellent science, no doubt; but the very last which I should have thought Annette Lislethorpe would choose.

It is the same with other people. In the most quiet and unconscious way he takes the lead in whatever he is talking about. He was having an argument with Dr. Byte this morning, in which Mrs. Flexon's favourite conspicuously came to grief. If he had been a gentle, quiet sort of man—though in that case Mr. Justin would never have put him to such confusion—I should have been really sorry for him, because one cannot enjoy seeing a man like that utterly discomfited. But Dr. Byte airs his opinions so very freely, and with so little respect for those of other people, that human nature could not resist a certain satisfaction at seeing him put into his right place. And I suppose I have not quite forgotten the way he behaved to me when I went to ask about the envelope. Shall I ever have common sense and Christianity enough, I wonder, to consider men and women according to what they are in themselves, and not according to what they have been or done to me? I am afraid not.

It was rather a public discomfiture, too, for our doctor is not a man who does anything quietly, and his angry way of conducting the argument had drawn quite a circle of listeners round the combatants; amongst them, of course, Mrs. Flexon, who was exceedingly

anxious for the honour of her cavalier. When the
discussion was practically put an end to by Dr. Byte—
who is a capital gymnast—jumping from the poop to
the lower deck, and going to smoke a cigar with the
first mate, Mrs. Flexon looked at Mr. Justin severely,
and walked away with one of the young men, saying
something about " insufferable impertinence."

I am not quite sure to what the "insufferable
impertinence" applied, whether to the manner in which
our audacious little Esculapian had been floored, or to
the subsequent conduct of the victor. For after the
sudden disappearance of the adversary from the scene
of conflict, Mr. Justin quietly walked across to Annette,
who had been taking no interest in the proceedings,
and said :

"Miss Lislethorpe, you have not had your usual
exercise this morning. Put your book away and come
and take the thirty minutes' dose with me."

He took the book from her, put one of the shawls
over her, for we are beginning to feel a touch of northern
coolness in the air now, and conducted her away

Perhaps this was the "impertinence" to which Mrs.
Flexon referred. I think, practised upon herself, she
would rather have enjoyed it ; for I heard her say once
to Mr. Justin, when he was holding her quoits for her,
that she did so dote upon masterful men. She said a
man was worth nothing if he could not make a woman
do what he liked. But her opinions vary according to
circumstances. When talking to the chief engineer
once, who, though clever, is very mild and shy, she
could not endure men who had too much self-possession.

To obtain her favour, she said, they must be humble
and modest.    Which Mr. Justin is not, to any great
extent.

Annette takes it all very quietly.    She struggled
through her walk of thirty minutes, Mr. Justin making
her rest now and then, or lean on his arm ; and then
she came back to me, apparently neither glad nor sorry
that the thing was at an end.    I believe it is a good
discipline for her to have the force put upon her which
Mr. Justin exercises.    She wanted somebody to shake
her out of that dreamy indifference which was becoming
a habit.    I could not do it—I have not will enough.    I
can order my own life, but I cannot touch the lives of
others.    I could never keep a school, or be a matron, or
a lady-superintendent, or anything of that sort, for nobody would obey me.    I used to suggest exercise to
Annette over and over again, but she only looked wist-
fully at me, and gave herself an extra curl up amongst
her shawls.    If she had done so when Mr. Justin
suggested it, he would just have shaken her out of her
shawls, picked her up, carried her to the middle of the
deck, set her on her feet, and told her to walk up and
down until she received orders to stop.

That sort of treatment does Annette a world of good,
and I am very glad she is having it.

I hope we shall be able to keep up this pleasant
friendliness with him when we are settled at Abbotsby.
Of course it will depend upon the Rose or Violet who
is at the head of his house then.    If she happens to be
one of the stylish, fashionable sort, I am afraid it will
not last very long.    But if, as I hope, and yet am almost

afraid to believe, she should be a quiet, pleasant, home-loving little body, what enjoyable times we shall have together ! How she will like to hear what I can tell her about the boyhood of her husband, how we used to play together, how even then he had begun to show his superior, overmastering spirit ; how he was the leader of us both, though younger than either of us, how his quick, active intellect used to find out ways and means which ours, slower and more plodding, carried into effect.

I think it must be so pleasant for a wife to hear that sort of thing about her husband, supposing she has not known him all her life. But I have been writing here until the twilight has fallen. How like England the air begins to feel ! The captain says we shall be there in nine days.

# CHAPTER XVII.

AM awake in our cabin in the early dawn of the morning. All would be so still, were it not for the labouring and panting of that restless steam-engine heart below, whose every pulse is sending us so much nearer home.

Greatly to our disappointment, the captain found that we need not touch at Malta. We passed it last night in a cloudy moonlight, which only let us see the heaving outline of the island upon a gray sky. Our young men, who had reckoned upon making a night of it amongst the questionable amusements which are so plentiful at Valetta, looked dreadfully crestfallen, though I dare say next morning their pockets would be considerably heavier in consequence of the involuntary self-denial.

"Here St. Paul was shipwrecked," said one lady, sententiously, whereupon Dr. Byte, who never lets a statement pass if there is the least excuse for contradicting it, pounced upon her, and requested her reasons for the fact. The poor lady, not being prepared with proofs of what she had all her life simply and unhesitatingly accepted, was as much puzzled as though she had been called upon to resolve a problem in algebra or trigonometry. The doctor took advantage of her simplicity, and very soon showed her, according to his own logic, that that brief and touching history must be relegated to the limbo of vague possibilities, into which the annals of the Hebrew people have so satisfactorily resolved themselves. I wonder why it is that Dr. Byte believes all other history except that which is given to us in the Bible. You have only to say that a statement is contained in the books of the Old or New Testament, and forthwith he begins to pick it to pieces. But this was a great triumph for him, and I think a little consoled him for the flying leap he had been obliged to make a day or two before to escape from Mr. Justin's inexorable logic.

I did wish Mr. Justin had been there this time, not so much to protect St. Paul from the imminent danger to which he was exposed at the hands of this mighty man, as to give Dr. Byte the opportunity of another jump. It must be such good exercise for him!

"The barbarous people showed us no little kindness." What would not one give to know all that was said and done by Paul during the three months he and his comrades spent on that little island whose dim gray outline we passed last night, which I can see now, a mere film on the horizon, as I sit up here in my berth? What a different life it must have been from that which priests and bishops live nowadays! Yet not altogether without its gentle courtesies, for that Publius must have been a true man, able to see beneath the guise of an out-worn and shipwrecked prisoner the make of a hero whose peer the world had scarcely seen. I am afraid, in this nineteenth century, we should be slow to recognise

our great ones in such fashion.  We should pause before
"honouring with many honours" a man who came to us
under such untoward circumstances—nay, would he not
rather be bidden by our vigilant police to "move on,"
and carry his wondrous message to a land where "sus-
picious characters" were not so jealously reconnoitred?

Four o'clock, and just a few crimson streaks upon the
awakening east.  It is no use getting up, for in half an
hour the sailors will begin to wash the decks, and then
the only place of rest for me will be up in the rigging, for
at this time in the morning the saloon smells too strongly
of the night before to be at all a comfortable locality.
So there is nothing but to stay in my berth, which, being
the upper one, has a port close to my elbow, and amuse
myself as well as I can with my own thoughts—always,
when I can fix them on this home-coming, sweet and
pleasant to me.

What a difference between the within and without
which this little port-window separates!  On one side,
the six feet square cabin, with its meagre belongings, its
scanty attempts at gilding and decoration, its confused
mixture of odds and ends, the comical result produced
by squeezing the greatest quantity of things into the
smallest quantity of space.  On the other side, the great
wide sea, the gray horizon line which divides the seen
from the unseen, the breaking splendour of the unrisen
sun, the white sails of far-off vessels, with their freight
of human souls, each carrying its own separate share of
joy or sorrow.  So like the little life of things we see
and touch around us, and the great life which lies
beyond, parted from us by the narrow port-window of

death—this life so crowded, so over-weighted, so filled with necessary trifles, which we would gladly cast away; that life so vast, so silent, so full of beauty and majesty, which we cannot understand, only long after.

Sometimes I stand on the bulwarks, so near the ocean that its spray dashes on my face, and look from that side into this little cabin. It is so mean and petty then, though myself and my interests, when I am in it, make it the centre of my world. I wonder, out under the great wide sky, how I could ever crowd into it at all. Will it be so with us when we stand in the new life, and look back to this; when the little cabin is done with, and the infinite hereafter is all our own; when with untold space to work in, and untold time to become acquainted with it, we remember the crushed up, crowded life on the other side the port-window—how we fretted and worried in it, how we longed for more room to breathe and work, how impatient we were to break away the little casement, and let in the whole wealth of air, and sunshine, and beauty, which could but struggle so feebly through it? The little we could see through our window, the much there was to see when we could only get outside; what we saw only suggesting what we might see, what some day we should see. It is all a picture of what is and what is to be.

It seems to me, and Annette says it is just the same to her, that we have been quite six months living in this ship, and yet it is not three weeks since we lost sight of the purple headlands of Bombay. I suppose it is because everything is just the same day by day; no new people, no new interests, so little to concentrate

one's attention upon, no news of how the great tide of
life is going on elsewhere.   I look upon the faces of the
five-and-twenty passengers, and it seems utterly impossible that they are strangers of less than a month.
The junior chaplain's wife, who sits opposite to me at
the end of the first long table, is it really true that
she has sat there only three times a day for only three
weeks?  It cannot be.  I know every separate fibre
in the curls which stray out underneath the coils of
her back hair.  I have counted the buttons up and
down the front of her dress as many times as ever in
my childhood I counted the knobs on Mrs. Justin's
mirror, or the separate little points of the dog-tooth
ornament upon the Norman archway opposite our pew
at church.  Three weeks!—nay, those buttons are
acquaintances of six months' standing at the very least.
And so are the masonic studs, with the square and compasses graven upon them, which Mr. Brevitt, one of our
unemployed young men, wears.  I have watched them
also regularly three times a day, at breakfast, tiffin, and
dinner, throughout a period which stretches now into
the remote past.  Sometimes they are put in properly,
the compasses pointing down, as they ought to point.
Sometimes Mr. Brevitt is careless, and lets them tilt, in
a manner suggestive of loose habits.  Again they point
upward, in act to pierce his youthful chin, and I can
scarcely help reaching across the table to put them
straight for him.

And the captain, too, broad-faced, sunny, smiling,
with his question put regularly every dinner-time to
the chief engineer, who sits at our end of the table :

"Well, Mr. Enfield, how many knots have we made to-day?"

Is it possible I have heard that question asked and answered only twenty-one times? The almanac says yes—my internal consciousness says a thousand times no.

The chief engineer vexed me very much at first by always addressing me as "Mrs." when he wished to know what I preferred; whereas the junior chaplain's wife, who is, I suppose, about eight-and-twenty, and tolerably pretty, was as regularly called "Miss," because, as he said, she looks too young for a "Mrs." Of course, he meant no harm, being one of the most good-natured men living; but still I had my feelings about it, though generally I am rather proud than otherwise of that generous amplitude of build which causes me to be taken for a matron, and which, in my early days, obtained for me the dear old name of Fudge. Yes, it was a dear old name. Even now, when we are talking about those early days, I can see Mr. Justin's lips getting ready to pronounce it, instead of the orthodox "Miss Brown" by which I have been known for the last five-and-thirty years, and which, I suppose, now will last me until the day of my death, none being left to call me by any other.

Mr. Justin and Annette and I, and the chief engineer and Mrs. Barrett form a little society at the end of that dinner-table. Annette is a great deal better now. The regular exercise which she is obliged to take does her good. Only yesterday I heard Mrs. Mateby saying to Mrs. Marsham:

I

"It is really quite astonishing how Miss Lislethorpe
has picked up, poor thing! Sometimes she gets a colour
into her face, which makes her look almost pretty. I
really should not be very much surprised, now, if——"

Here they moved away, and what possibilities lay
hidden behind that "if" I shall never know. Perhaps
Mrs. Mateby was thinking that Annette would like now
to resume the most eligible post of companion to Mrs.
Marsham ; but if so, I am quite sure she is mistaken.
If nothing better than that remains for her, the child
shall stay with me always, and be unto me as a daughter.

# CHAPTER XVIII.

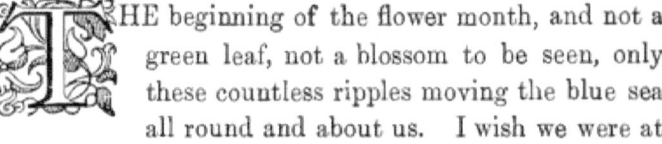HE beginning of the flower month, and not a green leaf, not a blossom to be seen, only these countless ripples moving the blue sea all round and about us. I wish we were at the end of the voyage. Being on board ship is like living under a microscope. Everybody knows so very much about everybody else. People make a point of finding out who you are, and what you are, and where you come from, and where you are going, and if you have any property, and if not, what you intend to do for a living. Your age, too, and your personal appearance, and your dresses come under inquisitorial supervision ; and, in a word, if you want to see yourself as others see you, you have only to take a long voyage and keep your chair always in the same place, a little out of observation. I do not say that the results will be flattering to your pride, but they will certainly throw a new light upon your character.

I hear many curious discussions amongst the men, on social, political, and religious subjects. People talk much more freely on board ship than they do at Indian or English dinner-tables. I suppose this is because they

I 2

are so entirely independent of each other. A little extra
Radicalism, Toryism, Scepticism, or Ultramontanism will
not interfere with their "prospects," and so they say
just what they think. The most inane talk is between
the ladies and the young men, much more so than
between the ladies themselves. I wonder what sort of
wives these men will choose if they think that women
must have such twaddle talked to them. But the ladies
like it, judging from the pretty little peals of laughter
which ring out whenever the unappropriated young men
congregate round them.

I should not care so much if they would only let
their fellow passengers alone. What spiteful things have
I heard said about Mr. Justin—who is worth all the rest
of them put together—just because he will not put himself forward and be flirted with, like the rest of the
gentlemen. But I was most indignant this morning to
hear poor Annette thrust through the mangle of feminine
criticism, Mrs. Flexon and Mrs. Marsham turning the
machine between them. Perhaps I was more vexed,
because during the process I came in for my own share
of flattening; but however that may be, I had great
difficulty to keep from breaking in and telling them
exactly what I thought.

"Engaged, did you say?" remarked Mrs. Marsham.
"Dear me! I should not have thought she was the
sort of girl to get off so quickly. Such an exceedingly
washed-out and listless-looking creature. I was sure
from the very first time I saw her that she would be of
no use to me. I will never engage another companion
without a personal interview."

" Oh ! but I assure you," said Mrs. Flexon, " that in her prosperous days she used to be one of the gayest of the gay. Never a ball or badminton or anything of that sort without Miss Lislethorpe. And such a flirt ! I believe she was engaged to half the gentlemen in Moorkee. But you see it has ended as such conduct generally does."

"Of course. I believe I heard something myself about her behaving very badly to a Captain Asperton, who left the place soon afterwards. A good-hearted, gentlemanly young fellow, I believe, and a very nice match for her, only a rich old man came in the way, and then there was no chance for the other. She must feel now that she was atrociously foolish."

What a good thing for Mrs. Flexon that our " burra mem sahib " is not on speaking terms with any of the ladies of the opposite faction, or the glass of public opinion might be turned upon her own conduct in a most unpleasant manner. With what entire satisfaction could I have brought forward a certain envelope at that particular stage of the conversation, and begged for further information respecting it. There was not the least change or sign of discomfort in her voice as she replied :

" Oh ! yes, you mean that poor old Mr. Moberley. What a ridiculous old man he was, to be sure, but enormously rich, and ready, I dare say, to do anything in the way of settlements. But, you see, Mr. Lislethorpe dropping off so suddenly, quite altered the state of affairs. I have no doubt he was very anxious for the match, more so, perhaps, than the young lady ; and I

believe, if he had lived a few weeks longer, things would
have been settled between them."

"Poor creature! Well, it served her right for
behaving as she did to Captain Asperton. But I don't
think she has quite forgotten how to play her cards,
even yet. That Mr. Justin seems wonderfully taken
with her!"

"Yes," replied the other, with now a perceptible
flavour of spitefulness in her manner. "He walked
into the snare from the very beginning. You know he
is just the sort of man to be taken by weakness and
helplessness in a woman. Miss Lislethorpe knew very
well what she was doing, when she took the part of the
interesting invalid so prettily, and used to be reclining
on deck from morning till night, with that dreadfully
commonplace Miss Brown as a foil to her own elegant
appearance."

How hard women can be to each other! But I
went on knitting my stocking in perfect silence. Annette wanting to make an impression on a man like
Mr. Justin, such nonsense! Mrs. Marsham then took
up the thread of discourse, or, I should rather say, the
handle of the mangle.

"Poor Miss Brown! As you say, so exceedingly
commonplace, and so very fond of interfering in other
people's affairs."

"Yes, indeed," said Mrs. Flexon; "I never saw
such a meddlesome woman. One might think she had
appointed herself censor general of the ship. Do you
know, she actually came to me the other day and asked
for an explanation of the writing on a bit of paper I had

thrown away, and when I ignored the whole affair, she was quite impertinent about it ; in fact, almost threatened me with proceedings. Dr. Byte, who was with me at the time, was excessively amused."

" Really ! " said Mrs. Marsham. " But, do you know, I think if Mr. Justin means anything by his attentions to Miss Lislethorpe, it will be rather a disappointment to poor Miss Brown. The old lady was evidently bent upon a conquest in that direction. To hear her talking with him, and putting on such an appearance of youthful anima- tion, was almost too funny ; as if, you know, any- thing of the sort could ever have been possible. But some people *are* so ridiculous ! "

" Exactly, dear Mrs. Marsham ; that is just what some people are," thought I, poor Miss Brown, to myself. And then I did get up and walk away to another part of the deck, for I was afraid, if I heard anything else, my self-love would be too severely wounded. But I am sure I was as much amused as they could possibly be at the picture they had suggested. I only wish they knew how comfortable I hope to be without any of the arrangements which they appear to think I am proposing for myself. I wish they knew how to dwell among my own people is all I care for, ten times better than "conquests" in any direction whatever, except, perhaps, the conquest of one's own ill temper at hearing such things said.

But their idle gossip about Annette *did* give me a touch of anxiety. Of course it is only gossip.

Annette is perfectly unconscious. I should have
thought a duller woman than Mrs. Flexon might
have found that out. Even a stupid old creature
like myself can, I think, see the difference between
listless, involuntary submission to the influence of a
stronger will, and the coquettishness which lays
itself out to attract and receive attention. If I
know Annette aright, nothing is farther from her
thoughts now than to lay a snare for anybody.
The only thing about which she talks with hope
or interest, is our life together at Abbotsby. She
*does* seem to enjoy the thought of that, and of
finding something to do, so that we may keep
together. As for anything else—— But about
Mr. Justin !

Here I fell to thinking. What did he mean
when he said, in that curious, quizzical way, that,
even with my very wide-open eyes, I did not see
everything? Is he quietly making himself master
of so much heart as poor Annette has to give ? Is
*that* going to content him? Is Annette to be the
violet ? But if Mr. Justin does not marry a woman
to be proud of in some way or other, he must marry
a woman who will worship him, look up to him as
a sort of idol, and I am quite sure Annette does
not do that. Perhaps, like men who have always
been accustomed to rule, conquer, succeed, he is
taking it for granted that Annette cannot refuse
anything he condescends to ask. Or, perhaps, the
man's self-love is blinding him, and he thinks her
listless submission is a sort of homage to his

superior strength, a homage which will be only too glad, by-and-by, to give up everything. Mr. Justin is mistaken. At least, I am almost sure he is.

But what ought I to do? "Meddlesome woman," Mrs. Marsham called me, and there is a fibre of truth in almost anything one hears about oneself, though often not more than a fibre. I suppose she was referring to the part I took in getting Annette freed from the companionship affair. Now must I meddle again? If Mr. Justin has any thought of Annette, and I believe, as I certainly do believe, that she has no care for him, is it right for me to take her away from her own people and keep her at Abbotsby, where he will have constant opportunities of seeing her? Ought she not to go to this aunt in Cheltenham, who doubtless knows a great deal more of the world than I do, and who, under these circumstances, is her proper protector? At this point I got into a tangle and left off.

Leaning over the bulwarks, and looking away westward to my home, I tried to think things into shape. After all, what right have I to make myself a providence in the affairs of other people, putting my little influence in to shape or alter them? A wisdom wiser than mine does that. If, having any private schemes of my own, I had asked Annette to come with me to Abbotsby, with Mr. Justin's possible proposal as an eligible background to the arrangement, I might reasonably feel that I had taken a great responsibility upon myself, but I did it having no thought of the kind, having, indeed, no thought of anything but Annette's

comfort, because the child loves me, and feels at home
with me.  So then my coast is clear.  I need not go
back from what is a genuine kindness, because of what
is very likely a needless fear.  The gossip of these
women shall be to me as though it had never been.
Annette shall go to Abbotsby.  The great things of life
do not fall out by chance in this way.

So the knife of common sense cuts the Gordian knot,
and what Mrs. Marsham may think, or what Mrs.
anybody else may think, shall not interfere with what
I believe to be the best home now for Annette, mine
at Abbotsby.

# CHAPTER XIX.

*May 4th.   Off Gibraltar.*

 NEED not have troubled myself about it; it is all settled now. The Gordian knot has been cut in quite another fashion, though I am very glad that I did cut it for myself, after my own fashion.

What trouble we take, what thought we spend, over things which neither thought nor trouble of ours can alter! I might have spared myself all the worry which Mrs. Marsham's gossiping tongue caused me. Perhaps I had no right ever to have listened to it. If we could hear all that is said about us, and about other people whose interests are in some way knitted up with ours, we should get into such a tangle that action of any useful sort would be impossible. Therefore one must go straight on, brushing these chance threads of opinion aside, like those gossamer films which in autumn mornings vex us so by constantly spinning themselves before our faces.

After that waspish little bit of conversation, which cost me so much uneasiness, and which I wish now I had never heard, things went on quietly enough for a day or two. Mr. Justin and I had our pleasant little talks together as usual, not even Mrs. Marsham's

criticisms making me, I think, any less animated
when we got upon the subject of old times. Annette
was generally with us. When the twelve o'clock bell
rang, Mr. Justin used to rouse her up, and send her
for her twenty minutes' promenade up and down the
deck, not always going with her himself, but watching
her all the time, ready, when she looked tired, to fetch
her back, or give her the help of his arm for a little
while, or, when the walk was over, to wrap her up and
settle her comfortably down again in her place beside
me. If she was not with us—and lately I have noticed
that she sits alone rather more than usual—he would
often ask me questions about her, what she was intending
to do in the future, and so on. Sometimes he would
ask me—when he found I had been at Moorkee—about
her father and the sort of life she led, up in that
fashionable hill-station. I could tell him little. The
most of what I knew was not mine to tell. I used to
describe her to him as I remembered her in church,
with that wistful, half-satisfied look in her eyes, but
not as I had seen her on the hillside, full of hope
and happiness, with the beauty of unspoken joy glowing
through her smile and deepening the colour on her
cheek. To make him understand how beautiful Annette
Lislethorpe could be, I must have told him of something
which I think he has never yet reached, perhaps never
will reach.

As for Annette, though I watched her closely, I
could find no change in her. If sometimes I saw her
face in repose, it had a quiet, restful look as of one who
has no longer anything to search for; but not the

beauty of one who has found the best thing earth has to give. However, I made no remark, I asked no questions. My heart is full of good-will to the child. I knew that when she needed a friend she would come to me. And so she did.

Last night there was a concert on the poop, which drew away all the passengers, Mr. Justin included, for he has the best voice amongst them. I, not being disposed for gaiety, went to my own corner, where I could hear without being seen. I began to build castles in the air about my life at Abbotsby, so peaceful, so pleasant, as it is to be a life where the gossip of strangers will no longer vex me, and where I shall be able to rule my own affairs without meddling with those of other people. This seems a selfish way of looking at things, but at the present time nothing is so delightful to me as the prospect of doing as I will with my own. I am so tired of having to live in public, being able to shut no door behind me, and with it shut out the tongues and opinions of that busy world which never thinks itself so well employed as when turning the mangle of hostile criticism, after the fashion of Mrs. Marsham and her friends.

I was so busy with my own thoughts that I did not know Annette was sitting by me, until I felt her hand — what a thin little hand it is! — laid upon my arm.

For a while we just sat there quietly together. Once or twice I began to talk about something, but her answers showed that her thoughts were far away. I felt that she had something to say to me, which would not say itself until we had come entirely into sympathy with each other. I just drew her a little closer to me and waited. Somehow I felt what she was going to tell me, but I could not help her at all. She must come to it in her own way.

"Miss Brown," she said at last, very quietly, "I want to say something to you."

"I know you do, my child. What is it?"

The little hand scarcely trembled at all as she said :

"Mr. Justin has asked me to be his wife."

It was said in a low voice, but then Annette's voice is always low. And besides, we have got into the habit of talking in an undertone, both to avoid disturbing other people, and that we may not be overheard by them.

I only put my own hand on the hand that was resting on my arm, holding it steadily for a while. I need not have done so, I think, for it did not tremble at all.

"And then, Annette?"

"I said I would."

That was all. I could find nothing to say. I had no gladness to express. If Annette had but said it a little differently. It was not the tone of one who wraps up in the words a whole future of hope and happiness. If she had been telling me of her re-engagement as companion to Mrs. Marsham, she could scarcely have spoken the words more quietly. And yet they had bound her to an untried something which only death would end.

"I said I would."

How it all made me think of my own little romance, folded up and put away so long ago, so long, long ago, yet I think fresher and sweeter to me now, even in its memory only, than the page which Annette was just turning. I had not been so calm when I told my mother that Gilbert Ross had asked me to be his wife. Calm? Why, I remember now the tumult of joy and wonder which stirred all my life when I first knew that he loved me. Nothing seemed the same to me after that—how could it be? Commonplace, practical, housekeeping girl though I was, I felt that a glory had arisen upon me, and I think something of it must have shone through my face. And though that is seven-and-twenty years ago, I have never forgotten it. And though death came so soon between us, death itself could not take away what love had given. My life took on a new meaning then. I came into possession of my inheritance. I broke through the little port-window, and found that the wide, beautiful world outside it was all my own. Ever since, though people pity my loneliness now, and talk of me as out of date, and all the rest of it, I look back to my life before Gilbert Ross and I loved each other, just as I look from the bulwarks of this ship, with their infinite prospect of sea and sky, into the narrow little cabin on the other side of the port-window, and pity its smallness.

Does Annette feel anything like this? And if she does not, is she giving what a man like Gregory Justin will always prize? That is what I am afraid of. But we must not judge others by ourselves. It may be her way to hide much.

Meanwhile, the concert was going on briskly. Mrs. Flexon and the doctor were singing a duet, as Annette told me in so few words of the strange thing which had happened to her. The sailors had gathered on the lower deck to listen, one or two of them putting in a deep bass note now and then. In the distance we could see the lights of Gibraltar, which we passed at midnight, and its great rock looming heavily upon the scarcely dark sky. On the other side of the Straits was the little African town, nestled in amongst rocks and headlands. It gave one a curious feeling to be touching so nearly the two great continents, one of which seems to represent the past, the other the future, of the world. Africa, with its elder civilisation, full grown and ready to decay when baby Europe, a half-clothed little savage, was scarcely learning the letters which should afterwards compose its history. One was for Memory, the other was for Hope, and between them, in the darkness of the night, we rushed along towards the younger, better land. Was that a good omen for Annette? I do not know. Everything seemed so dim, and I could but remember the great calm of the words—

" I said I would."

# CHAPTER XX.

N the dead of night, with a huge black rock looming in the distance, and the sails flapping about like the wings of some evil-brooding vampire, one naturally feels disposed to look on the dark side of things.

Until the dawn of morning twilight, I lay awake, thinking about Annette's engagement, and finding in it nothing but a dim foreshadowing of trouble. I felt so sure she did not love him properly. I felt so sure he was looking for something in her which she would not be able to give ; and that after a while, when the very moderate amount of sunshine which attended her affection for him now had departed, there would remain for them both nothing but a long, weary stretch of life, unwarmed by enthusiasm or romance or anything else to make it interesting.

Long after Annette's quiet, regular breathing told me she was asleep, I kept turning over and over, trying to find some bright side of the picture, and finding none. What a weight of care seems to come down upon one in the silent watches of the night ! Listening to the ceaseless plash of the waves, and the heavy pulse of the engine, which sounded like

K

the labouring breath of some human heart, I felt as if I was responsible for all that might happen to those two people ; as if the step they had taken was in some manner of my bringing about, and as if the trouble—for I could not think of anything else but trouble — which might follow it must be borne by myself.

I had heard and read many times that a person's first thoughts about anything were the right thoughts. So it seemed impossible to me that Annette's engagement could ever appear other than the, at best, half-satisfactory thing which it certainly was at present. I pictured to myself all sorts of things that might happen. Suppose Captain Asperton should not have gone to Canada, and should turn up accidentally, just when his turning up would be too late to be of any use. And then, after he had turned up and gone away again, suppose some malicious reports, concerning Annette's previous relations with him, should reach Mr. Justin's ears, and he, with the pride and fastidiousness of a man who must have the best of everything, should begin to think lightly of a love which had not from the very first been his own ! How would it all end then, and what would there be for them both then—for him with his unsatisfied present, for her with her unsatisfied past ?

And then — for until sleep came I must go on plaguing myself — I wondered if Annette had told him anything about Captain Asperton, or whether that would be a secret kept even from her husband ; and I pictured to myself all the uncomfortableness which might arise from the finding out of it afterwards, until the burden of life's possibilities became altogether too heavy for me, and from sheer weariness of brain I slept.

Next morning everything was so different. Sunlight swept all the cobwebs away. Out on deck, with little waves plashing and sparkling in the ship's track, white-winged sea-gulls skimming over the foam, big vessels with outspread sails shining like silver in the distance upon the clear line which divided blue sea and blue sky, I was able to laugh at myself for having indulged in such sad-coloured imaginings. They were only—so I thought and think still—the result of over-anxiety and excitement.

For Annette came to me, looking brighter and happier than I had seen her for many a day, and then Mr. Justin joined us, and we all had a quiet little talk before any of the other passengers came on deck. Of course, he knows that I know all about it. Annette told him she would not keep it from me for a single hour ; and being able to talk to him frankly and freely on the subject is a new bond between us. I think his engagement has already improved him. He wanted something to touch him a little more closely than social science and health of great towns and public education, and all those sort of things, would do. Before, he was too much like a room lighted by un-coloured windows. Annette has turned the sunlight upon him as through rich purple and gold of cathedral glass, and everything about him is transfigured—at least, so it seems to me.

K 2

I wish Mrs. Marsham could know how much we enjoyed that talk together ! I think it would be a most convincing proof to her that I have not suffered severely from the success of Miss Lislethorpe's "snare."

"And so you thought you knew everything that was going on on board the *Nawab* ? " he said, when Annette having slipped away, we talked more freely about this new turn in his life, and I could give him my good wishes and congratulations. " I knew all the time I was preparing a surprise for you. You have been so busy writing that book of yours about Zenana work, and all the time a far prettier story has been going on at your very elbow."

Yes, indeed, literally at my very elbow. What a goose I have been, to be sure ! If I had been half as clever as a woman ought to be, I should have had a suspicion of it long ago. So I pleaded guilty, and I let the Zenana hypothesis pass muster too, for a man naturally likes to think he has hit upon the right thing. And then he told me how he had watched Annette from the very beginning, and studied the womanly simplicity and purity of her character, and determined at last that, when he had made his home at Abbotsby as beautiful as it could be made, she should be the mistress of it.

This was very like a man. I suppose the possibility of Annette not meekly acquiescing had never entered his mind. But Gregory Justin always had a way of taking success for granted, and I believe that is the reason he has so often achieved it. Not that he could give any one the impression of a stuck-

up or conceited man, but he has a masterful way about
him, which is its own reward, like the virtue of the
copy-books.

And then he went away to have his cheroot on the
lower deck, and Annette came back, and we had it
all over again, seen through the light of the woman's
window this time. I had a sort of motherly feeling
towards the child. I think any woman, be she ever
so far past the season of romance for herself, has yet
a sympathetic chord for it in those who are dear to
her. Though as to romance in this case, I must say
I seemed to have the greater share of it myself. It
was I who built the castles in the air, and enlarged,
as I most honestly could do, upon Mr. Justin's good
qualities, and made all manner of pleasant imaginings
for their future happiness, when that beautiful old
house in the Northgate should be refitted and finished.
And I described the place to her, and the old garden
sloping to the river, and the elm-trees, and the rooks,
and the chime of bells from St. Boniface Church,
which played hymn tunes every Wednesday night ;
and we both agreed that the lines had fallen to her
in pleasant places, and that it was far better to be
Gregory Justin's wife than Mrs. Marsham's companion.

Annette listened quietly, as though to something
which did not quite belong to herself; but I think
under this passive manner, which has now become
natural to her, there is a true pride in the man to
whom she has promised so much. It is not her way
to make much ado about anything. Looked at from

a simply material point of view, she must be very
thankful for her prospects.  Mr. Justin does not seem
to have told her much about his position in Abbotsby.
She has no idea of what an important person she will
be there—quite the leader of society, if she likes.  I
think he has a sort of pride in letting her find it out
for herself.  Gregory is just the man who would enjoy
disguising himself like an artisan, and winning the
affections of some gently born girl, who thought she
was reaching far down to take his hand, and then
bringing her to his beautiful home, and telling her who
he was, and feasting upon her look of sweet surprise.
Only girls do not do that sort of thing in these days.

But, oh, dear! how that half-hour's talk with
Annette brought back the time when I told my
mother of my own engagement to Gilbert Ross!
How that Sunday stands out from all the other days
of my life!  What a difference it made to me!  What
a sudden burst of sunshine it brought up over everything!  Though I was not making what the world
calls a very good match—not half so good as Annette's,
Gilbert being only clerk in a bank, with no great
prospect of preferment—I suppose it was the loving
each other very much which made the difference.

So it is to be the violet after all.  I am heartily
glad of that.  I was afraid Mr. Justin might look for
a wife who, as the phrase is, would help him to rise.
As if for a man's heart to be ever growing upward in
the sunshine which a good woman's love can make
for him, is not better than the extremest heights of
social position to which a magnificent devotee of

fashion could lift him. It was Annette, my child
Annette, whom Gregory was thinking about when
that tender look came into his face the other day.
I might have been sure that no woman of the world
could bring it there. Instead of his marriage putting
me away from him, it will bring us all more closely
together.

If it had been given me to choose a wife for him,
as women are so fond of choosing wives for their men
friends, I could not have found one more after my
own heart than Annette Lislethorpe. If only I were
quite sure that she is giving him all she has to
give. That "if" still makes me just a little bit
uncomfortable.

But, as I said to myself before, what right have
I to set myself up as a providence to other people?
Or why should I assume that, because everything is
not just as I would have it, therefore it is not as it
ought to be?

# CHAPTER XXI.

*May 6th.*

NE advantage of Annette's undemonstrative-
ness is that none of the people on board
have the least notion of what has happened.

There is no retreating into unoccupied
recesses of the deck, behind the supernumerary water-
casks, tarpaulins, or sails ; no clasping of hands in the
dusk, no glances of mutual absorption, no unconscious
attitudes for the benefit of the rest of the passengers,
especially the young men, who are always ready to
find out anything of this kind, and amuse themselves
with it. Indeed, I think Mrs. Flexon and Dr. Byte—
who really must be engaged to each other now—might
take a lesson from the admirable deportment of my
affianced pair.

Everything goes on as usual. Annette has her
daily constitutionals upon the deck, Mr. Justin taking
care that they last the proper time, and are gone
through with proper rapidity. Sometimes we all
three promenade together ; sometimes he takes us
one at once, so that I don't think either Mrs.
Marsham or Mrs. Flexon can make much of it.
When the walk is over, we take possession of our
usual corner, and have pleasant little chats about

the future. The only external difference is that Annette talks a little more than she used to do.

It is all settled now. At first we thought that as this engagement to the Recorder of Abbotsby has cast an air of importance over the bride elect, which as a homeless young person in search of employment she could scarcely have assumed, she ought to go at once to her aunt in Cheltenham, ask that excellent woman's blessing, and remain with her until the orthodox carriage and pair convey her with due pomp and ceremony into the matrimonial estate. In the meantime, of course, Mr. Justin would present his credentials, state his prospects, request in due form Mrs. Vermont's consent to his suit, and make any little money arrangements which might be necessary. This would, as we all very well know, be the proper thing to do.

But as that letter received at Port Saïd so completely handed Annette over to the tender mercies of any respectable lady who was willing to give her board and lodging and a trifling sum in return for her services, and as Mrs. Vermont so carefully shielded herself from any responsibility respecting her niece, except in the case of illness or urgent need, we have agreed now that I am quite justified in stepping into Mrs. Marsham's place, so far as providing a home for Annette is concerned; the only difference being that I receive her as my loved guest, instead of my hardworked dependent, and shall consider how much I can put into her life, instead of how much I can take out of it.

So Annette still goes with me to Abbotsby, and
as soon as may be, after Mr. Justin has presented
himself at Cheltenham, she will be married from my
house.  She is of age, and can decide for herself how
it is to be.

I am wondering very much what sort of a letter
we shall have from Mrs. Vermont when the engagement
is announced.  A very different one, most likely, from
that which greeted Annette at Port Saïd, with such
scanty assurance of good-will, such very lavish com-
mittal of her to the care of an all-disposing Providence,
which would give her a portion along with the ravens
and sparrows, though scarcely, one would suppose,
quite such a portion as she might have hoped to enjoy
at the table of her nearest relative.

Poor Annette !  What a chill that letter gave her !
How completely it would have kept her out in the
cold if we had not learned to love each other, and
if I had not had a home to offer her !

But this engagement will change things wonderfully.  The affianced wife of Gregory Justin will be a
much more welcome guest at Cheltenham than Mrs.
Marsham's invalided companion.  Most probably Mrs.
Vermont will request that the wedding may take
place from her house, and then, during the summer,
she will come to Abbotsby to see how the young
couple are getting on.  A visit to the Recorder will
be quite the correct thing.  However, the wedding
will *not* take place from her house.

I believe I have spite enough in my nature to wish
that Mrs. Marsham and Mrs. Flexon could know about

Annette's prospects. It is so pleasant, when people have been pitying and neglecting you, to throw up the blinds, and let them see what a pleasant prospect your windows command. To think that "poor Miss Lislethorpe" will so soon be lifted out of her friendless, dependent condition, and placed at the head of society in an average country town, would, I am sure, be a great blow to these two ladies. However, we will bide our time. They will see it in the papers. I wonder how many times during these last four days I have mentally composed the paragraph, and comforted myself, wicked woman that I am, with the thought of the vexation it will cause to some of our fellow-passengers.

Mrs. Flexon has had a deep grudge against both Annette and myself since the finding of that envelope. She appears perfectly unconscious of our presence, if ever we happen to be in each other's neighbourhood, ignores us as completely as though we belonged to the sweeper caste, and she were a thrice-born Brahmin. Yet, from the manner in which I find her occasionally studying us from a distance, darting her eyes away as soon as she is observed, I feel quite sure that her mind is not at rest. She would be much more comfortable if she had that envelope in her own possession. I suppose now, except for my own satisfaction, I need not make any further inquiries, though I should very much like to know all that can be known about it. Annette has never referred to it again.

I wonder what the effect of a very long voyage, say three or four months, under our present conditions, would be? Christians though we call ourselves, I am afraid we should be anything but a happy family at the end of the time. I can understand now, though, when I heard it, it seemed very strange to me, the exclamation of an old coast-guardsman with whom I had a talk, years and years ago, before I went out to India. He had served his time in Her Majesty's Fleet, and on one occasion had been for three years in the same ship, with the same crew. I remarked how sorry they must have been to part, for that three years' service together would have made them like brothers of one household.

"Law bless you, miss!"—it used to be "Miss" then—"Bless you, miss, I was never so thankful in my life as when I saw the last on 'em! I wouldn't ha' gone with that lot another three years—no, not if it was ever so."

I thought at the time he was a very ungracious old man to say so, but now I know too well I should say just the same myself.

However, it will soon be over. The captain thinks that early in the morning of the day after to-morrow we shall sight the English coast, or even to-morrow night, if we get a good wind all the time until then. The ladies are already beginning to gather up their odds and ends. I saw that memorable tobacco-pouch in the doctor's hands yesterday, well filled with the weed of which he is so fond ; so the lady who backed the chief engineer will lose her pair of gloves. I wonder if a more important gift has accompanied that of the pouch !

To-morrow Annette and I are to take turns in having the cabin to ourselves. It is so small that we are obliged to make this arrangement, or our possessions would become inextricably mingled. So I shall have a long quiet morning up here by myself, for Mr. Justin will be busy, and no one else now takes any notice of poor little me. Not that I complain, far be it from me ; only I think sometimes how pleasantly I used to get on with every one in India, and how very much the reverse of pleasantly I have got on with many of the people here.

I have come to the conclusion that men and women are different under different conditions. What elements shall be brought out depends entirely upon what influences shall be put in, at least, almost entirely. If you put salt into your coffee, and sugar into your soup, is it the fault of the coffee and the soup, or your fault, that both are anything but a success? Right things in wrong places produce the misery of life. In our own homes, and in our own little circles, we are all—Mrs. Marsham and Mrs. Flexon perhaps excepted—the pleasantest of people. There we are like sensitised photographic paper, upon which the sunlight of congenial surrounding brings out a pretty enough picture. Here, the sunlight being wanting, the picture can scarcely be called satisfactory. But is it quite the fault of us, or the sensitised paper ?

Then it is a dreadful trial for five-and-twenty people to be together for a whole month, with nothing to do. After all, my old coast-guardsman had not that trouble to baffle with, when he went through his three years' service with the same set of comrades. Occupation is the yeast which makes the dough of human character rise. It is the compressed air which gives to the social champagne its refreshing sparkle and vitality. We here, without it, and, alas! also, for the most part, without that originality which can create it, have become like flat wine and bad bread, a trouble to ourselves, and a trial to each other. I tremble to think what a hopelessly disagreeable woman I might have become, had it not been for the trifle of compressed air which the writing of this journal has put into my life.

But it will soon be over now. Let us hope that the sight of land to-morrow, or the day after, will restore us, at any rate, to our normal condition, even if it does not succeed in making us all that we ought to be.

# CHAPTER XXII.

NNETTE amongst valises and portmanteaus. Mr. Justin, and most of the other passengers, ditto. I up here on deck, with that indefinable shadow of sadness creeping over me which comes to most of us when any period of our life, however small, is coming to its end.

I think, sometimes, what a mercy it is that disease and decay gradually weaken our power of realising things, before death, the most decisive change that we know of yet, closes the period of our existence in the present state. If with every faculty of mind undimmed, we could think of all that we have left undone, or even quite understand what the ending of our time here meant, what a great shadow of sadness would rest upon the holiest of us. But the soul slumbers towards its great change, and none have come back yet to tell us what the waking is like.

Sitting here alone, and remembering the past month, a sort of reproachful feeling comes over me, as I think of the end drawing so near. Those two lines,

All that thou mightest have been,
All that thou mightest have done,

keep saying themselves over and over again to me. I cannot put them away. Perhaps I had better not try to do it.

But human nature loves to justify itself. Here I paused a long time, thinking of many things. Am I so bad, after all?

In biographies of colonial bishops and archdeacons, going out to take possession of their preferments, one reads such beautiful accounts of how they managed to keep straight with everybody on board, and how they always manifested such a Christian spirit, and how a sort of influence radiated from them which made everybody feel that they belonged to a superior order of created intelligence. I never took a voyage with a bishop or an archdeacon, so I cannot speak from actual observation ; but the biographies say so.

Now how much of this enviable state of things arose from intrinsic excellence of character, possessed or acquired by these dignitaries, and how much from extrinsic circumstances, which made it comparatively easy for them to be good? For one thing, I am quite sure they sat at the top of the table, and sitting at the top of the table makes a great difference : witness Mrs. Marsham, who beams upon the rest of the passengers with a benignity which only the equatorial zone of the captain's right can produce. Would Mrs. Marsham have beamed at all, if she had been put half-a-dozen seats lower down, in what might be called the extreme temperate, or almost antarctic regions of position? I believe not.

It is a vast help to superiority to have no superiors.

This sounds commonplace, but it covers a deep truth. It is comparatively easy to be good when nobody sits above you. Could I not be as Christian as any of them, if my opinion was asked about everything, if somebody was always ready to fetch my deck-chair when I wanted it, and also to put it in the most comfortable place for me, so that I might be cool and good-tempered when other people were broiling in the heat, or snugly wrapped up on the sheltered end of the poop when they were shaking in the teeth of the north wind? I am quite sure that I should be the Christian then, even perhaps to the extent of asking the " others " sometimes to change places with me for a little while, which is what Mrs. Marsham has never done.

It is true that all this month I have been of not the slightest use to any one, except Annette Lislethorpe, and I am afraid not much of an example either, except in the matter of keeping myself to myself. I have not even attended daily service regularly, which Mrs. Flexon has always done. Except during those first three days, when I was so ready to offer lime-juice and smelling salts to the sea-sick ladies, and find out for them the pleasantest places on deck, have I in any sort "radiated" what could be called a wholesome influence? I doubt it.

I come back to my favourite theory : that people, as well as things, are only useful or beautiful in their right places. Yonder, at the other end of the deck, is something, namely, a piece of coal, which certainly ought not to be in its present situation. If I had been a thoughtful woman, I should have picked it up and

L

thrown it enginewards when I came on deck a couple
of hours ago.  I suppose the sailors missed it when they
were clearing up after those young men, who amused
themselves this morning by tying an empty canister to
the jib-boom, and aiming at it with little lumps of
coal, by way of practice, maybe, for the hitting of that
indefinite something which is to yield them a livelihood
in the future.

The next person who comes on deck will kick away
that piece of coal as an insult to the passengers.  Mrs.
Flexon has just appeared, and with her dainty little
patent leather balmoral has done the deed.  But if,
instead of being kicked ignominiously into the Bay
of Biscay, it could have been placed with others of its
own sort in your cosy little fireplace some winter
night, how you would have blessed its warmth and
glow!  And yet the thing itself would have been
just the same.

I am like that lump of coal.  I am in my wrong place
here.  Somehow or other I cannot get on with other
people when I am thrust in amongst them in this way.
I see only their angles, and they see only mine.  If
Annette and I had not happened to occupy the same
cabin, I dare say we should have been strangers too.
It was just that chance revelation of herself which
gave us to each other.  As for Mr. Justin, I suppose
we should have found each other out anyhow, the
foundations being already laid.

Here comes Annette herself.  I may go to my
packing now

# CHAPTER XXIII.

OME, sweet home!

We saw the English coast in the distance last night, just like a gray cloud after sunset. Night hid it from us before we could know it for our own country, but this morning it is clear and fair, as I have seen it many times in my dreams.

As we neared the Isle of Wight this morning, there passed us the most imposing sight I have witnessed during the whole voyage — an outward-bound emigrant vessel—what a stupid I am to say outward-bound, when it was an emigrant vessel—which had just landed her pilot there.

A splendid ship, with all sails spread, even to the sky-scrapers, and the English flag flying at the mast-head. She passed so near us that we could see the people crowding her decks, and with a glass distinguish the name written in great white letters on her bows—*Good Hope.*

Well, God grant her name may not be there for nothing! What a thing of beauty she was, riding so proudly over the breakers, with the broad sunlight upon her sails, and glistening upon the foam that marked her track! Such a queen, looking so majestically down upon us, little black, wriggling ant of a steamer that we are, with our stumpy masts and

stumpier funnels, and flapping bit or two of dirty
sail, and long, straight hull, lying so low in the water,
and no sort of comeliness or dignity about us at all.
This magnificent creature, this ocean princess, sat upon
the waves like a monarch upon her throne, sheet after
sheet of dazzling white canvas bending to the breeze,
and flashing to the sun, her infinite, sweeping curves
of rigging flung upon the sky, like the lines of some
mighty, celestial problem.    Such grace and majesty
I have never seen in anything fashioned by human
hands.    Such royalty of dominion she seemed to assert
over the little pigmies who made her.    It did seem
as if for once the thing formed might say to him
who formed it, " What hast thou done ? "

Only she was outward bound, carrying with her a
good five hundred of emigrants to New Zealand ; and
I pitied the men and women who were crowding her
landward side to get a last look at their country,
for well I knew how many a pang of loneliness they
must suffer, and how many weary days and nights
would be appointed unto them before that narrowing
line of coast would be seen again, except in dreams.

I watched the *Good Hope* until she was just
a white speck in the distance, the sun shining on
her all the time, though we were for a while under
a cloud.    But let me be under English cloud rather
than foreign sunshine.    I would not take the glow
and glory of any southern land to have before me
again all that lies behind me now.

Steamers and merchant vessels are thickening
around us.    We shall soon be in the midst of the

forest of masts which marks the outlet of London's great river. All is bustle and confusion, sailors drawing up the baggage out of the hold, and depositing it on deck, stewards running about with bills, passengers settling accounts with each other, and inquiring after missing property. The young men are getting up an "anchor lottery," as it is called. Yesterday they ascertained the probable time of the casting of the anchor, and having secured twenty subscribers to the pool, they divided the time on each side this given hour into as many portions, which were drawn by lot, the shares being half-a-sovereign each. The lucky subscriber in whose division of time the anchor actually is cast pockets the whole pool.

"Such is life," says one sententious lady passenger. I do not see the analogy. I think she means that it is wrong to have lotteries. If so, I agree with her. Most of the subscribers are at loggerheads with each other, fancying they may be possessed of private information, or be bribing the engine people to advance or retard our speed by a few minutes, so that the anchor may be cast at the time that will best suit themselves. It is well they do not make an "anchor lottery" at the commencement of the voyage as well as at its end, or I fear there would have been still less of unanimity amongst us during this month past.

And now I will put this little book away, until I open it again under my own roof-tree, to tell the sweet story of my home-coming. Perhaps next Sunday I shall say my prayers in the old church of St. Boniface at Abbotsby.

# CHAPTER XXIV

THOUGHT I should have told the story of the home-coming sooner; but it is pleasanter to live one's happy life than to write about it day by day. However, I mean to continue writing the story of the weeks as they slip past, leaving such pleasant memories behind.

How seldom it is that one's dreams come true, as mine are coming now! Ever since my brother Mark died, more than fifteen years ago, it has been my one wish to come back to this old house, and live out my days in such quiet, useful fashion as might be possible. Night after night, through those sultry Indian summers, I have lain awake, listening to the measured swing of the punkah, and thinking how much of Eastern luxury I would give for the comfort of an English cottage. And day by day, when my work was done, I have sat in the verandah, and looked westward past tamarind and palm-trees, and the broad-leaved plantain and the waving bamboo, to the red sunset, and pictured to myself this little garden with its old-fashioned beds of lavender and clove pink, its trimly bordered gravel paths leading through homely rows of carrots and cabbages and rhubarb, its cosy side entrance, where of an evening, when her work was done, Keren, in the cleanest of print gowns and the whitest of caps, used to sit knitting. How much more wholesome to look upon that well-washed old woman than the coolies and bearers, and khansamas and chuprassies, and all the rest of the other people, brown-skinned and white-turbaned, that crowd round one's bungalow in the sunny clime of India!

And now, thank God! here I am, my years of labour ended, sitting in the chair my mother used to sit in, at her own favourite bow-window, looking out upon the flowers she used to tend, and the trees, fair blossoming lime and chestnut and sycamore, which my father planted. And life has no more any hard toil for me, and my work lies close to my hands; and needing nothing from the great world of society, I find within my own little possessions all that I desire.

We landed six weeks ago, in the early dawn of a Saturday morning. Mr. Justin gave our things into the charge of an agent, and brought us at once, Annette and myself, to Abbotsby. Mrs. Proud had got her rooms ready for us. It was quite late when we arrived, so that I could see nothing of the old place as we rode along from the station; but just as we reached the door of our lodgings the Abbey clock struck ten, and the dear familiar sound, which I had known since my babyhood, seemed like a welcome home. And truly I think we all felt—Gregory, Annette, and I—that we *had* come home.

Very early next morning, the sweet Sunday morning,

before any of Mrs. Proud's people were astir, I got up and went alone to the old house.

Only once in a lifetime can the feeling come to any one which came to me as I turned the corner of this quiet, out-of-the-way road, and saw the boughs of the lime and chestnut-trees, which overhang the palisades, moving in the May sunshine. My childhood and my girlhood, with all the holy memories of father and mother, were rushing back upon me more vividly with every step I took. One tree after another, under whose shadow I had played, came into sight. At last I could discern the gable-end of the house through the branches of the big old apple-tree in the corner of the garden, the tall gable with its very tiny window near the roof, belonging to the room where I slept when I was a child, the window from which I have watched with such wonder and delight the scarlet-coated huntsmen riding after the hounds, disappearing amongst the copse on the other side, and then flashing out again, with whoop and call of bugle, on the common beyond.

Rapidly, as in a dream one lives through the events of years in a moment, there came before me the joys and sorrows which, as a child, I had gone through in that gable room. Sorrows of darkness with which I had struggled alone, whilst the nurse lay sleeping behind her curtained partition; joys of the early morning, when I watched the red sunrise over the bridge, and the sheep nibbling the dewy grass by the river-side, and the milkmaids tripping off with their pails, singing as they went, and the terrors of

the night before seemed so far off, so unreal ; hours
of banishment to that little room, when I would not
learn my lessons properly, or had appeared in the
presence of my various masters with unwashed hands
or untidy hair ; hours of other banishment, self-
imposed, when I used to shut myself up there to
build castles in the air, or pour out my thoughts into
the diary which I had bought with the careful savings
of many weeks—how it all came back upon me now !

Silently I opened the gate, and found myself face
to face with the old life. It would not have seemed
strange to me then if I had seen my father himself,
with bent head and hands loosely clasped behind him,
sauntering down the worn path under those trees ; or
my mother trimming the rose-bushes on the bed in
front of the bow-window. I was so completely in
possession of the past. It seemed so much more
real to me than the life I had been living on board
ship, or in India during the last twenty years.

There was the little winding walk, leading through
clusters of lilac and elder-bushes to the old seat under
the apple-tree, where I used to go and sit alone on
Sunday afternoons, thinking my own thoughts, while
in early summer the pink-blossomed branches dipped
almost to my face, and through them I could see the
rich purple of the scented lilacs and the golden glow
of the laburnums, upon the sombre background of
chestnut and sycamores beyond. There was the old
sun-dial on its carven column of stone, once, they
said, a pillar in the Abbey church ; there was the
gnarled willow - stump behind which, doubled up

amongst trailing branches of ivy, I generally found little Mark when we were playing hide-and-seek on holiday afternoons. There was the very apricot-tree, quite past fruit-bearing now, I should think, but not cut down on that account, which formed the boundary between my bit of garden and Mark's, and at whose roots I always buried, wrapped up in white writing-paper, a flower-bud of some kind when any of my friends died. It was always a bud, let the friend have been young or old. Was this, I wonder, because of a dim, childish notion that death, the mysterious disappearance of a familiar face, was an unnatural and premature thing? I have often asked myself that, for it was a strange thing for a little child to do.

All was so exactly the same. And I, too, coming back again, felt the child-heart unchanged through all that had come since.

The side door of the house was open, the door at which Keren used to sit when her work was done. A little path between the currant and gooseberry beds led to it, passing first the tool-house where, in my young days, Waggit, the old man who cleaned knives and shoes, used to live. That side door always stood open for the benefit of us children, who were allowed to run in and out at our own sweet will, the only restriction being that we must always wipe our feet on a mat placed there for the purpose. Going in there now, after a lapse of twenty years, exactly the same impulse came over me to wipe my feet upon that mat; and with the impulse came the thoughts which had usually attended these childish entrances and exits, a certain longing for slices of sweet brown bread which were always ready for us at eleven o'clock, and a vague feeling of uncomfortableness about verbs and exercises, the consumption of the brown bread being followed by the advent of our French master, who troubled us sadly by his particularity about our lessons.

Keren was not there. Most likely she was reading her Bible up in her own room, as she always used to do on Sunday mornings, getting up half an hour earlier for the purpose. I don't think she ever read her Bible more than once a week, but she would not have missed that one reading on any account, and she always read as many verses as she was years old; so that by this time, making allowances for failing sight and an average of difficult words, I judged that her retirement would be lengthy.

With a curious reverent feeling, as though entering the portals of a church, I went through the little parlour, our usual sitting-room. There, fronting the door, was the old bookcase, with the cupboard under it, out of which in days gone by I had had many a lump of sugar and handful of currants given me. Over the fireplace was my father's picture — opposite, his geological charts which he had made when preparing some lectures for the Museum. And the old-fashioned sideboard fitted into a recess in the wall, with a square, empty place between the two wings of it, where Mark and I, and even Gregory Justin himself, used occasionally to be sent when we were naughty. For my mother had a singular feeling of justice in punishing children. Those who came to her as guests

used to fare exactly like ourselves, if they misbehaved;
and we in our turn were never allowed in the presence
of our little visitors to assume any license which would
not have been allowable at other times.

How strangely, looking upon these things, the
blank of twenty years passed away, until that which
had been memory so long became real again.

Then, still unseen, I went up into the room where
my father and mother died, from which I had seen
them carried to their resting-place under the churchyard grass. And there, as in a sanctuary, blessed by
holier hands than of priest and bishop, I knelt and
gave God thanks that He had brought me home
again.

And so quietly back into the garden, for I knew
old Keren would be startled if she heard strange
footsteps about; and after a spell of sweet thought
amongst the familiar paths, thought which was sweeter
for its very sadness, I bade good-bye for a little while
to the past, and remembering myself again as a
middle-aged woman, who had been for twenty years
engaged in zenana mission work in India, and was now
returning to take possession of her ancestral home, I
went boldly up to the front door and announced
myself by a proper knock.

Keren knew me, despite my gray hairs and crows'
feet and the slightly wizened appearance which the
balmy breezes of India's coral strand had produced.
After giving me a hearty welcome home, she began
to tell me all about my Aunt Miriam, going with
singular minuteness, as is the manner of her class,

into every particular of her last illness and death, together with the arrangements of the funeral, and the mourning that was worn by the followers. But she asked me nothing—and I have noticed since that very few of my poor people ever have asked me anything —about the sort of life I had lived out in India. Not, I am sure, from any want of interest in what I might have enjoyed and suffered there, but simply because those who have to struggle hard with the little pinchings and worries of poverty, or whose life is spent in the lower cares of providing for food and raiment and lodging, lose the faculty of imagination or realisation. They are intensely curious and speculative with regard to things which touch their own little round of experience, but beyond that they cannot picture to themselves, and therefore cannot feel interest in, anything.

But she was never weary of answering my questions about the past, giving me the history of all that had happened in the house since I had left it, and that was far better to me than having to tell her my own doings during that long, long toil and exile.

And so ended my first coming to the home where I am now at rest and content.

# CHAPTER XXV

E are quite settled down now. We took possession of the house the Monday after we arrived at Abbotsby, and since then Annette and I have been busy making preparations for her wedding, which is to be on the 7th of August. Until then, as there will be plenty of work for everybody, I have an experienced servant to help old Keren; but I am on the look-out for a nice stupid little girl to train for domestic service. I should like her to be rather stupid, for the clever ones can get on well enough without any training of mine. I want to save some poor, ungifted little pauper, if I can, from a life-long drudgery of ill-done scullery work, and cuffs, and blows, and scoldings, such as I am afraid go on in many a big, rich household where the mistress never sees the inside of her own kitchen. I went to the Abbotsby Union yesterday, and a child named Stump was brought to me by the matron, warranted to be a dolt pure and simple, with no bad in her, but absolute absence of ability to be taught; obedient as a dancing bear, almost as awkward —short, stout as I used to be myself in my childish days, with a good square chin—there is hope in that

chin—and the plainest, roundest, full moon of a face that ever was seen. I have a fellow feeling for Stump. I will take her, and see what can be done for her. The only thing in her favour is that she washes herself whenever she can get a chance, a peculiarity which the matron looks upon as indicating aberration of mind.

Mr. Justin comes in two or three evenings a week. At least he is supposed to do so, and Keren prepares a special supper for him on those occasions; but he finds excuses for quite doubling the number of times, so that scarcely a day passes without a visit from him. He has his whole heart in what he is doing, whatever may be said of Annette. I think, however, Annette is happy in her own way, though most likely I shall never again see upon her face that glow of joy which made her look so beautiful when I met her on the hillside of Moorkee, with Captain Asperton by her side.

Oh, how I should like to know the truth of that! And yet what would be the use of knowing the truth now? What difference could it make?

Mr. Justin is very busy, as busy in his way as we are in ours. The beautiful old house in the Northgate is being entirely refurnished, but not in the modern style. Gregory has too much good taste to put new wine into old bottles, as is the fashion of so many people nowadays. He was up in London last week, buying furniture, and hangings, and china to match the date of the place, and a lovely home it will be when it is finished, quite meet for the Recorder and his young bride.

Annette, with a pretty shyness, will not so much as set foot in it until she goes as a bride. I like that, and so does Mr. Justin. It is all very well for middle-aged women, when they are going to marry widowers with grown-up children, to enter boldly into their future husbands' homes, and discuss linen, napery, kitchen-towels, and crockery. But I think a girl-bride's home should have a pleasant touch of mystery about it, which is brushed off by every step she makes into it before she is a wife.

Of course I go in and out, and give my opinion like a regular old friend. I have a fine Indian extravagance about household linen. I am making him get heaps and heaps of it. I have a word to say, too, about fittings, which he would prefer rather sombre. His taste, in the matter of light, is entirely mediæval. He wants the drawing-room windows filled in with stained glass, so as quite to cut off any view of the street, with its busy coming and going. But I tell him that will not do for Annette. She wants a great deal from outside bringing into her life, to keep her from dwelling upon that which is within. It will never do for her to be thrown in upon herself. A room may be ever so beautiful, but still one likes occasionally to see what is outside it. Have not I had enough of that in India, where for four months in the year one cannot get a peep of what is outside, except in the half dark of morning or evening twilight? How weary one becomes, under such conditions, of the loveliest pictures and the richest draperies! One would so gladly sweep them all away for a touch of English life!

No; it will do Annette a world of good to get up a little interest in what can be seen in the old North-

gate. She must amuse herself by watching the groups
of well-dressed people that lounge about the "Star
and Garter" Hotel at race and ball times. And then
there is the engraver's shop next door, with its fine
old etchings and lithographs, as good as any to be seen
out of London ; and on the Judge's Sunday I dare
say there is still a little bustle and parade to be seen
round the Residence, though Mr. Justin tells me the
halberd men do not walk on each side the High
Sheriff's carriage now, with their tin battle-axes, as
in the days of yore. Of course the chairing at election
times is gone, but the yeomanry have their annual
review yet—a pretty sight for grown-up people as well
as children ; and I dare say now there is always a
tide of life ebbing and flowing in the narrow street
to look out upon, which will be ten times better and
healthier for Annette than turning in her thoughts
upon the past, as she sits, saint - like, behind the
loveliest of stained glass, in diaper work of crimson
and purple.

I said as much as this to Mr. Justin when he was
advocating the filling in of the drawing-room windows
with designs from one of the best houses in London.
He replied, in his own quick, argumentative way :

"Why, what nonsense you are talking! One
would think I meant to let little Annette sit in that
room by herself from morning to night, without ever
speaking to her! We shall be always together, of
course, when I am not wanted at the Guild Court.
You don't suppose I am going to condemn my wife
to solitary confinement, do you?"

"Not exactly," I replied, with a glance across the hall—we were going through the Northgate house together then—to the study, which was being made a marvel of comfort in maroon leather and oak, reading-lamps, lounging-chairs, writing-tables, despatch-boxes, reference-shelves, and all that sort of thing. "But, you know, you talked of devoting your spare time to literature, writing for the reviews and newspapers, and of course, if you do that, Annette will be obliged to spend a good deal of time alone."

"That was before I was engaged," he said, with just a touch of annoyance. "A man's first duty is to his wife."

I quite agreed with him, but I had my doubts whether, in months to come, he would see matters in exactly the same light. Gregory Justin is a man of ability and ambition. He will want to make himself a career. I fancy he has not enough of the domestic element in him to be content with home life, and I doubt if Annette has enough public spirit in her to be glad that a great name shall be purchased by him at the cost of loneliness for herself. Of course he thinks now that they will always spend their evenings together.

"We shall read aloud, you know," he said, "and I shall form her mind, and teach her to be interested in my pursuits; and she will be able to help me by-and-by in my literary life, copying and correcting, and writing out references for me. She has a correct and intelligent mind, though half enough has not been made of it."

I had my doubts, too, whether Annette would ever find much delight in copying manuscripts and writing out references, but I said nothing. I had my own way, however, about the drawing-room windows. They are to be left to their pristine light and cheerfulness, whilst the dining-room, which has a blaze of southern light upon it, is to have stained glass put in, and is to be fitted with dark oak. Annette ought to be dressed to correspond, with elbow ruffles and mittens, and powdered hair, and a muslin kerchief over her pretty white shoulders.

I feel a real woman's delight in this marriage. But, apart from my love for both the people interested in it, it will, looked at from a merely selfish point of view, link me with the social life of Abbotsby. Otherwise I should almost have dropped out of that life, having so little sympathy with it. The few friends of my own class whom I had when a girl, have mostly married and left the place, and the remainder have drifted into quite a different track from myself; so that, but for Gregory Justin and his wife, I might be left almost alone.

They will take care of that. As long as that old house in the Northgate belongs to Annette's husband, I shall not want a friend at whose fireside I shall be welcome. And the child is almost like a daughter to me now. I hope she will be happy.

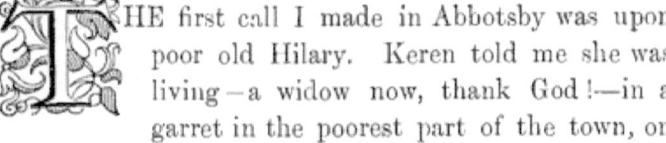

# CHAPTER XXVI

THE first call I made in Abbotsby was upon
poor old Hilary. Keren told me she was
living—a widow now, thank God!—in a
garret in the poorest part of the town, on
half-a-crown a week, one shilling of which she spent
for rent, and eightpence for coal. The remaining
tenpence, supplemented by frequent doles of broth
and tea from Aunt Miriam, and, since Aunt Miriam's
death, from Keren herself, kept body and soul together
in, I should think, rather an unsatisfactory manner.

How my heart yearned to the poor old woman,
who in her more prosperous days had always picked
out for me the most geometrically correct gingerbread
horse, with the most brilliant pink comfit eyes, and
the most glittering of gilt paper bridles; or if it was
a biscuit that I longed for, had invariably selected
the one with the amplest scattering of sugar upon its
delicately browned surface. I went to see her as soon
as I learned that anything was left of her to be seen.

Alas! what a blank she had drawn in the lottery
of life! How very, very far away from her particular
slice of time had the anchor been dropped! She was
living in Forbes' Buildings, a tumble-down place in one
of the very oldest parts of the town, long since given

over to dirt, and misery, and vagabondism. I remembered, when we were children, our nurse had orders never to take us down the street out of which Forbes' Buildings opened, such a nest was it of filth and disease, though cheaper for rent than any other place in the town. Later on, when my brother was home from college, I used sometimes to go there with him to see his old pensioners; but I am afraid my benevolence never overcame a certain innate love of fresh air, which made me long to get out into the street again. It was not until the six months in which Gilbert Ross and I belonged to each other that I ever went into that street with any delight in the errands which took me there.

Inquiring for Hilary in a huckster's shop, on the ground-floor of Forbes' Buildings, I was briefly directed by a woman, who was strongly perfumed with red herrings, to number twenty, right hand, top landing, and after climbing the narrow stair, found myself in a little sloping-roofed room, as clean as a woman's hand-labour could make it. Hilary, patched to the limit of patching possibilities, and bent almost double, but neat and tidy as ever, was creeping about, gathering together the materials for her evening cup of tea. The hands, once stout and strong, which had so often been stretched across the counter of the little shop at the bottom of the lane to give me my dole of sweets, were knotted and drawn with rheumatism; the face, which I dimly remembered even yet rosy and winsome under its Sunday white straw bonnet, was very wrinkled now, and had that look of patient hopelessness which is often all that the aged poor can win when the toil of a dutiful life is nearing its end. But still there was just enough left in the form of the features, and the dim sweetness of the blue eyes, to tell me it was the Hilary who had made my childish days happy.

She made no great professions of astonishment or delight. The "rough carrying on," as she termed it, which she had had for so many years with that drunken husband, poverty, pain, the continual fight with dirt, hunger, and disease, seemed to have cramped and drawn her imagination, just as rheumatism had cramped and drawn her body, and she could no longer see things as they would have appeared to her in her younger days. But still a spark of brightness came into her withered face when I had made her understand who I was, and her poor bony fingers clung tightly to mine as she got hold of my hand to give it a shake of hearty welcome.

"And so you're come home, Miss Hester. Well, thank the Lord, He's spared me to see it, and me the old woman that I am. Keren told me you was a-comin'; but, law! ma'am, I never thought to set eyes on you, and you as good as dead and gone this twenty year past; for it stands to reason when folks is shifted off to them foreign parts, they'd as well be buried for any chance there is to see 'em again. It's a big way off is India, ma'am, isn't it—a bigger way nor what London is? My husband had a cousin once lived maid-of-all-work in London, and it took her a vast of time comin' and goin'"

I told her it took a whole month going to and

coming from India, but I think she mildly disbelieved me. And then we had a long chat together, which convinced me that old Hilary, up there in her garret, with nothing beautiful about her but the sunshine which sometimes struggled in through the little window, was still the same in goodness of heart and simplicity of purpose as the bright, open-faced girl whom my father and mother had cared for. Sad that her seventy years of toil and endeavour and self-denial had brought her to no pleasanter asylum than this at last!

"Well, Hilary," I said, as I got up to come away, "I wish I had found you somewhere else than here. I should like to see you with a bit of garden round your door, as it used to be in the old times when you sold gingerbread horses in the little shop down the lane. Couldn't you find a room somewhere out of the town, where you could get a breath of fresh air now and then, instead of always smoke from your neighbours' chimneys?"

A wistful smile came over Hilary's face as she remembered the little shop down the lane, with its garden full of lavender and roses and marigolds. I expect the life she lived then was almost clearer, more vividly present with her, than the darker days which came after.

"Well, Miss Hester, for that matter I expect I'm where God a'mighty put me, and I don't see any way of shifting; though I don't misdoubt but what it 'ud be a rare thing to have a bit of garden to the front, and me that fond of the fresh air as I didn't think I could ever have kep' my health without it, but I've learned myself to do without a vast o' things since them there times, ma'am, and now I don't wish for nothing, if only I

could be a bit lower down the stair. It would make a
deal of difference to me, ma'am, if I was a bit lower
down the stair."

"Why, Hilary," I said, "you would be ever so much
worse off then. The lower down you go, the nearer you
are to the dirt and smoke. You do get a whiff of sweet
air here sometimes, when the wind does not blow across
the town."

"So I do, ma'am, and wonderful good it is, and
sometimes when the rheumatiz isn't over bad, I make
shift to stand up on that there chair and get a look
out of the window, and I can see away to the green lane
where father and mother's little shop used to be afore it
was pulled down for the new public-house, same as I
couldn't ever do if I was nearer the bottom; but,
ma'am, it's the getting up and down as shakes my old
bones so as I scarce knows which of 'em belongs to
which. I don't never try it only once a week, of a
Sunday morning when I go to church, and of a Friday
when I get my 'lowance from the Board, and then to
your poor aunt Miss Miriam, for the sup of broth as
Keren's give me it reg'lar ever since she was took.
And thinks I, ma'am, every time I come back up these
stairs, and there's five-and-forty of them, I wouldn't
wish anything more in this world only I could be a bit
lower down."

"Well, Hilary, suppose we look about and see if we
can find a cheap room anywhere else."

"Yes, ma'am, that's what I've oft thought, if I could
only have somebody of the quality to speak for me to
Mrs. Byles, her as lives at the bottom of the stair, ma'am,

and keeps the shop, I don't doubt but what I could manage it. And it 'ud be a deal comfortabler for me."

"Does the place belong to Mrs. Byles, Hilary, then?" I asked.

"Oh, no, ma'am! only she's got a shed to the back as she keeps boxes and such-like in, same as she could heap 'em up in the yard just as well, and. I've been at her this many a week past, to see if she would let me have it for what I pay up here, but she says it's more into her pocket to let it to them as comes about hayin' and harvestin', and then it's clear all winter for faggots, which takes a deal o' room."

"But, Hilary, you would never get any sun at all down there, would you?"

"No, ma'am, not much, but them stairs would be such a weight off me; and if I could only get her spoke to about it, and me paying my rent regular, as there's a many here doesn't do it, I don't doubt but she'd be willing, for she's a woman as thinks a deal about the quality, is Mrs. Byles, ever since she lived maid at the Deanery, when mother and me kep' the little shop. If you wouldn't mind the trouble, ma'am, as you go down, just to look into the shed, you'll see it's wonderful handy, and I could be as contented as a queen once I got there, because of not having to come up the stair."

So I left her, promising as I went past it to look into this *ne plus ultra* of poor Hilary's earthly ambition. But as I was groping my way down the dark stair, a much better plan came into my mind, and delighted me so that I cannot help writing down the whole story of it.

# CHAPTER XXVII

I DID look into the shed, though, just to see how far my idea of a haven of rest for Hilary was better than that which had shaped itself in her own mind.

Fancy any lover of God's green earth living there, any one who had once watched the buttercups and daisies spring, or looked at sunrise and sunset through leafy summer trees! It was a little room about ten feet square, with a window, consisting of four small panes of glass, just under the roof, and a rusty fireplace in the corner. Through the window one could only see a dirty brick-wall, culminating in a stack of chimneys belonging to the next tenement. The open doorway commanded a prospect of Mrs. Byles' pleasure-ground, a square courtyard about as large as the shed itself, containing a clothes'-line, two props, a heap of coals in one corner, a heap of faggots in another, and a pile of empty bloater and blacking-boxes in the middle. And this was where Hilary Bennet, after seventy years of honest industry, asked leave to end her days, asked it as a boon, which, if granted, would make her as contented as a queen.

I don't think I ever felt much happier in all my life, certainly never during the Indian part of it, than I felt as I hurried back home to reconnoitre the little lean-to on one side of the greenhouse, which I thought of turning into a room for Hilary. It was originally, I suppose, a potting-shed, and there had been a stove in it, connected with the greenhouse ; but we were never rich enough to keep a gardener, or have bedding-out plants for the summer-time, so my father had put in a window and fireplace, and made the place comfortable for the old man who cleaned knives and shoes for us. Aunt Miriam kept the old man on until he died, and since that time the room appeared to have been used for empty flower-pots, bean-sticks, and such things, which could now be stowed away somewhere else, and then what a magnificent apartment the lean-to would make for Hilary, rent free too, so that she would have an extra shilling a week to spend upon a bit of " butcher's meat " now and then, or a cup of tea to brighten her poor old intellect.

I took counsel with Keren before coming to any decision, for I knew well enough that my faithful help would look coldly upon the execution of any plan which had not previously been submitted to her own approval. Fortunately she took to it as kindly as I did myself, observing, with a certain air of pride in her own discernment, that she had long looked upon Hilary Bennet as one of the excellent of the earth, a city set upon a hill, and a light shining in a dark place ; a testimony which, considering the number of steps leading to poor Hilary's garret, and the scantiness of window accommodation in the neighbourhood, I could not in any way dispute.

Having once taken kindly to the project, Keren

gave herself no rest until she had cleared out, and neatly stowed away in some fitting place, every bean-rod, flower-pot, and useless tool from the little lean-to, blackleaded the grate, scoured floor, woodwork, and window, and made the whole look like an empty temple of cleanliness. Then came the most delightful business of going over the house and considering what we could spare in the way of furniture. Keren soon produced from the lumber attic a most respectable square of carpet, an old table, which had long been discarded from the kitchen, but never sold, because Aunt Miriam had made me a faithful promise that she would never part with anything left in the house by my father and mother—a chair, a fender, a three-legged stool, and a folding iron bedstead, which was kept for lending to any one who might happen to need it. She then produced from the linen-chest a pair of chintz curtains, with which we divided Hilary's new abode into a bedroom and sitting-room; and then out of some Turkey red, Annette, who soon took as much interest in the proceedings as any of us, made a most tasteful drapery for the little window.

I wonder if three people were ever happier than we were—Annette, Keren, and myself—during those days when we were fitting up the lean-to for Hilary? I don't believe Gregory Justin himself, amongst the stained glass and brocaded curtains and carved oak furniture of the Northgate house, was more busily content than were we, turning that empty shed into a comfortable home for an old woman, and putting into it as much convenience, with as little expense as possible.

But I should wrong Gregory if I said that he took
no interest in the proceedings. He gave himself no
end of trouble in contriving an iron rod to stretch
across the room, instead of the rope, which was all our
feminine ingenuity could devise ; and he fastened it up
for us with his own hands, and provided it with rings
for the curtain to slide upon, so that at night, or in
hot weather, Hilary might have the benefit of all the
air that could find its way into the place. But, more
than this, having a dim notion, derived, no doubt,
from tracts read in his youth, that aged and respectable
female poverty enjoys nothing so much as the washing
of its own clothes, he made us a present of a wash-tub
and stand, clothes'-pegs, props, lines, and everything,
with a wooden packing-case, in which they could be
stowed away behind the shed when not wanted. And he
even went so far as to want to buy the dear old lady a
washing-apron of brown holland, after the pattern of
those he had seen in Germany, bound with scarlet
braid, and ornamented with pockets ; but we felt that
would be offering her too much temptation to set her
affections on this world, so we declined it.

Everything was finished by Thursday, the morning
on which Hilary came for her weekly mess of pottage.
Instead of having it ready for her in the accustomed
blue-striped yellow jug, Keren had spread a cloth on
the table in the lean-to, and arranged a comfortable
meal upon it, and she had laid what she called a "cold
fire"—that is, a fire ready for lighting—in the grate,
and put a mug full of sweet-smelling flowers on the
window-shelf, and a very coloury picture of Samuel

and Eli over the chimney-piece; and altogether the little room, though a trifle scant of furniture, space having been left for Hilary's own special household goods, looked as bright as sunshine and good-will could make it.

When the poor old lady hobbled up with her tin can, we all three of us took her down to behold the finished result of our labours, the use for which the room was intended being kept a secret until she had expressed her opinion as to the general effect.

" Well, Hilary," I said, " you see I have begun to make improvements already. This is the shed where we used to keep flower-pots and bean-rods. What do you think of it now ? "

" Well, ma'am," and Hilary tried to straighten her bent old back to get a look all round, up and down, and everywhere, "it's a right comfortable little room, and as fresh as a palace. I lay, miss, you mean to come and take your vittles here of a summer day, as I know there's a many of the quality likes to do it that way, and rare and pretty too, with the green grass in front, same as it used to be when I lived here maid in your poor mother's time, and many and many's the night I've set myself out here with my bit of sewing when the work was done, and was as happy as a milkmaid. Law! ma'am, I was a fool not to know when I was well off, but young folks will have their way."

"So they will, Hilary," said I; "but let us hope you will have a comfortable ending after all the worry and trouble you have gone through. It is never too late for the sun to shine, you know."

" No, ma'am, that's what your poor mother used to say when Bennet had took to his unsteady ways; but he went as quiet as a lamb at the last, and, thank goodness! I've got all his debts paid, and I'm standing straight up on end again, and wouldn't wish for nothing, only there wasn't so many stairs to climb, which I don't doubt but Mrs. Byles will let me have the shed when you're kind enough to say a word for me. And I wish you joy of the little room, Miss Hester, and I hope you'll have your health to take many a pleasant hour in it among your books and things, as the quality has them."

" Thank you, Hilary, and I'm very glad you like the little room. But I didn't have it tidied up for myself, and so you will have to make another guess."

" Didn't you, ma'am ? Then maybe you've invited some of the quality to the flower-show, more'n what the house can put 'em up convenient. That was the way with your father and mother, Miss Hester; they'd always a rare houseful when anything was going on past the common, though they'd never so many as to put up beds outside for 'em, like that there."

And Hilary peered behind the curtain, where stood the little iron bed, covered with a patched quilt of Aunt Miriam's work.

" Wrong again, Hilary," I said. " The room is neither for myself nor for flower-show company. Keren has helped to get it ready, and so have Miss Lislethorpe and Mr. Justin, and it is for *you* to live in. I don't 'like to see you in that sky parlour up at the top of Forbes' Buildings, and it would be worse still for you to be buried alive in Mrs. Byles' rubbish-shed at the bottom, and so, as this little room was of no use, I thought perhaps you would like to have it, and you are not to pay any more rent, and you will not have so far to come for your broth once a week, nor to break your poor old knees either in going up those rickety stairs. Now sit down and drink your broth, and we will leave you for a while to think about it all."

I thought perhaps she would have begun to cry, or something of that sort ; but no, she just looked up at me with a kind of blinded wonder in her dim old eyes, and then round the little room, and then up into my face again.

"I—I return you many thanks," she faltered out at last, but apparently with a great reserve of doubt. It was all very misty to her as yet. I fancy she thought she was only changing landladies, and possibly at an increase of rent, too. However, we left her to think it into shape by herself.

Going quietly to the door half an hour later, I found her kneeling down in front of the three-legged stool, with tears trickling down through her wasted fingers. Whether they were tears of joy or regret I could not tell, for I came away again without disturbing her.

Later on I sent Keren, who, I thought, would explain everything to her better than I could myself, and then they went back to Forbes' Buildings to pay up the rent, and bring away such pieces of furniture and household effects as Hilary did not like to part with. Before nightfall she was comfortably settled, with a bit of fire burning in the grate, and a supply of bread and tea and sugar and soap in the cupboard, and her clothes "put to steep," in readiness for a wash on the morrow; for Mr. Justin was quite right, that was the first thing she thought about when she got into her new quarters.

So now Hilary lives on my "estate," and will do, I hope, until her death, and many a pleasant chat we have as she stumbles through her knitting, or bends over that washing-tub, "the beautifullest ever was seen," which Gregory's care supplied. It was a long time before I could persuade her that I did not want any rent for the lean-to, and that the extra shilling a week might be spent as she liked. For many weeks, Keren said, she stored the money up in a tin mug in the cupboard, lest at any time I should change my mind and call round for it. But she was always of an independent turn of character, slow to accept anything for which she could make no return in kind.

Poor old Hilary! I am glad that, after the long toil and trouble of its midday, she is likely to end her life as she began it, where the green grass can refresh her weary eyes, and God's sunshine look broadly into the little room where she kneels to say her prayers. I feel that her presence here is a sort of blessing on the place, because of her gratitude, which springs like a fountain day and night. Now, while I live, that little room shall be a home for some decent old Christian woman, who I know has lived honestly, and worked faithfully, let her creed be what it may. And God grant that here, in my native town of Abbotsby, I may never fail to find such a one.

N

# CHAPTER XXVIII.

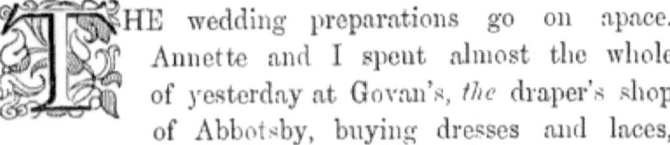HE wedding preparations go on apace. Annette and I spent almost the whole of yesterday at Govan's, *the* draper's shop of Abbotsby, buying dresses and laces, and various bits of finery. I had to do it all myself. Annette just left me to pick and choose as if it had been my wedding, and not her own, which was being furnished. She sat there amusing herself by making up bouquets of artificial flowers, and arranging the ribbons in pretty varieties of colour, whilst I rubbed the silks between my finger and thumb, and pulled them, and held them up to the light, and criticised the Valenciennes, and examined the handkerchiefs, like a regular matronly expert. I never laid out so much money in one morning before, but Mr. Justin says that everything is to be of the best kind, and Annette submits.

I do wish the child would brighten up and take a little more interest in things. Only once, since I have known her, has she kindled up into real animation, and that was when we were getting the house ready for Hilary Bennet. I never saw her make up a bow for herself with half the delight she showed in stitching

those Turkey red curtains; and she has never asked
me a tithe of the questions about her own lovely home
in the Northgate, which she asked about the placing of
the furniture in that little lean-to. I could shake her
sometimes, and yet I am sure she loves Gregory in her
own quiet way.

It is to be a perfectly private wedding, no bridesmaids,
and only two guests invited, Mr. and Mrs. Vermont, from
Cheltenham. Mrs. Vermont wrote with great cordiality
when the engagement was announced. She said she
should be delighted to have the wedding take place from
her own house; but when we said we had made other
arrangements, she accepted them quite pleasantly, as
also my invitation for herself and Mr. Vermont. At
first, after that letter from Port Saïd, Annette was inclined to have nothing more to do with her; but I don't
quite like young people throwing their relations over-
board in that way, and so I prevailed upon her to let
me ask them here for a week.

Keren, Hilary, and the temporary servant, who is
with me now, are to have new dresses for the wedding,
from Mr. Justin. Poor old Hilary has been making
three yards of worsted pillow-lace for the bride, as
costly a gift, I dare say, time and eyesight counted, as
the dainty little trifle of a pocket-handkerchief-case
which has just arrived as a present from Mrs. Vermont.
My gift is a curious, and, I think, rather choice tea-
service for two, which I brought from India. It will
show to more advantage in one of Mr. Justin's carved
oak cabinets than in my old-fashioned little parlour.
As for the bridegroom's offerings, they are simply out

of count. Scarcely a day passes without some piece of lace or jewellery arriving from him.

If only Annette would be a little brighter, I should feel quite right about everything ; but I can never make out whether the child is really happy or not. For hours together she will sit still, apparently absorbed in meditation. Perhaps she is only thinking of the important step she is about to take, and if so, I would not on any account disturb the current of her thoughts ; for marriage *is* a very serious thing, and young people cannot enter upon it with too much consideration. But sometimes I cannot help fancying that it is the past, and not the future, which brings that steadfast look of musing to her face. I wish I could be quite sure that she has done with that past. Only last night I had been having a talk with Hilary, and came back quietly into the parlour. Annette was sitting in the bow-window, with Mrs. Flexon's envelope in her hands. When she saw me, she put it hastily out of sight, and began to talk about some entirely indifferent matter. By-and-by she said she had a headache, and went off to bed, though she must have remembered that it was one of Mr. Justin's nights for coming in.

So he and I had to entertain each other, which we did by talking about the old times, when we were children, and used to make houses under the big table in this very room where we now sit, grave middle-aged folk, with all the responsibilities of life upon us.

I enjoyed that long quiet talk with him, though probably he was disappointed enough. It is very pleasant to say what we like without any fear on either side of being misunderstood. Of course, since his engagement to Annette, we have been able to do this even more than when we first met. And then we fell to talking of our voyage home, our finding out each other on the deck of the *Nawab*, his introduction to Annette as she and I sat under the shade of that skylight, and the quick growth of his love for her, until he felt that she was the one woman out of all the world who could make his life complete.

How curiously one thing leads on to another, and we find ourselves saying, "If it had not been for this—if it had not been for that," we should never have been where and what we are. As if anything went by chance at all; as if the great interests of our lives did not depend upon far other than these little comings and goings, and meetings and partings. I like more and more to think that it is all arranged for us. In God's great plan of the future there is neither maybe nor perhaps, only one great and merciful *to be.*

How strange that, whilst talking over some of his Indian experiences, Mr. Justin mentioned Captain Asperton, whom he had met at the beginning of the cool weather, somewhere during his travels through Bengal.

Suddenly startled out of my self-possession, I exclaimed :

"Why, is it possible that you know Captain Asperton ? "

" Yes, why not ? " replied Mr. Justin, coolly, fixing upon me those quizzical blue eyes of his. "Have not I as much right to know Captain Asperton as anybody else?"

I was so vexed with my own folly that I could have wished myself at the bottom of the sea. I am sure I don't know how I floundered out of the subject, but when he saw my confusion he very quietly, like the gentleman he is, changed the subject.

Of course it was only my own self-consciousness which made me think that Mr. Justin could know anything about the friendship between Captain Asperton and Annette, or that my involuntary exclamation could have betrayed her. I am beginning to feel positively guilty upon that subject. Sometimes I think I ought to tell Mr. Justin about it. And yet what do I know, and may I not be building a castle in the air upon no reasonable foundation? When I come to think quietly about it, it is as clear as daylight that words of mine on that subject could only do harm; and yet it is also as clear as daylight that something ought to be said. I cannot enter upon it with Annette, for I only know by a sort of intuition what the past has been to her; and until she chooses to do so, I do not think any one else has a right to enter upon it with Mr. Justin. I must just let things arrange themselves without interference of mine.

But I was very thankful when the talk came back to stained glass and the old oil paintings which Gregory has been buying for the dining-room.

They are to make a tour through Germany for their wedding trip, remaining abroad for about a month. Mr. and Mrs. Vermont will stay with me a day or two after the wedding. When they are gone, my temporary maid takes up her abode at the Northgate home, and

I have arranged with the workhouse authorities that Stump is to come to me, to be trained under Keren's superintendence.

What a comically uninteresting household we shall be then ! Keren at sixty-five, wizened, parched, and practical, with little of the loveliness of old age about her — I speak only of externals — and much of its angularity ; Stump, my little pauper girl, most rightly named, the veriest unshapen log of humanity that ever waited lifting up of axe and hammer of life's teaching upon it ; myself to complete the trio, middle-aged, unromantic, unhopeful, the foam of youth gone, the clearness of advanced life not yet attained ; in outward appearance, at any rate, just what Mrs. Flexon described me, " a commonplace old stupid." To any outsider who may do us the honour of calling, what an utterly humdrum co-operative society we must appear !

Yet how this commonplace external husk encloses, like the rough, swollen seed-pod of the peony plant, something not lacking a certain beauty and fineness of its own. What a delight it was to me, as a child, to break open that rough husk and count the rosy-tinted, glistening seeds, sleeping like little buds of coral within their silken fine white fibre ! Thank goodness that our home here will be something like the home of those little coral buds, the roughest on the outside. Within, I hope there will ever be found a glow of quietness and content which the hand of the spoiler cannot mar. Keren is as good as gold, though not as fine as paint. Her memories go side by side with mine to the days of my youth. She loved those whom I love. Her faithful service saved my mother's life from many a care. She scolded and petted us when we were children; she shared our little joys, and comforted us in our little troubles. She remembers, too, the bright young face which once made sunshine for me, and sometimes his name is spoken between us, the only time I ever hear it now.

Hilary's gratitude seems like a benediction to the house. Already some of the weary lines have smoothed out of her face, and a sort of moonlight reflection of the brightness which once used to be there is coming again, that sort of after-glow which is so beautiful in old age. I think Hilary, when Annette is gone, will monopolise the good looks of the entire household.

It remains to be seen what qualities Stump will evolve. Brilliant and clever she certainly will never be; but I think I see a stratum of honest, good sense under the coarseness of her exterior, which may develop into something as useful as either cleverness or brilliance. Anyhow, we will try to make this a home for her. She will learn, so far as I can teach her, what love and confidence mean, better, perhaps, than she could have learned in workhouse wards; and knowing what these two things are, she will not want a foundation upon which to build a good life.

She has come over to-day from the Abbotsby Union to have her tea with Keren, and go over the house, and be told what sort of work is expected from her. She and Keren are in the back garden now, admiring the cabbage beds. What an affluence of solidity, what a superfluity of substance there is about her, as she stands there with her arms a-kimbo, her broad, gray-stockinged feet firmly planted on the ground, the square, massive outlines—not curves—of her short figure admirably defined by the indigo blue gingham of the workhouse dress. Stump, one might make a butcher's block of you, or your width is so liberal that if, like the *Elle* maids of the Scandinavian legends, you were hollow at the back, you might serve as a magnificent horse trough! Whether you will ever become such a maid-of-all-work as to meet the requirements of Keren and myself, only time, that great prover of all things, can tell.

# CHAPTER XXIX.

ELL, it is over! The sun shone bravely upon them. Annette, in her simple muslin, of the whitest and finest, with the set of Roman cameos which the bridegroom gave her, looked just as I expected she would look. She shed never a tear, nor was there the least tremor of excitement in her voice, and her eyes had a wistful, far-off expression which I would fain not have seen in them, as she gave to Gregory Justin what can be taken back no more now, until death do them part.

"Decidedly interesting and stylish-looking," was Mrs. Vermont's verdict, as the bride, enveloped in her filmy, cloud-like raiment, came into church. And then she said what a good thing it was that the dear girl had chosen a man with comfortable means, as she was evidently not fitted to grapple with the difficulties of a small income. I think she is very proud of the match, and proud of her nephew, and especially proud of the Northgate home; with its beautiful stained glass and carved oak furniture, "so much better," as she whispered to me when the newly married couple had gone into the vestry to sign their names, "so much better, you know, than the poor dear girl could have expected when she was left without a penny of her own, and nobody in the world to whom she could justifiably look for a home. And, indeed, my dear Miss Brown, Mr. Vermont and myself are so infinitely obliged to you for all the kindness you have shown her. You have really been like a mother to the poor thing ! "

How coolly and pleasantly she said it, just as if that Port Saïd letter had never been written !

Mrs. Vermont is a clever, wide-awake woman of the world. She beamed upon us all with the greatest complacency, said my cottage was the sweetest little ideal of comfort in the world, promised to visit Mr. and Mrs. Justin some time during the winter, hoped they would consider her house their home whenever they needed a change, and assured me that if ever I came to Cheltenham nothing would delight her so much as to renew her acquaintance with me.

It is not impossible that I may go to Cheltenham some day. Though I never kept up any correspondence with my cousin Delia whilst I was in India, she has written to me very kindly since I came home, and asked me to spend a week or two with her, after Christmas. I don't think it is well for people to lose sight of their relations, so probably I shall accept the proposal, especially as I think she may enjoy coming to see me here in the summer-time.

It is certainly not from her father's side of the family that Annette inherits the simplicity and unworldliness which are so attractive to us who know her. I think I never saw a woman who is so utterly, openly, and I may almost add delightfully, of the earth, earthy, as Mr. Lislethorpe's sister. Exactly the woman to have recommended a West End fashionable school for her niece, and to have left her on the hands of any charitable friend, when she came home, an orphan and dependent, to struggle with the world as best she might. I suppose Annette has her mother's character—the mother whom she can scarcely remember now. How strange and sad it must be not to remember one's mother! How it must sweep away from life some of its best and fairest colouring! The whole landscape of my childhood and girlhood is so dependent upon the sunshine which my parents shed over it, that I can scarcely realise any condition from which that light should be absent.

Mrs. Vermont is a woman who rejoices in eligible marriages. She openly expresses her conviction that an early settlement is indispensable to a woman's success in life, she having achieved matrimony herself at the age of eighteen ; and she enlarges so innocently upon the ways and means by which a woman of the least common sense may secure a husband for any girl committed to her charge. So clearly did she state these convictions that I could sometimes have owned myself guilty of unpardonable stupidity for being, at my present mature age, Miss Brown still.

But no condition of human life is without its compensating balance. Mrs. Vermont falls into the megrims if left to herself for half an hour. She must have society—continual society. It is as necessary to her as the air she breathes. What she will do when her husband is dead, if he dies first, I cannot imagine, for I am sure no companion will sit with her day in and day out, as she expects him to do. She told me the greatest trial of her life was being left alone of an evening, when Mr. Vermont went to a committee, or anything of that sort. She was always obliged to have somebody for company—one of the servants, if she could raise no one else.

Now that is a condition as utterly unintelligible to me as not being able to remember one's parents. My very sweetest hours are those which I spend with no other companionship than that of memory. I have a perfect delight now in looking forward to the long winter evenings, when I can draw up my arm-chair to the fireside, and put my feet on the fender, and call up one by one sweet pictures of the past, beyond that spell of hard work which I call my fifteen years in the wilderness. And yet, but for those years of toil, would these of rest have been so sweet? That part of my life is like the somewhat grave-coloured middle distance of a picture, giving tone and beauty to all the rest.

Mrs. Vermont and her husband left me the second day after the wedding. I fancy, though she expressed herself much to the contrary, that she found my quiet life rather slow; and having, before the bride and bridegroom went away, secured an invitation for the winter, there was no need for further delay on her part than absolute courtesy demanded.

I got on better with Mr. Vermont. He is a quiet, meditative man, fond of rambling about amongst libraries, which also is my delight. We had very little conversation, however, because Mrs. Vermont did not like to be alone, and she hates to hear people talk about books. I equally dislike hearing them talk about other people; so that, when the wedding was exhausted, our facilities for social intercourse were somewhat limited.

Now I am left alone. "Poor dear Miss Brown!" as Annette's aunt said when she bade me good-bye, and

I am sure she meant it. She was far sorrier for me
than I was for myself. I wish nothing better than that
my days should go on to their end in the quietness to
which the departure of my guests has consigned me.
If I want society, I can go to Mrs. Carbery, my mother's
friend. What a wonderful old lady she is, really, as
Mr. Justin told me, at eighty reading the papers and
reviews, and keeping up with the interests of the day
like any one in the prime of life, only with this superiority,
that her opinions have the mellowness of age and experience, and that her judgments are tempered by a charity
which has gone on widening with her knowledge of life. To
hear her and her son, the London doctor, who comes down
twice a year to see his mother, have a discussion on politics,
or some social question, is one of my greatest treats.

Always excepting, however, her recollections of my
parents. She remembers them when they came as
bride and bridegroom to Abbotsby, and took possession
of this house, which was their home quite on to the end.
Mrs. Carbery was the friend consulted by them in all
domestic difficulties ; the first to come, the last to leave,
when death or sickness visited the family. At other
times, how her entrance was hailed by us children !—
for she never came unprovided with some delightful
little story to tell us, or some picture-book, or paper of
sugar-plums hidden in the depths of her great sable
muff. She tells me that, when she rides out in the cold
weather, she wears that muff still, its pristine proportions
never having been curtailed to meet the requirements
of fashion. I wonder what little children get the sugar-
plums and picture-books now, and if they enjoy them
half so much as brother Mark and I used to do ?

Then I have Stump.

Stump is delightful. As for her outward appearance, she is like a palm-tree, exactly the same thickness all the way up, though without any of the aspiring elegance of that magnificent endogen. At the top she throws out a shock of yellow brown hair, which, being stiff by nature, and frequently cut by art, utterly refuses now to adapt itself to the downward sweep called for by neatness. Her only resource is to gather it all behind, and tie it round with a piece of string, leaving the ends to stick out like a bottle-brush. She came to us the evening after the wedding. When I went into the kitchen to receive her, she was sitting very far back in one of the biggest chairs, her feet dangling backwards and forwards within six inches of the floor, her short, stout arms, guiltless of anything like tapering towards the wrists, embracing affectionately the bundle which contained her worldly goods. There was a look of vacant wonder in her face, as of one who, without regret for the past, or hope or fear for the future, has been launched into an entirely untried state of being.

"Get up and drop a curtsy to the missis, ye mannerless little hussy," said Keren, not unkindly ; and then, turning confidentially to me, she whispered :

" Law, ma'am, she be a rough sort, and no mistake, but there's a deal of her for her years."

The bundle was tilted over to one side, the straight round ankles planted firmly on the floor, the curtsy dropped with as little of grace as was possible, and then Stump got on the chair again, shuffling herself back as far as ever she could, until her feet were dangling at the proper height.

" Please'm, is there aught else to do ? "

This was addressed to Keren.

"Yes, there is," said the old woman, good-humouredly. "Go your ways to the pump and fill yon cistern. I reckon it's fitter work for your arms nor for mine."

Down came Stump again, and off to the pump in the corner, from which the cistern which feeds my patent cooking apparatus is supplied. Here, heedless of ulterior results, and knowing no more than that Keren had told her to pump away, she *did* pump away with such might and main that in two moments the cistern was emptying its surplus all over my kitchen floor, Stump seeing nothing but the work immediately before her of using the pump-handle as vigorously as possible.

" Laws a massy me ! " she said at last, when, startled by Keren's shouts of dismay, she turned and saw the mischief she had wrought. " I've done it overmuch, I lay." And with an agility scarcely to have been expected from her build, she seized upon one of my best glass-cloths, and began to mop the floor with it, until called to order by renewed screams from Keren.

" Ye little ne'er-do-weel ! Is that what you've been brought up to, and them cloths the best linen to be bought in Abbotsby town for love or money ? Ain't you ashamed of yourself, then, to know no better, and you the size you are ? "

" No, ma'am," said Stump. " You should ha' told me when to stop. I've been brought up allers to go on while I was told to stop."

I retired, feeling that I could laugh with more comfort in the parlour. And so ended Stump's first evening in her new place.

# CHAPTER XXX

UT still I am bound to say that she is delightful. Her ignorance is of that robust and refreshingly primitive kind which never irritates any one. Indeed it rather gives me the feeling which a gardener must have, I should think, when he gets possession of a piece of utterly uncultivated, and therefore unexhausted soil, into which he can put almost what he likes, and be sure of its coming to something.

Was ever anything like her stare of astonishment when Keren took her over the house the morning after her arrival, to show her the different things, and tell her how they were to be kept in order? She evidently thought I must be a very selfish woman to require so much accommodation, so many plates, dishes, knives, forks, and glasses for my own individual use, besides the entire labour of two people spent for my convenience. Stump has imbibed a great deal of that sort of philosophy which makes wealth to consist in the fewness of one's wants. She rather scorns than is impressed by a multiplicity of requirements. One cup and one platter, one suit of clothes to wear, and another to wash, one room to live in, and a fiftieth share of a pump to drink

o

from—this is Stump's idea of the claims of the individual, and every one who exceeds it is, according to her system of social economy, taking more out of the common stock than she puts into it.

Viewed geologically, Stump consists at present of only two formations. The primary, or granite period, so to speak, consists of opinions like those above mentioned, deposited during her ten years' existence in the village of Wabblesthorpe, where she and her old grandmother lived on two shillings a week from the parish. The remains of this period are of the simplest description, but will nevertheless, I doubt not, heave up and overtop any other strata which succeeding periods may form.

Three years ago, the old grandmother died, and Stump was brought to the Abbotsby Union, where she has remained ever since, until, a week ago, she came to my house. At the Union began the secondary formation, a deposit of ideas widely different from the granite simplicity of the Wabblesthorpe period. Things at the "workhus" were done on a scale of unprecedented magnitude; coppers full of soup, cart-loads of loaves, puddings—when such luxuries made their appearance— as ample in proportions as that before which Jack the Giant Killer satisfied his hunger; boots and shoes like the rank and file of an infantry corps; wearing apparel in heaps as big as a haystack. But then, if the preparations were vast, so were the necessities which had to be met, so that Stump's philosophy easily rose to the occasion, none of the paupers getting more than was needful, and every one being rigorously compelled to put in a certain amount of labour for the food and

clothing bestowed. Here the Juggernaut of uniformity
began to crush poor Stump under its ponderous wheels.
She must eat, drink, sleep, wake, work, rest, think, like
every one else, and life resolved itself for her into a huge
machine, in which she and her companions were but
threads, flitting backwards and forwards, with no will or
choice of their own as to the pattern into which they
were being woven, or the uses to which they might be put.

"Heaps upon heaps of us, ma'am," as poor Stump
said when describing her "workhus" life, "and the bite
and the sup as reg'lar as clockwork, and always your
quantity, let you take it or leave it, and every one on
us with pinnies and petticoats alike, and a book apiece for
us when we went to the prayers, and never no difference
in nothing, only Chrissamus, when the plum-puddings
was agate. Law! ma'am, but it was a wonderful place,
was the workhus."

"And did you like it, Stump?" said I.

A strange look, as of some inexpressible but quite
understood thought, came into Stump's full moon of a
face as she replied:

"Well, ma'am, I can't say as I mattered it much.
I was kind of overmuch mixed up into all the rest, so as
I never knew for certain where I was nor what I was,
only when I said through my prayers of a night, same as
my grandmother always teached me. It never seemed
to come to me any time but then what things was all
going on to."

A curious remark, I thought, for a girl of thirteen to
make, and showing a fine field of meditative faculty
beneath that stupid, uncultured surface.

"But, Stump, wasn't it rather nice having so many girls to talk to? Don't you think you will perhaps be rather lonely here?"

"No, ma'am," said Stump, straightforwardly, "it wasn't nice. We was always overthick of a lump, ma'am, and I belonged as much to the whole lot on 'em as I did to myself, in a manner; and if I tried to do right it was no credit to me, and if I did my work bad, why, it got shuffled in among the ruck, out of sight, and nothing came of it; and that wasn't the way grandmother had used to teach me out of the Bible. She said we was all to do our own work and take our own blame, if we got any."

I was amused at the way Stump talked on to me, evidently without the least shyness, and glad to find some one who would understand the opinions which she had hewn out for herself from the rude materials of her life. And I, for my part, began to have a delightful dawning of respect for this girl, with her sturdy, square-built form, and her thick arms and legs, and her round tea-cake of a face, out of which the features seemed to have been shaped with some one's finger and thumb, and her stubby yellow-brown hair sticking out behind in bottle-brush fashion from the piece of string which held it together. "A most unhandy lump of a lass," said Keren, with a deprecating glance at the unlovely exterior; but there was a half-formed soul struggling for expression within, and a fine individuality of character which scorned to be "shuffled in among the ruck," even for the hiding of its faults. Stump's ethics, so far, were about as good as any I could teach her. I might perhaps be able to instil new ideas into her mind relative to the proper management of pump-handles, but I don't think I could suggest a better foundation for the building up of a useful life than that which the old grandmother had already laid—doing her own work and taking her own blame if she got any.

But I see that Stump has a reserve of doubt. A third stratum of ideas is being deposited in her mind. In the first stage of life at Wabblesthorpe, and the second at the Abbotsby workhouse, small and large means were adapted to proportionately small and large ends. Here, that principle is being entirely overthrown. I am absorbing, to my own private uses, an amount of labour, money, and material which, according to Stump's preconceived notions, is entirely disproportionate. What right have I to such an unlimited number of plates, knives, and forks, and such ample accommodation in the matter of space, to say nothing of two women to fetch and carry for me, and a pump to my sole and separate use? The girl looks at me with misgiving, though she sees I am kindly disposed to her. I am taking more out of the world than I am putting into it.

I heard Keren explaining it to her last night, by the help of the Catechism, which hitherto Stump has only learned parrot-like at the "workhus," without any idea of its application to the daily routine of life. Keren argued that there was a certain class of people, broadly described under the term "betters," towards whom it was the duty of girls like Stump to order themselves "lowly and reverently," not taking it amiss if the betters did fare a little more sumptuously every day, or absorb a little more of the floating labour of their fellows. Furthermore, Keren insisted that the Apostle Paul himself exhorted servants to be obedient to their masters ; that from the days of Abraham downwards it had been a generally accepted law that some people should have more things than were absolutely necessary for their daily wants, and that other people should gain an honest living by making and keeping those things clean.

At any rate, Keren had one advantage. She could clinch her argument by personal example, her whole life having been spent in faithful ministration to those whom she had been taught to esteem as her betters. And so far that ministration had issued in a fair share of comfort to herself.

When the homily was over, I heard Stump say, and I could just fancy the mixture of doubt and dawning perception with which she said it :

" Well, there's no telling. Maybe if folks can pay for it, they've a right. But it's a queer world."

# CHAPTER XXXI.

INCE then we have got on beautifully. The irrigation of Keren's common-sense arguments has left a sort of alluvial deposit upon the previous foundations in Stump's mind, out of which the vegetation of a useful life is slowly developing.

But she takes on the amenities of civilisation very slowly. She has a great objection to doing anything, the reason of which she cannot thoroughly understand. Especially she dislikes what she considers useless outlay of time or labour. She will persist, whilst waiting upon me at dinner, in carrying on an animated conversation with Keren in the kitchen, relative to the change of plates and the successive stages at which I have arrived in the meal.

"Keren, haul out the pudden, missis is nearly through with the mutton shoulder." Or: "Look alive, Keren, and get up the cold pie. Missis don't matter the warm meat to-day."

In reply to which, muttered growls of monition come from the kitchen, or Keren herself advances to the parlour door, and fires off a hissing cannonade of reproofs.

"Hould yer whisht, can't you, you ignorant little baggage? Do you think that's the way the quality has their vittles served? Come your ways right off to the kitchen when you've got aught to say."

"And keep missis waiting," rejoins Stump, with fearless confidence in her own way of providing for my comfort. " Why, she'd never have done dinner at that gate."

But Stump yielded to persuasion. At first, when I had taught her that my dining-room was not the place whence she should issue information to the presiding genius of the kitchen, she would go out, shut the door carefully behind her, and, still with her hand upon the latch, shout hastily to Keren, coming back with the proud consciousness of one who knows at last how to do things properly. But after patient explanation, the truth dawned upon her mind ; and now when she has anything to say to Keren during meal-times, she goes quite away to the kitchen and carefully shuts *that* door behind her, too, before she begins to state the facts. Dear little, ugly Stump ! If she errs at all, it is not from want of will to please.

It is curious, too, to watch how she sticks to the principle which she asserted at first as the reason of her behaviour at the pump, namely, going on with a thing until she is told to stop. Give Stump a bowl of potatoes to wash, and she will go on scrubbing, scraping, polishing, lustrating, until each separate tubercle is as clean as the face of a new wax doll. The idea of finishing never enters into her mind, only of making her work as perfect as it can be made. So of black-leading. Seeing her one afternoon in want of occupation, I sent her into the drawing-room to brighten up the grate, and after the lapse of three hours found her there still, burnishing away with might and main, though there was not a square inch of the whole surface in which her conscientious little dab of a face could not be seen as plainly as in a looking-glass. The good child! and she would have gone patiently on until midnight, if nobody had stopped her.

But Stump prospers both in body and mind, and is, I believe, quite content. Every night she comes to me to read her chapter, write her copy, and do a sum in simple addition. Then I have given her a little bit of garden for her own, close by Hilary's door, and there she digs and waters, and puts in and pulls out, just as she likes, with a big pinafore tied over her afternoon frock, whilst Hilary sits in her arm-chair outside, with —must I confess it?—a pipe in her mouth! For who am I that I should damage the old woman's declining days by denying her that comfort? She deserves it more than I deserve any of mine.

Then on Sunday evenings they all three of them come into my room, Hilary putting her best bonnet on for the occasion, and we have a little church to ourselves, followed by what they seem to enjoy very much—a look at the pictures in my great illustrated Bible, about which I encourage them to make their own remarks, and express their own opinions as freely as they like. I think, on the whole, Stump is happier with me than she was at the "workhus," for she knows now where she is, and what she is, and takes her own blame if she "gets ony."

Of course this sort of thing would not do at all if I were, what is called, in society. Fancy a dinner-party made up of people like Mrs. Vermont, Mrs. Flexon, Mrs. Marsham, waited on by Stump, with a flying visit occasionally from old Keren in her thick white cap and kerchief! How the guests would laugh—inwardly, of course. But, thank goodness, I am not in society! I can arrange my life according to my own fashion, and

be happy in my own way. Mr. Justin and Annette
understand my peculiarities, and I am quite sure when
they come they will not laugh at me.

They soon will come now. They have already left
Paris on their way home. Phillips, the new maid, has
been in the house a fortnight, making everything ready.
To-morrow I go to arrange flowers and put those
little finishing touches which the hands of a hireling
never seem to do quite rightly. Stump and I are off
early to-morrow morning for grasses and bulrushes from
the river-side, to be mixed with ferns which we shall
gather from Barlby Planting on the hilltop. Annette
has such a passion for ferns, though certainly not
because she was brought up amongst them, for I question
if she ever saw a living one until she went to Moorkee.
I sometimes wonder if she loves them so because they
bring to her remembrance the mountain paths there,
and the days when she wandered so happily among
them. But I will not let myself think of that now.

7th.

The bride has taken possession of her new home,
and very bonnie and wife-like she looks in it. I went
in last night to give them a welcome, as they said they
should like me to be their first guest

Oh dear, how things change, and the world changes
with them, and we change too! There seemed nothing
the same last night but the great star and garter over
the door of the inn opposite, which caught my eye as
soon as I went into the drawing-room. The place does
look very beautiful now, and Mr. Justin has brought
something quaint and curious from nearly every one of

the old German cities where they stopped. Up the staircase and on the landings are arranged the Indian things which he collected last year, and a little sort of corridor, through which you enter the drawing-room, is entirely filled with the loveliest ferns and mosses, in compliment, I suppose, to Annette's taste for them. The house gives one the impression of being presided over by refinement and plenty of money; but somehow it has lost the delicious feeling of homeliness which I remember long ago. And Annette?

Well, I suppose nothing will ever make her flash and sparkle again. I must not look for it. But somehow one expects, in calling upon a bride, that happiness itself will be embodied in her smile, and a sort of queenliness of delight ray out in every tone of her voice. Annette was not at all like that. I could see nothing but old cathedrals and altar-pieces reflected from her eyes. She seemed to have put on the repose and almost a little of the melancholy of the mediæval cities from which she had just come. It suits her wonderfully well, I must say. just as does the costly Belgian lace with which Gregory Justin has adorned her pretty throat and wrists, if only one could forget that it is a bride of scarce six weeks upon whom such utter serenity has fallen.

But what Annette lacks in animation, her husband supplies. He seems brimful of happiness and good spirits; positively insisted upon giving me a kiss of welcome when I crossed the threshold; has brought Hilary a bran-new shawl, and Keren a merino gown; is proud of his home, proud of his wife, and ready, in his overflowing content, to do a good turn for anybody. So I hope all will be well.

# CHAPTER XXXII

November 28th.

DON'T often get time to write in this little book now. Somehow, things are always coming up that must be attended to, and I never can settle down to writing unless I have a clear, undisturbed spell of quietness before me.

We are nearly through November now, that month which Mrs. Vermont says she dreads so, but which—this year, at any rate—has been pleasant enough to me, spite of its fogs and fallen leaves, and general reputation of melancholy. I do so enjoy the long firelight evenings. I tickle the coals into a playful flicker, and then turn down the lamp, and put my feet on the fender, and think over the old times, and enjoy the perfect rest of being able to do just as I like.

The luxury of being let alone! After all there is none like it. I wonder sometimes how I went through all that zenana work out there in India. I think of the poor little woman toiling away year by year, with scarcely any one to say a kind word to her, or pity or caress her, and I do feel so sorry for her. I can scarcely realise that it was myself. I have heard about my Indian women once or twice. They have somebody else now to talk to them. I hope she won't pull down all that I tried to build up, but I think Mr. Grant would not let any one do that. I have this comfort, that some seeds of truth have been dropped into their minds, and I think no truth can ever die.

Mrs. Vermont paid her promised visit to the young people at the beginning of this month, and there were some very elegant dinner-parties consequent thereupon. Mr. Justin is fond of entertaining—much more so than Annette. I believe he thinks what is the use of a large house and beautiful furniture and a pretty wife, unless you can gather plenty of people round you, to show them how well off you are? I did not mean to put the case quite so barely as that, but still so it is. Mrs. Vermont says Annette is a most fortunate girl—quite a credit to the family; but she thinks she does not rise sufficiently to her position. She ought to give frequent dinner-parties, she says, have "at homes" every now and then for an unlimited number of people, make herself a sort of centre of society here, and get herself looked up to as an acknowledged leader. As if simple-minded little Annette could ever get herself looked up to as anything of that sort!

I was quite vexed to hear Mrs. Vermont talking in this way to Mr. Justin, one day when his wife was not present, and still more vexed to find that Mr. Justin did not fling back the remarks as they deserved. Gregory is a man who is very open to judicious flattery. Mrs. Vermont knows how to flatter him judiciously. I believe, if she had stayed with them much longer, she would have succeeded in convincing him that he was quite an ill-used husband, because his wife did not give dinner-parties twice a week, and talk herself hoarse in trying to be a leader of society  Such nonsense ! I have no patience with women who will meddle in that way.   I am heartily glad Mrs. Vermont is gone, though before she went away she managed to get an invitation for next summer.

When I have an evening to spare, Annette implores me to go and spend it with her.  Of course this would not be the case if Mr. Justin had kept to his purpose of reading aloud to his wife every night—but I never ex- pected he would keep to that purpose.  He generally spends the evenings now in his luxuriously appointed study, where he is going into the subject of the ventila- tion of public buildings.  He says it is just the same as sitting with his wife, because the rooms open to each other, and she can call to him whenever she likes ; but I don't think Annette sees it in that light.  I am sure I should not if I were a wife, however much I respected ventilation.  But still they are very fond of each other.

Stump takes a great deal of teaching.  Fortunately, when an idea once works itself into her mind, she holds to it as persistently as a mongoose to a snake.  After nearly four months' patient training, she can now wait at table with tolerable neat-handedness, and as for her washing up of glass and china, it is beyond all praise, though in that, as in all other things, she takes her own time, and will not be hurried for anybody.  She has quite accepted the fact which I mentioned before as the tertiary stratum in her mind, that there is a class of elders and betters, who have hereditary or acquired rights to an unlimited number of properly-paid-for

plates, knives, forks, and other things ; and that there
is a second class of youngers and subordinates, whose
equal right, hereditary or acquired, it is to keep these
things clean ; and that, whether the duty exercised be
of owning or cleaning, it is equally honourable in the
Great Master's sight. So that Stump's self-respect is
no longer wounded by the position in which she finds
herself.

Her attachment to Keren, and myself, and Hilary,
whom she considers as one of the family, has a sort of
dog-like faithfulness about it which is very touching.
She will let us do nothing that she can do for us. She
is continually on the watch to prevent old Keren from
carrying anything, and if she sees me with a brush or a
duster in my hand now, she almost looks upon it as an
insult to herself. I never knew a girl with so much
consciousness of responsibility about her. Slow at first
to learn her duty, she is more vigilant in the doing of it
when learned than any up-grown woman I have met.

I heartily respect little Stump, though no one knows
what I have gone through in the cultivation of her
intellect. But so long as her moral qualities are so
satisfactorily developed, I care not if she comes to adult
years before she masters the intricacies of spelling and
subtraction, or is able to write her own name without
such putting forth and contortion of her tongue as make
me doubt whether that unruly member will ever recover
its proper position.

Hilary teaches her sewing. It is such a delight to
the dear old woman to think that in this way she can be
of any use in the world. Scarcely a day passes in which

I do not have a chat with Hilary. Her little room does look so nice and cosy, with its red curtains and cheery bit of fire. And then back again to my own comfortable parlour, which Stump keeps as clean as a new pin, always watching her opportunity, when I am out, to pop in and clear away every speck of dust she can find.

And her broad, genial smile of welcome, if I am away but half an hour, the innocent, unsophisticated satisfaction with which she relates to me her various achievements in the kitchen ; her look of content when, having finished her work, and " cleaned herself," she comes to me for the loan of a *Band of Hope*, or *British Workman*, and relieves herself of her superabundant gratitude by an expressive :

" Law, ma'am, but I *is* glad I was took in here !"

It is worth all those long years of exile from home and country to feel that, resting at last, my life is not entirely wasted ; that, with talents neither of money, intellect, nor position, I can yet gather a few people round me to love me, and be sorry when I am gone.

After Christmas I visit Cousin Delia at Cheltenham. I cannot say I much like the prospect of leaving my own fireside at that time of year ; but, as I told myself before, one must not let one's relations quite slip out of sight, and my cousin has been very kind in writing to me since I came home.

I am to eat my Christmas dinner with Gregory and Annette ; and Keren and Hilary and Stump will have a merry-making on their own account in the kitchen here.

# CHAPTER XXXIII.

HE world is really not so very large.

Mr. and Mrs. Justin—I like to write the words in full sometimes to see how they look—were at the county ball last week, and Annette danced in the same quadrille with Mrs. Aberall, the lady who wanted to be the "burra mem Sahib" of the *Nawab*. Afterwards they had a little chat together, the Colonel's wife being able to unbend to the wife of the Recorder of Abbotsby, as she could not be expected to unbend to "that poor Miss Lislethorpe," who was returning from India without a penny to bless herself with.

She has been spending the summer and autumn at Cheltenham. It is astonishing what numbers of Indian people go there. But she intends to winter at Mentone, and I am glad of that, for I believe my cousin Delia goes out a great deal, and I really should not care to renew my intercourse, or, to speak more correctly, want of intercourse, with Mrs. Aberall; though Annette says she inquired very kindly after me, was delighted to hear that I was so comfortably settled in Abbotsby, and said she would have been very glad to call upon me, only her time was so limited. It seems she was visiting some of

P

the county people in this neighbourhood, and so was included in their invitation to the ball. I can fancy how she would have laughed at Stump and Keren if she *had* called. At myself too, perhaps, afterwards; for I think we are all very much of the same pattern.

She told Annette that Mrs. Flexon is living in St. John's Wood, not married yet. Dr. Byte is settled in a practice in the neighbourhood, and Mrs. Flexon finds the air agree with her so well that she has no intention of removing for the winter. But I have heard that St. John's Wood is a very sheltered situation, and reasonable, too, for rents, so perhaps she has chosen wisely. It was curious to have that old ship-life brought back. It does seem so far off now, quite distanced from me by the calm bright reaches of the life that I live day by day in my own home.

Annette does not often come to see me, but generally I spend a couple of evenings in the week with her, when Mr. Justin is at his Club. He has taken to going there a good deal lately, having developed a taste for politics. I should not wonder if he becomes an important man in that direction. Mrs. Carbery was telling me the other day that people begin to speak of him as a likely member for the borough at the next election. Nothing would please Gregory better than that, but I don't know how Annette would like it. She is not an ambitious woman.

I feel now about Gregory Justin that he will not be content until he has made for himself a career of some kind. More than this, he must not only feel that he is working to some definite end, but he must feel that his work is acknowledged and appreciated. He is not one of those men, grandly independent of externals, who, having set before themselves a worthy thing to do, do it quietly, measuring themselves by what they are, and not by what the world's praise or blame makes them appear to be. He has great activity of mind and great love of approbation; so he must work, and he must be praised for his work. Then he will be happy.

Something of this came out the other night when he was bringing me home, after I had been spending the evening with his wife. I could see that he is already chafing at the extreme quietness of his home. I suppose quietness was not what he aimed at when he furnished it so beautifully, and spent so much money over stained glass and brocaded damasks and seventeenth century tables and chairs.

"You know, Miss Brown," he said, "I do wish Annette was just a little bit more fond of company. Goodness knows I don't want her to become a fashionable woman of society, or anything of that sort, but with the position I have in the town, don't you think now that it would be better if she could come out a little more in the matter of entertaining? Nobody dislikes formal company more than I do, but if she would let us give a good handsome dinner-party once a fortnight or so, during the winter, it would only be what people have a right to expect from us."

This was the springing up of the seed which Mrs. Vermont had dropped into his mind. How that clever woman did find him out, and flatter him on those points where a man of his character is so susceptible! Gregory likes to be thought brilliant in conversation. Mrs.

Vermont made him believe she had never seen any one to equal him in that respect. He loves popularity. She told him he ought to be at the head of society in his native town—would be so, if only "dear little Annette" would come out of her shell and live up to her position. How vexed I had felt with her when I heard her say that!—how ten times more vexed I felt now, when the words were beginning to bear their evil fruit!

I said something, in a feeble, inefficient sort of way, about people not being able to change their natures. Somehow I can think of excellent remarks when I am holding imaginary conversations with people, but when it comes to putting them into speech, the sound of my own voice makes me the veriest idiot. How often, since Mrs. Vermont's visit, had I argued out this very subject mentally with Mr. Justin, and retired triumphant from the field, having convinced him that Annette as she was was infinitely better than the Annette he would make. Now I could not get a word out. I had a curious feeling of sympathy with him from his own point of view, combined with antipathy, which arose out of my love for Annette. The two feelings clashing with each other made me as helpless as a dumb animal. I believe I came out at last with a feeble little bit of sentiment about home being a woman's sphere.

"Oh, yes," he replied. "I should hate to see Annette flaunting about, always calling and being called upon and thinking of nothing but what dress she would look best in, or who admired her most. I only want her just to take a little more interest in things, and look animated when people come. Of course, you know, on board ship one could account for her being quiet, and all that sort

of thing, because she had had such a hard time of it
before, poor darling, but I quite hoped she would get out
of it when we were settled down here, and she had so
many things in her favour. I fancy, however, now, that
she will always shrink from society, and so, you see——"

Gregory stopped to take a comfortable whiff or two
at his cigar.

"I—I think it will be better for me to see my friends
at the Gentleman's Club. Of course, if I mean to do
anything for the place, I *must* see people, and hear what
is going on, and get myself known amongst the men of
the neighbourhood, and that seems the simplest way of
doing it. An evening in the week, and two or three
afternoons, will be quite enough. Indeed, I could not
afford the time at night oftener, because I am reading
up so hard now for that paper I want to send to the
—— *Review* next month. I had no idea the subject
would take so much mastering. I have been at it every
night this week, and I am only just beginning to see my
way through it properly."

Every night! and little more than six months ago,
Gregory Justin was so very sharp with me for suggesting
that the drawing-room windows should be left plain, so
as to afford Annette the resource of looking through
them, if she did chance to be left alone sometimes of an
evening. But idiot though I am upon some subjects, I
am too wise a woman to "rile" a man, especially a man
of Gregory Justin's temperament, by so much as suggesting to him that any of his splendid purposes have come
to nothing. I only condoled with him on the difficulties
of arriving at anything like a satisfactory conclusion as
to the best method of ventilating public buildings.

"Yes," he said, evidently glad of even the little sympathy I could give, and pleased to be able to talk to me as a woman largely ignorant upon the subject—knowing, in fact, nothing whatever, except that it is a good plan to keep one's windows open top and bottom—and, therefore, willing to listen to his theories, instead of disputing them as an intelligent man might have done, "I have ransacked the library from end to end, besides borrowing books in every direction, and I don't find any theory which on the whole appears to me more capable of being carried into practice than this one that I want to write into shape for my article."

And then, with his own masterful clearness and accuracy, he set out the whole thing clearly before me. I say clearly, for I am sure it *was* clear, though I could not understand it. He evidently enjoyed talking about it, having some one who would listen patiently, with unwavering faith in his own superiority. I have no arguments, and Gregory hates to be argued with by a woman. I have little skill in conversation, especially on scientific subjects, and he dearly loves to lead the battle himself. I am sure he enjoyed that walk home.

For myself, I was conscious all the time of a vague, half-acknowledged feeling of hopelessness. I was sorry for him, sorry for Annette, wishing she could come out of herself a little more to meet his tastes, wishing he could understand her life better. And yet how could he understand it without knowing what apparently she wished to keep buried in her own thoughts?

Pondering and vexing myself with this undercurrent of meditation, I still replied as intelligently as I could to Mr. Justin's theories about currents of air from above,

and rushes of heated foul air from beneath, and valves
and siphons and perforated zinc plates, and all the rest
of it.   He was still deep in the subject when we reached
my garden gate.

"I should like to go in and finish it with you," he
said, taking the cigar out of his mouth in an undecided
sort of way ; " but, perhaps, Annette would like better
for me to go back and keep her company.   You know
I've been out a good deal to-day, at the Club, and one
thing or another, and it doesn't do to——"

"No," I said, promptly, the last thing in the world
necessary just then being an apology from Gregory Justin
for going home to his wife.   " You had much better go
back.   Annette does not care to be left by herself these
winter nights, and I thought she looked just a little out
of sorts."

" Did you, though ?   I am sure I hadn't noticed it.
You know she never has very much of a colour, and so
people fancy she is delicate.   I will go back and sit with
her as soon as I have put my papers straight.   And do
come in and see her whenever you can, will you ?   I
know she enjoys it so much, and somehow she doesn't
*take* kindly to the people here.   She was only saying the
other night that you always brightened her up so.   Just
ask that little Stump of yours for a match before I go
away ; my box is empty."

I promised to come.   The match was found.   Gregory
re-lighted his cigar and went off, looking back, however,
as he closed the gate, to say :

" Now don't forget to come in as often as you can.
You are really the only person Annette cares to see
quietly of an evening."

# CHAPTER XXXIV

*Christmas Eve.*

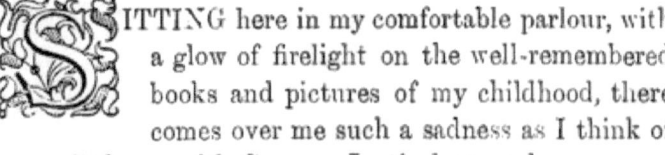

ITTING here in my comfortable parlour, with a glow of firelight on the well-remembered books and pictures of my childhood, there comes over me such a sadness as I think of my walk home with Gregory Justin last week.

I felt in his words so much more than came to the surface. They told of the "little rift within the lute," which may in years to come quite silence its music. And then in that outwardly so pleasant home what will be left?

Annette's mind, I can see, is fixing itself more strongly upon the past. She lives in it more than in the present. Almost always now, when I go to spend an evening with her, she turns the conversation upon Moorkee and the people we knew there. Lately she has often spoken to me about that affair of the envelope. I think she would be more at rest if it were settled. Of Mrs. Flexon's double-dealing in the matter there can be no doubt. Yet perhaps after all the letter may have contained nothing of importance. It may have been an acceptance for a Badminton party, or putting off or planning a riding excursion, though Mrs. Flexon's guilt in opening the letter would be just the same, however trifling the con-

tents. I wish we could know. I wish it may prove to
have been a letter of the merest common-place. And
yet no, I do not, for that would leave a dark stain upon
Captain Asperton's honour, and I cannot bear to think
of Annette giving her preference to a man who would do
anything dishonourable.

But supposing it should have been something of importance, something whose interruption must have made
a great change in Annette's life, and if Annette ever
finds that out, how will she bear it? I fear, in that case,
poor Gregory will have to complain more than ever that
his wife does not care for company. For she is not one
of those women who can brave a thing out, and cover up
with a froth of pleasant manners the depths of yearning
and emptiness beneath.

So whichever way it is, I seem to see only sadness.
She will just wear herself away by brooding over the
past, and her husband, who is rather the man to weary
of a wife of whom he cannot be proud, will go more and
more into public life. We shall hear of him as a great
man in the town, the leader of its public improvements,
chairman at all the Liberal meetings. By-and-by, if
things go on favourably, we shall hear of his trying for
a seat in Parliament, and I fancy Abbotsby would return
him, too. Who knows, if only the good times had continued forty years longer, but I might have sat at the
Northgate house drawing-room windows, and watched
the little Gregory of my childish years, chaired in triumph
through the streets, bowing and smiling from his dizzy
altitude to the cheering multitude around? And all the
while there will be a sad-faced woman pining at her

lonely fireside, with the light of her life gone out, and no more any warmth left but that of memory.

Things like these I seem to see so clearly as I think over my talk with Mr. Justin. He is beginning to have a dim consciousness of rebuke, but he will not listen to it. The career to which he looks forward is so pleasant, and his wife's want of sympathy is in itself a reason for throwing himself more vigorously into it. If she had made his home brighter, it will be so easy to say he would never have sought interest beyond it.

Since then I have tried to be with Annette as much as possible when her husband is away, though I am not sure that even in this I am doing her a real service. Mr. Justin, who, when he *is* in the house now, seems most at home in his study, where he is still working away at the ventilation of public buildings, comes into the room sometimes, with that curious look of doubtful self-reproach upon his face, and seeing me ensconced there by Annette's side with my knitting, brightens up directly, and says :

"Oh! all right, delighted to see you, Miss Brown. You'll keep her company, won't you, whilst I see what they are doing at that committee? Good night, pet."

And with what appears to me a delightfully affectionate kiss upon the pretty, yet half-pouting lips, away he goes to one of those everlasting meetings, leaving us to the mild twaddle which women almost of necessity drop into when they have no strong man's influence to lift them out of it.

But Gregory will not let himself think that he is doing anything wrong. He does not notice, seeing it every day, that Annette's face keeps getting just a little paler and thinner, and that there is scarcely any sparkle now in the soft eyes which he used to praise so much. I suppose, too, he does not notice the listless way in which she moves about ; or if he does, he puts it down to that " want of energy " which is beginning to be just a little tedious to him.

Perhaps if an illness were to come, as illnesses always do come so conveniently in story-books, and poor Annette's spark of life were to be blown nearly out, that of his watchfulness would be proportionately rekindled. He would have dreadful spasms of repentance, call himself an unworthy wretch, and no end of bad names, and be the most devoted husband in the world—for the space of six months. But I am afraid, when her health was quite re-established, his notions of " a career " would revive, and he would take to public affairs with as much zest as ever.

I suppose he will not be content now until he has become what is called a leading man in the place. People have begun to praise him up in the papers, too. Once or twice I have read leading articles in the *Abbotsby Gazette*, in which " our talented fellow-townsman, Mr. Justin," has been spoken of as destined to no very distant honours. And Gregory is just the man to be flattered by that sort of thing. I believe, much as I like my old playfellow, that he would spend a good many evenings away from his wife, to secure another article of that kind. His faith in himself is much influenced by the faith which other people have in him. Praise will spur him to great endeavour and great doing.

Last time I went to see Annette, she broke through the ice a little more than usual. Not in respect of her past, she never does that, but of her future life, and she let me see the faint touch of disappointment which is creeping into it.

She had been showing me, with genuine wife-like pride, one of these newspaper articles about her husband, and had also told me, as a great secret, that a paper on which he had been working for some time, in fact, throughout the autumn, on the sanitary arrangements of great towns, would appear in the next number of the —— *Review*. And I had told her, half in jest and earnest, that she would by-and-by be the *burra mem Sahib*, not of the *Nawab*, but of Abbotsby itself.

"If Gregory becoming famous, would make me so, I dare say I should," she said, with a half-sigh; "but do you know, Miss Brown, such dreadfully stupid thoughts do come into my head sometimes? I think Gregory ought to have married some one else. I mean somebody different, grand and stylish, and fond of fashion and talking, and going into company, and things of that sort. You know he wants a wife who can be at the top of everything."

"My dear," I said, seeing that contradiction, not sympathy, was just what she wanted then, "you are a little goose! Your husband is a man of talent, and influence, and ambition, and so he, not his wife, must be at the top of everything. He would not love you half so much, if you were just the same sort of person that he is himself."

"No, you don't understand me. He wants a wife who can help him to get to the top of everything, and keep comfortably beside him when he has got there. He would like me to give dinners and entertainments, and make up parties when any one grand is stopping in the place. You know his writing brings him into correspondence with a good many literary and influential people, and he says if only I would wake up a little, and get hold of them as they pass through here on their way north or south, we might have no end of a circle of friends. But, oh! Miss Brown, it isn't a bit of use. I couldn't do it, if I tried ever so much."

" Of course you couldn't, my dear, so don't trouble your little head about it. If your husband is destined to great friendships, he will work his way up to them without any painful efforts of yours. I don't think much of friends who come in that way."

Though, at the same time, I knew very well that a brilliant series of dinner-parties, especially if presided over by a clever woman with plenty of talk, *do* help a man up wonderfully to eminence and position. It would have made all the difference to Gregory Justin in that respect, if his wife had been a rose, instead of a violet.

" You child," I continued, " just keep on looking as bright and bonnie as you can, and always have a smile for him when he comes in, and dress yourself prettily, and you don't know how proud he will be of you. Remember how he looked at you when you came into this room dressed for the county ball. Why, you ought to be the happiest little woman in the world ! Don't go troubling yourself about such nonsense as talents, whilst you can look as pretty as you did that night."

" Ah ! yes," and a faint smile of pride passed over her face. " I know he likes to see me nicely dressed, and he

was so pleased when somebody asked at the ball who
that elegant girl was. But then, you know, one can't
always be dressed for a ball, with white satin and flowers,
and be walking through quadrilles, and smiling and
looking pleasant. That sort of thing lasts such a little
while. I believe he would be ten times better satisfied
if I were just decently plain, but could entertain well
and make everybody say what a clever woman Mrs.
Justin was."

"No, you little goose, he wouldn't, because then his
own cleverness would not be noticed so much ; and a man
like your husband always likes to be number one. I
don't blame him for it, either, because I think he is born
to the position. What you have to do, Annette, is just
to be as bright and pleasant as you can in your own way,
and have a smile always ready for him ; and when he
wants to have a friend or two in to dinner, don't make
a difficulty about it, even if it does give you a little
trouble."

"Oh ! but," and Annette's face put on that weary
expression which I know so well now, "he knows I hate
dinners so. I wish he would not fix upon that one thing
out of all to wish me to do. What interests have I in
common with any one here ? What can I talk to them
about ?"

I was beginning to feel a little bit out of patience
with her. If Annette wants to be happy, she must
cultivate the habit of looking at things in the light of
other people's ideas as well as her own.

"You must make interests," I said, "and then you
will soon find something to talk about. I suppose if you
hate dinners, you also hate being left by yourself at

night. Now if you would sometimes indulge your
husband's taste for society by making up a nice little
dinner-party for him at home, you would find that he
would not go out half so much, just because he could see
the people here instead, and see them all at once, too.
Don't you understand ? "

" I understand that you are a dear, good, sensible
thing, and that I am the stupidest old goose in the
world," said Annette, putting her arms round my neck
and giving me a kiss. " Next time Gregory asks me to
have a dinner-party I'll say 'all right.' Will that do ? "

" Yes ; and the next time you ask him to spend an
evening at home with you, you will find that he will say
'all right' too. Now let us talk about something else."

For I don't like a wife to make her husband a subject
of conversation, unless the remarks are all in his favour.
This is an excellent principle, one that I should certainly
have acted upon myself, if Providence had placed me in a
position to do so.

I wish Annette had " internal resources," as people
call them, but her mind does not seem to turn to any one
subject with sufficient zest to make it supply the manifest
void in her life. She takes strangely little interest in
anything that goes on around her. That delightful outlook from the drawing-room window into the Northgate,
which to some people would be like a perpetually open
story-book, full of romance, mystery, probability, and
excitement, is just nothing at all to her. If sometimes
she gazes out, it is with eyes that see nothing but the
past.

The only thing I have known her really give her
mind to was the turning of that tool-house in the garden

into a room for some possible old woman, after I told her how well the experiment of having old Hilary with us had answered. Gregory, who is only too glad to do anything for her which does not involve spending all his evenings at home, or giving up any of his cherished plans, promised to find an old woman for her, just as he would have promised to look out for a dog, or a kitten, or a parrot ; but nobody turned up who appeared in all respects suitable, so the plan fell through. The room is to be turned into an aviary now—he thinks that will amuse her as much as anything. Somehow, I begin to have an uncomfortable feeling as I think about them both. Gregory has his face set towards the hill-top of ambition ; Annette stays in the valley, not with good words cheering him on, but rather wearying that he does not stay by her in her lowlier path. And for neither of them is there any true rest.

So I sit here in my quiet little room on this Christmas Eve, when in so many a home loved ones from far and near are gathering ; and I can feel thankful for the loneliness which keeps back from me much of life's bitter as well as its sweet. Not for me the joy of being worked for, tended, prized by some one cleverer and stronger than myself ; but not for me, either, the restlessness of a heart unsatisfied from itself ever looking back towards something the present has failed to give. Of the past I wish nothing again. It has gone, as all time must go, but only for a little while, carrying my treasures into a resting-place, to which by-and-by I myself shall win. And, having that hope, which no spoiler's hand can touch, my Christmas Eve is full of peace.

# CHAPTER XXXV

T last I am home again, after that dreadful three weeks in Cheltenham. Never before have I been so entirely convinced of the truth of what my dear mother used to say—that the pleasantest part of a visit is the coming back. Oh, the rest, the peace, the stillness of my own fireside!—the delight of being able to sit still and think my own thoughts!—the relief of having no longer to put myself *en rapport* with new characters, to shelve my own individuality, and accommodate myself to theirs! This is surely the most wearisome thing in the world. It always produces in me a kind of bewilderment, similar to that which poor little Stump experienced in the Abbotsby Workhouse. I don't know where I am, nor what I am, and I get too much mixed up with everybody else.

It is strange that, after knocking about for so many weary years in India, where home is like the shell on a snail's back, carried about from place to place at a moment's notice, I should now be so loth to leave my own fireside ; but so it is. I think in India I lived a temporary life, adapting myself so patiently to necessary evils, that I quite forgot to bemoan them as evils at all.

Q

Now that I have returned to England, my real self has returned to me, and being able once more to have things as I like them, I find less willingness to endure having them as I don't like them.

And then with me it is not merely leaving one's own fireside, it is leaving one's habits, occupations, associations, everything, and turning out into a new world, so entirely different from this prosaic, old-fashioned spot where I hope to end my days. I wonder if my cousin Delia had the least idea what it cost me to go and visit her? Did she know the days and days I spent in putting myself into proper trim for that circle of society in which she lives, moves, and has her being? Can she realise the feelings which possessed me when I beheld myself in a "low black body," that mysterious style of costume which the dressmaker imposed upon me as the only thing admissible at an evening party in a place like Cheltenham? Does she know how pitifully I begged for plenty of matronly black net to cover my arms and shoulders, and how resolutely I fought against the "plain fronts" which are just now coming into fashion, and which are so exceedingly uncomfortable for a well-developed person like myself, especially in the position of sitting down? And those evening caps!—oh! what they did cost me! I don't mean in money—I could have paid that willingly, for I am no niggard—but in thought and consideration, and deliberation, and vigorous intellectual efforts to realise the effect which the dress-maker described with her little bit of pocket-handkerchief as pattern. My dismay, too, when they were sent home, and I first saw the change they produced in juxtaposition

with my solid, unromantic old face. I say Cousin Delia
must take all this into account before she knows *how*
much that visit to Cheltenham cost me, and when she
does know it, I don't believe she will ever ask me
again.

At least, I hope she won't. I am not made for
society. I do not adorn it. Neither—which is more to
the purpose—does it bring out what is best in me.

And then I did get so tired of being asked about
India. Some excellent people proposed my holding
meetings, drawing-room meetings—of course, for ladies
only—to give an account of my work in the zenanas.
Others asked me for "little sketches," to appear in
magazines. Others asked me to go to Sunday schools
and give addresses on Indian missions. Others, of no
special religious tendencies, trotted me out, or tried to
do so, on Hindoo social life and manners, influence of
civilisation and caste, etc., etc. As if I, who am
frightened at the sound of my own voice when I
try to string together three consecutive sentences in the
presence of as many people, could ever have done more
than make both myself and my subject ridiculous.

No. It has been my place to do, and not to talk.
Yonder is the work, a little lamp lighted here and there
in the thick darkness of the Hindoo woman's life, not
much attempt at what is called direct religious teaching,
for that means, to them, the absolute upheaval of their
whole family life, but only seeds of truth planted and
left to work their own way up through the soil, which is
already beginning to loosen and crumble round the
foundations of that hoary faith. By-and-by, when the

temples have quietly mouldered away, those seeds, having life within themselves, will bear much fruit.

But as for talking about these things, I never could do it. I feel too strongly the difficulty of a subject before which clever men doubt and differ. The glib remarks I have heard sometimes from superficial, well-meaning people, who dispose of the great Hindoo race as easily as Dr. Byte disposed of the children of Israel, though after a different fashion, have made me very chary of venturing an opinion. And so people who came to meet "that excellent Miss Brown, from India, you know," would most likely go away feeling she was all a delusion.

The fashionable society was even more trying. Was I myself or was I somebody else, clasped by the above-mentioned "low black body" in some perfumed drawing-room or other night after night? Certainly I never felt such a stranger to myself before, if it was indeed I. I envy women who can move through these crowded rooms with that apparent unconsciousness which is the highest pitch of art; women who can stand like paintings in an exhibition, knowing that their dresses are of the best material, that the set of their trains is faultless, that the manner in which their draperies are looped behind can excite only admiration and envy, that the crimson curtain before which they have taken up their position is bringing out into more effective relief some favourite line of check or forehead, some coil of braided hair, some fresh beauty in the round white arm which rests so carelessly on Diana's pedestal, and which is daring even Diana's proportions to rival it. Such women must be supremely

happy. They make me wonder whether my stupid little
Abbotsby life is not all a mistake, whether I had not
better upset Keren and Stump, let my house, live in
fashionable lodgings, and learn what existence really
means. Such women ought to have rays of light
emanating from them. Wells of unfathomable content
—not to say lakes or oceans of the same—ought to
gleam beneath the lustrous brightness of their eyes. The
adoration paid to them in the great temple of Mammon,
which is their shrine, ought to produce the sublime,
lofty, indescribable calm which is the inalienable attribute
of an idol. There should never be any wrinkles at the
corners of their eyes, never anything but sweetness upon
the lips to which so many worshippers bend for smiles.

I wonder if it is so. Of course, not knowing, I cannot
say. But from the little I have heard I could almost
fancy that the destiny of these magnificent women of
fashion is something like that of the goddess Doorga,
who has such a great " pooja," or worship, offered to her
every year in Bengal. The rich people dress her up—
she is only framework underneath—heap upon her as
much tinsel and finery as she can carry, set her up in
their family temple, pray to her, feed her with richest of
cakes and sweetmeats for the space of a certain number
of days, then take her to the river, and quietly tumble
her in. Next year another framework is made, clothed,
fed, prayed to, petted, and drowned, in just the same
manner. So perhaps I am safest in my quiet little
Abbotsby home.

Mrs. Vermont invited us to what she said was a very
small dinner-party, and there I had to turn back again

to a page of events, the reading of which has already
given me a great deal of trouble.

But here comes Stump for her evening diet of reading,
writing, and arithmetic.   Oh! Stump, from what depths
of perplexity, wonder, and uncertainty does that wholesome vegetable life of yours preserve you !   How little
you know of idols, or the trouble one is put to in wor-
shipping them, or of " pages " which must be read again
and again before their meaning is discovered, or of the
whips and stings which wait upon the sensitive soul as it
remembers the past or dreads the future !   Your calm
amplitude of content looks neither before nor after, and
sums up its simple story in the words :

" Law, ma'am, but I *is* glad I was took in here."

# CHAPTER XXXVI.

WAS going to say that I met Captain Asperton at Mrs. Vermont's dinner-party.

If I had known that I should meet him there, should I not have put the length of the London and North Western Railway between myself and Cheltenham? I do not know. If my theory is true, that things in this life do not come and go by chance, then why need I trouble myself by asking at all? I am but the hook to which the chain is suspended, or the scrap of paper—for that figure only too naturally suggests itself to me—upon which the skein is wound.

Enough that at Mrs. Vermont's dinner-party I *did* meet Captain Asperton; and our hostess, supposing that we should have some Indian remembrances in common, so arranged it that I should be taken into the dining-room by him, which involved a couple of hours of such conversation as came uppermost. He has sold out of the army, his health having broken down, and is now spending some time at Cheltenham, that refuge for Indian invalids. So is Mrs. Flexon, I am told; not that *her* health has broken down, people say she looks charming; but probably she found St. John's Wood cold when the east winds set in.

She is not in Mrs. Vermont's "set," nor in my cousin's, and Cheltenham is a wide place, and I am too small a person for my comings and goings to be talked about ; or, doubtless, if Mrs. Flexon had heard that Captain Asperton and I were likely to sit side by side at a dinner-party, she would have put double the distance of the London and North Western Railway between us before any such catastrophe should have happened.

Of course I did not know who the guests were to be. So far, I had been conscious of little else than a blaze of light, a hum of voices, a multitude of bare-shouldered, much be-flowered ladies, and the pressure of my low black silk, which I was wearing then for the first time, when Mrs. Vermont came up to me, all smiles and animation, bringing with her a quiet, gentlemanly-looking man of eight-and-twenty or thirty. After introducing us she said :

" You know, dear Miss Brown, I was sure you would be delighted to have a chat with Captain Asperton, so I have arranged that he shall take you in to dinner. It will be so interesting for you to talk over all those curious temples and idols and things that we stupid English people don't know anything about. Mrs. Dorrison "—this was to my cousin Delia—"do let Captain Asperton have your end of the couch, and I will take you off to old Major Fitz-James. He has found out that you know some friends of his up in the north, and he is dying to have a long talk with you about them."

Upon what slight reasons do people nowadays resign the thread of life, thought I to myself, as Cousin Delia hurried away—no, she did *not* hurry, she paced leisurely along by Mrs. Vermont's side, the beautiful folds of her purple silk gleaming beneath the chandelier—to rescue Major Fitz-James from an untimely end, and Captain Asperton took her vacant place, the man of all others whom I wanted and yet did not want to see.

He is pleasant-looking, with what ought to be a good face, except that there has crept into it a bitter expression. Not a man to play fast and loose, I should think, with any girl's heart; and not the man, either, to forget if deceit or wickedness left its mark upon his path. There is, of course, nothing military about him, except his upright bearing. He rather lacks the frank, genial manner which most men in the army generally acquire; indeed, there is a sort of reserve about him which rather keeps one at a distance, just at first.

Somehow I felt, as one does now and then feel things for which there is no definite argument, that I was speaking to the man who ought to have been Annette Lislethorpe's husband.

After the first few minutes I got along with him very well, better, I think, than with most young men, because of the gravity and half shyness of his manner, and the entire absence of that kindly condescension which an unfashionable woman like myself generally meets with in society.

We were still buzzing like flies round such Eastern recollections as suggested themselves to us, when dinner was announced. After we were arranged in our places, I found myself face to face with a jolly, good-tempered old lady, all smiles, white hair, and Honiton lace, whom I already knew pretty well from having met her several times at my cousin's little afternoon teas. We had taken very kindly to each other, she being, like myself, unfashionable; and she lived alone, and trained girls for service, which was another bond of union between us.

"Miss Brown," she began, as we were playing with our soup, "I don't suppose you care about gossip, but still you will be glad to hear of the prospects of one of your companions on board the *Nawab*. Mrs. Flexon is engaged to be married to Dr. Byte."

"At last!" I replied, rather spitefully, I must own, for one never quite forgets being treated as that fascinating woman used to treat me.

"Well, yes," said the lively old lady, "*at last*, for they do say she has made one or two attempts before. She has come to Cheltenham now, to stay for a few weeks with an old aunt, and be married from her house. Shall you not call upon her?"

"No, thank you. I think not."

"Do you know Mrs. Flexon?" said Captain Asperton, facing round upon me in rather a determinate manner.

"Yes," I replied, "we came home together in the *Nawab*, and she used to be particularly disagreeable to my friend, Miss Lislethorpe."

Captain Asperton devoted himself assiduously to his soup for a minute or two, and then said, in an undertone scarcely noticeable through the hum of conversation:

"I don't wonder. Miss Lislethorpe deserved nothing else."

"Miss Lislethorpe deserved everything else," I replied, "and, at any rate, under the circumstances, common politeness was due to her. But," I added, seeing that the old lady's quick little gray eyes were upon us, "this is not the place to talk over the merits of one's friends. Miss Lislethorpe was a lady, and ought to have been treated as such. Did you ever see the Taj at Agra?"

Captain Asperton took the hint, and we were soon discussing Hindoo architecture with an interest which lasted until the ladies rose from table.

As I expected would be the case, we found each other out again after dinner. He came to me as I was turning over some photographs in a quiet corner of the room, and after a little conversation gradually leading up to the subject, he said:

"Miss Brown, I always like my friends to have justice done to them, and apparently you have the same feeling. If I am not trespassing too much upon our short acquaintance, I should like very much to know why you do not appreciate little Mrs. Flexon. Of course you said nothing that you had not a perfect right to say, but I have never heard any one speak of her yet, except with interest. We used to be very good friends at Moorkee. She was always most kind to me."

Most, indeed, I thought. Even to the extent of separating you from the woman you loved. But she did it for your good, no doubt.

"I have nothing to say whatever about Mrs. Flexon," I replied, quite pleasantly, determined that I would not commit myself in any way just then, by making an opening which might let in so much new light upon Captain Asperton's mind. The whole thing had come upon me too suddenly. I did not know what to think

much less what to say or do. Perhaps I ought not to
have expressed myself as I did about Mrs. Flexon.
Perhaps, by indulging myself in that spiteful little de-
liverance respecting her conduct to Annette, I had
damaged my opportunity of becoming acquainted with
the real state of things. How seldom one repents oneself
of silence, how often the reverse !

This much was clear to me. Captain Asperton was
staying in Cheltenham for some time. I could easily
communicate with him, if, after due reflection, I thought
it best to do so. And so, with an air of knowing, as
Stump expresses it, " nuffin about anythink," I apologised for my hasty expressions, and said that perhaps
some day I should have the opportunity of talking to him
more fully than was possible just then, amidst the hum
and pleasant stir of Mrs. Vermont's drawing-room.

With that we began to discuss the beauties of
Cheltenham, a subject which lasted us until my cousin
came to tell me that the carriage was waiting.

# CHAPTER XXXVII

UT all that night I lay awake, thinking, thinking ; and the worst of it was that I could bring my thoughts to no practical result.

At first it seemed the most proper thing to write to Annette and tell her I had seen Captain Asperton. But then Gregory, who had met Captain Asperton himself, would naturally ask what she knew about him, and that, with Annette's strong instinct of reserve, would not be pleasant for either of them. Again, it was just possible that, as Mr. Justin had mentioned incidentally to me his meeting with Captain Asperton somewhere on his travels, he might have mentioned it also to Annette, with no acknowledgment on her part of having known him herself, and her husband might think that it showed a want of openness. No, I must not write to Annette.

Then I might send a note to Captain Asperton, asking him to come over to my cousin's house, and then I could tell him all that I knew.

Again no. That would be taking matters too much into my own hands. I could not ask him to come without telling him, when he came, all that he chose to ask—and I had no right to do that without Annette's permission. Finally I decided to do nothing at all until I came home, and could talk quietly to Annette about it.

I need not have troubled myself. Captain Asperton took the affair into his own hands. Early next morning, on the pretext of bringing some magazines which my cousin had expressed a wish to see, he came over to us, and I had a long conversation with him.

I suppose people who are to be friends to each other at all soon find it out. I began to have a pleasant, elder-sisterly feeling towards this man, whose life—if what I had heard was correct—had been spoiled by the contrivances of an artful woman, in whom he still believed. We had had a good deal of talk before Cousin Delia came in to us, though not about the matter which was uppermost in my mind. I found that in many things we could have real sympathy with each other, although his experience had taught him to doubt human nature ; and I was happy enough never to have been deceived in anything which touched my life closely and permanently. It was quite curious to me to find myself talking away to him as if we had known each other for years. He told me about his own Indian and Canadian experiences, and about his plans and purposes, now that his military career was at an end. He said he meant to take a little farm somewhere amongst the Surrey hills, and shut himself up there, and be independent of everybody.

"The less one has to do with the world the better," he said. "One never knows how things will turn out in it. I have found it a very great fallacy to suppose that in social life a man reaps what he sows. So far as I am concerned, it has generally been exactly the contrary, so

I am going to take to agriculture, just to see whether tares do come up as a natural result of wheat seed, or whether, when you have done your best, old mother earth mocks you, as the soil of human nature does—just slaps you in the face for your pains."

" You are bitter," I said.

" Perhaps I am. Thank heaven for yourself that you are not the same, for I can assure you it is not at all a pleasant state of mind. What wouldn't I give if I could trust the world as you seem to have done ? "

" Perhaps I waited rather longer before I *did* trust it," I replied, having Mrs. Flexon in my mind, of whom he had said, in the course of our conversation, that she impressed him as a woman of such a very simple and innocent mind. The fair complexion and the smoothly banded hair had done it, of course, combined with those pure white ruffles, coming out in such lovely relief upon the crape.

But just then Cousin Delia came in, and we returned to generalities. As he was going away, he asked if he might drive me to see some old ruins in the neighbour- hood ; and as I did not at all dislike the idea of bettering my acquaintance with him, I very gladly fell in with the proposal.

" And now, will you tell me," he said, as we were speeding along through the frosty January air, " why you spoke as you did about Mrs. Flexon last night ? It was not what you said. It was the way in which you said it."

So, being now prepared with what I meant to say, I told him of my coming home in the same ship with

Annette, and of Mrs. Flexon being one of our fellow-passengers, and of the little scrap of paper which she flung away, which turned out to be an envelope addressed to Miss Lislethorpe. How, when I showed it to Annette, she identified the writing as his own, but said that she had never received any letter from him, so that there must have been a misunderstanding somewhere. And then I went on to tell him how, when I asked Mrs. Flexon for an explanation, she had entirely refused to give me any, and had, moreover, been very rude to me, and had tried to get the envelope into her possession again, which of course I had declined to allow. I then told him the address, and the date in the corner, September 7th, which I had copied.

He was silent for a little while, as if trying to remember. Then he said that about that time he *had* written a note to Miss Lislethorpe, and written it from Mrs. Flexon's house, and entrusted it to her to be sent to the Parsonage.

"No doubt she sent it all right," he continued, as if making light of the whole affair. "But, you know, girls are careless creatures. They do let their letters lie about so."

And a very scornful expression came over his face as he said this.

"Most likely she stuffed it into that dainty little embroidered pocket she used to wear, along with a lot of other things; and next time she went to call upon Mrs. Flexon, she pulled it out with her handkerchief, or some of those specimens of moss and leaves she was always carrying about with her, and never missed it."

" No," I said, "it was not so. Annette Lislethorpe told me herself, when we were trying to find out some explanation of it, that she had never received a letter of any kind from you in her life ; and she should not have known the handwriting, except that she had seen it when you had written to her father about men in the regiment."

" That is curious," he said. " Are you quite sure she told you that ? "

" Quite sure," I replied. " I remember every single little thing which happened about that envelope, because I felt, somehow, that there was something wrong about it, and I wanted very much, for Annette's sake, to find it out."

" I should think there rather *was* something wrong ; but never mind, I won't trouble you about it. Just another instance, you know," he added, carelessly, " of sowing wheat and reaping tares. A dreadfully risky thing, Miss Brown, for an honest man to take to, *that* sort of farming. Then did you happen to know Miss Lislethorpe at Moorkee ? "

" No, not intimately. I used to see her riding about sometimes, but I went into company very little there. Shortly afterwards I heard of her father's death."

" So did I. Poor man ! But he had had his share of good things out of the world, and the Church too. I should not think it would make much difference to the young lady, either. She was just on the point of being married to that rich old civilian, Mr. Moberley, when I went away."

" Indeed, you are quite mistaken, Captain Asperton."

R

"No, I am not," he replied, almost rudely "They were engaged to each other—Mrs. Flexon told me so—and her father was delighted with the match. That is the way girls do who have been brought up at those fashionable London schools. I might have known ! A toothless old bit of parchment, as yellow as the scrip on which his money was written !"

"Well, I never saw himself, and it is not of the least consequence to me what colour he was, or how few teeth he had. But I do know this, for Miss Lislethorpe told me herself, that she never was engaged to him ; and I know her well enough to be sure that she never wished it."

"Oh, indeed ! So she became confidential with you —another pretty way that girls have—to match letting letters drop out of their pockets."

"Which they don't do, Captain Asperton."

"Very well, if you like to have it so. And, pray, did Miss Lislethorpe make any more confidences to you ?"

"No. Annette Lislethorpe is not a girl to make confidences to any one. And I think, Captain Asperton, you might have more charity than to thrust such insinuations against a girl who was coming home an orphan and poor and friendless, and with no one to speak a kind word to her."

"Was *that* it ?"

"Yes, that *was* it. Her father left her literally without anything, and she was working her passage home in the same ship I came by, as companion to the great lady who sat at the captain's right. At least, the lady called it companion, but it was really maid-of-all-work, for the poor girl never had a moment to herself. I suppose it would have gone on like that to the end, only her health quite broke down, and so the arrangement had to be given up, and I asked her to come and stay with me at Abbotsby instead."

"Poor Annette—poor Miss Lislethorpe ! I mean. I did not think it was so bad as that. What a brute somebody must have been ! Where is she now ? "

"She is living at Abbotsby. She is married to Mr. Justin, the Recorder."

"You don't say so ! I met him once, hunting in the interior—a capital good fellow too, only I should have thought him a great deal too old for her. And is she all right ? "

I said that probably she was, and there the conversation dropped. He kept on talking to me about other things, but I could see that his thoughts were far away Sometimes there were breaks of silence from which he would wake up with a start, and begin explaining to me the beauties of the neighbourhood, as if I did not know well enough that the neighbourhood was quite a secondary consideration now. As we were nearing home, he turned to me and said :

"You are quite sure that Miss Lislethorpe never had any letter from me ? "

"I am quite sure she said so."

"Then I must have it out with Mrs. Flexon."

And from the expression of his face, I should say he is an awkward man to have anything "out" with.

# CHAPTER XXXVIII

THAT was only two days before I came away from Cheltenham. Captain Asperton must have plenty of food for reflection now. I suppose I might reasonably have turned the tables upon him, and asked why he had been so bitter upon poor Annette, but it was not my place to betray any knowledge, either of her affairs or his. The affair of the envelope was now quite cleared up, so far as Mrs. Flexon's guilt was concerned. How I should like to have confronted her there and then! Without doubt she had opened the letter, destroyed it, and then, by one of those unaccountable pieces of forgetfulness which sometimes mar the most cleverly concerted schemes, had omitted to destroy the envelope too, and so the whole of the transaction had come to light, as such things generally do, sooner or later.

I wondered very much if I should tell Annette about it, but that too was settled for me. Captain Asperton came again next day, and told me that he should probably be coming to Abbotsby before long. He said he could make it out on his way to Edinburgh, where he was engaged to be groomsman at a wedding in February or March.

I said what was the least I could say under the circumstances—that I should be very glad to see him at my house, if he could put up with my primitive habits of life. He said he should be delighted to come. I don't feel at all afraid of him. He is not the sort of man that will laugh either at Stump or Keren. I think his experience, so far in the world, has taught him that it is not an unpleasant change occasionally to live out of it.

He told me, too, that he had called upon Mrs. Flexon, but she sent apologies for not being able to see him— she had such a wretched headache. He then wrote a note, asking her to name some time for an interview, as he had matters of business to talk over with her; and when I said good-bye to him, he was still waiting for an answer.

I must say I should like to be present at that interview. I fancy Mrs. Flexon's elegant self-possession will scarcely support her through the ordeal; and in this case the raillery which served her so well when I asked for an explanation cannot be brought into play. It is to be a matter of business. Most probably she will get over it by professing entire loss of memory—a most useful thing to profess upon some occasions. If that will not do, she is just the woman to face the thing boldly out by saying that she did give the letter; and as a gentleman rather naturally shrinks from accusing a lady of falsehood, the conventions of society will protect her. Anyhow, I am quite sure she will be protected. When did pretty ways like hers fail to serve the user of them? And when those round white eyelids are lifted for an appealing glance from the translucent orbs beneath, I am sure any jury of English gentlemen will give their verdict in the defendant's favour.

I cannot help wondering how much the loss of that letter may have meant to Captain Asperton. I have a very strong feeling that it was of no trifling moment—that it had some connection with the doubts which Mrs. Flexon had contrived to insinuate into his mind respecting Annette's straightforwardness. The conversation I heard between those two ladies on board the *Nawab* threw a good deal of light upon the transaction. My theory is now, that Mrs. Flexon worked herself into Captain Asperton's confidence, made him believe that Annette had just been amusing herself with him, whilst she was really engaged to the old civilian. Then she got him to write and remonstrate with the girl, and entrust the letter to her for delivery. Of course, she never sent it, and Captain Asperton, receiving no reply, would naturally think that his conjectures had been correct.

The only thing in which her machinations had failed was the transfer of Captain Asperton's affections to herself. She had very much mistaken his character there, but probably she had given up regretting that little awkwardness, as some one else quite as eligible had turned up, and the wedding had been fixed. In her search for a husband, Mrs. Flexon possesses the happy art, when she cannot have what she likes, of liking what she has, and doubtless she and Dr. Byte will be very happy in their own way, unless whispers should reach him of what she did at Moorkee.

Oh ! the wrong that a wicked woman may do ! To think of Annette and her lover as I saw them that sunny day among the pine-trees on the hillside, so ignorant of pain, so full of trust in their own happiness, and to think of them now—he old before his time with the age that bitterness and suspicion bring, spoiled for any more real rest or comfort in life, ready to doubt everything—love, religion, truth, honour ; she languid and unhopeful, for ever dwelling upon an unexplained past, wearying over what might have been, until all the sweetness is taken out of what actually is ; and then to think how different both their lives if only Mrs. Flexon could have let them alone !

If I had not a fast anchorage, I should begin to doubt too. Or if I believed it all, I should believe as Captain Asperton does, that the wicked have it their own way in this world, come what may in the next.

# CHAPTER XXXIX

O I am glad to come back to my own little home, which, having no dazzling sunshine upon it, can have no heavy shadows either, only that afternoon light of content, which, I am beginning to think, is best of all.

Stump was at the station to meet me, her face all one brick-red smile of delight. What a curtsy she did make, to be sure, and how she seized upon all my bags and boxes, and how she began at once to tell me all the small household occurrences, much to the amusement of a very stiff lady who had been my companion in the railway carriage. Probably the lady thought I was some country bumpkin who had been out for a Christmas holiday, and that Stump, who had put on all her best clothes, was my daughter. Well, never mind if she did. I could not find it in my heart to check the poor girl's honest expressions of satisfaction at having me home again.

Keren had made the house a perfect paradise of warmth and cleanliness. The dear old woman, in her white frilled cap, tied under the chin with substantial muslin strings, did look such a contrast to the flimsy Cheltenham maids who had vexed me with their endless flounces and furbelows. The first thing I saw when I went into the parlour, was a bouquet of ferns and flowers from Annette's little greenhouse, and whilst I was admiring it, Hilary came in with her duty and respects to "the missis," and would I accept of a dish of brussels sprouts which she had brought, covered with a clean white cloth.

"They've growed, ma'am, in the bit of ground you was so kind as to let me have, behind the little room, and I've been a-watching of 'em this fortnight past, and helping of 'em on as much as ever I could, thinking happen there might be a boiling ready against you comed home, if you wouldn't think it over-much making free to ask you to accept of them."

Dear old Hilary! She will be the same to her dying day. How many a backache she must have given herself in cultivating and planting out that little patch of sprouts, and "watching of 'em," and gathering them! It is her heart's delight to do anything for those who have been good to her. But indeed she does not confine her goodness to them. I heard, before I went away, of her going to sit up all night by the bedside of a man who had many and many a time tempted her husband away on his drunken bouts, and who is now dying of consumption. The world is not made up of Mrs. Flexons, after all.

When I was rested, Keren took me round to show how tight and trim she had kept everything during my absence. Keren begins to look like a winter apple towards the end of March, rather shrivelled and worse for wear, but I dare say she has some years of work before

her yet, especially with such a willing help as Stump,
who is able now to take most of the heavy work off her
hands.   I think Keren will be the next occupant of the
little room by the greenhouse.   Like myself she has no
near kith or kin, and she has been here so long that the
place would scarcely seem like home without her.

Oh ! the delight of being at my own fireside again !
After all, I do think I shall make a practice of going
away once a year or so, just for the satisfaction of coming
back.   It is so pleasant to be able to do just as you like,
to set yourself to rights, as it were, gather up the loose
threads and go on with the pattern of life again, putting
in a dash of fresh colour here and there, that you have
brought home with you.   How I smiled to myself as my
dear good cousin Delia, who really was most kind to me,
pitied me for having to come home to a lonely house,
with no one to welcome me, no one to whom I could
recount the little details of my visit.

"Really, Hester, my dear," she said, "I can't think
what you were about all those years, and in India, too,
where they say there are such shoals of unappropriated
men.   Why, if you had been half wide awake, you would
have picked up a civilian, or something of that sort, and
been coming home now on your fifteen hundred a year.
I must say, my dear, you have managed very badly."

Well, perhaps so I have.   I half thought it myself as
I watched those well-dressed women moving about in the
Cheltenham drawing-rooms, many of them wives of old
civilians of the type that my cousin would have liked
me to "pick up"; and so very well got up in velvet and
satin and no end of costly Indian jewellery.   But then I

remembered the image of Doorga, and how she was popped into the water when she was done with, and I must say that reflection restrained my feelings.

Then "nobody to welcome me!" As if Hilary's sweet old smile, and Keren's honest shake of the hand, and Stump's broad laugh of utter content, were not something of a welcome. And when I was left to myself at last, all the sweet memories of bygone years in this home came thronging round me, like birds that have been scared away for a little while, but are only waiting to return to the hand that feeds them. Nay, Cousin Delia, you need not pity me. I am really more happy than you can think.

You might with better reason pity Annette Justin in her beautiful home, with that bitter "might have been" always fretting at her heart, and her husband so busy now, making himself a great name in the world, that he has scant time left to spend with the wife who will perhaps not want him much longer.

Poor Annette! I went to see her last night. Gregory looked in in the morning to give me a welcome home, but said she was not very well and would be so glad if I would go and sit with her. He was going to the Club, where he had asked some gentlemen to meet him at dinner. The old story.

Of course I was only too glad to go, and glad that Mr. Justin should be away for once, as that gave me a better opportunity for telling all that I had to tell.

If one must go away from one's home for the joy of coming back to it, one must also leave one's friends sometimes to tell how the weeks and months are dealing with them. Poor Annette looks pale and thin. She moves about in a listless way which tells either of bodily ailment or of that mental weariness which is so much harder to bear. The servant told me she was in the drawing-room, so I went quietly upstairs and found her, with the lamps still unlighted, sitting in a great chair before the fire, her hands clasped in her lap, her head half buried in the soft crimson cushions, such an expression of languor and *ennui* in her whole attitude.

I felt very sorry for her. She ought not to be left alone in this way. I don't suppose her husband, with his full, eager, well-cultivated mind and animated interest in life, can quite understand what it is for her to be thrown in upon herself, with no food for thought except that which a past, whose bitterness he does not know, can supply. Annette is taking no root here in Abbotsby; she is gathering round herself neither interests nor occupations; and Gregory is so busy with his own that he cannot see the evil effect this sort of thing is beginning to have upon her. I did not see it myself really, until last night.

But I am sorry for him, too. It is hard for a man with so much power of work, so much lying around him to do, if only he could give himself entirely to it, to find no sympathy at home; to be able to kindle no ardour like his own when he talks about his favourite subjects, or the position he would like to make for himself. I don't wonder that he gets tired of it, and begins to build up the house of life outside of his own home. Gregory Justin must have both excitement and sympathy somewhere.

Annette did brighten up a little when I went in, and I sat down beside her there in the firelight, and we had a long talk about my visit, and Cousin Delia, and Mrs. Vermont, and the Cheltenham gaieties, before I came to the real kernel of my story.

"But come, Annette," I said, when I was quite ready to tell her about the most important thing, "has nothing happened all the time I have been away? Haven't you anything to tell me? I am sure I have given you plenty of news, and you have not told me a single thing.'

Annette stretched herself wearily in the great easy-chair, and crossed her little slippered feet, and turned to find a softer resting-place for the pretty head which was nestling amongst the crimson cushions.

"No," she said, "nothing ever does happen here. You know I have given up calling now, it was such a trouble, so the people don't come to see me, which is a great relief. And then Gregory is at work day and night over his writing. He says the farther he gets into it, the more difficult the subject becomes; and yet if he gives it up, all the previous labour would be lost, so he must go on. When he is not busy over that, he is seeing people at the Club. We have given over having dinner-parties now, it was more than I could manage. But I did try, Miss Brown, I really did."

"I know you did, darling," I replied, kissing her thin cheek, "and you kept to it bravely, as long as you were able. I am sure Mr. Justin saw that, and he does not want you now to do it any more. When we have got through this sharp winterly weather you will be ever so much stronger, and then company will not be such a weariness to you. What you have to do now is to take care of yourself, or somebody will think his little wife is losing all her roses."

For indeed I noticed, after three weeks of absence, what had never really struck me before, how something seemed to be eating away the roundness and youth from Annette's face. She is letting her life slip away from her, simply because she has not enough interest in it to hold it fast. She might be bright and strong and happy, if only she could live in the present and make its opportunities her own; but she is gradually losing the power to do this. A little more consideration from Gregory, a little more stooping from his own level of intellectual life to supply the needs of her entirely different nature, just a little more effort on her part to meet him on his own ground and give him a companionship which would keep its interest when the first charm of beauty and grace had passed away, and all would have been well. Now an uncomfortable feeling creeps over me that it is too late.

"But, Annette," I said, "I have kept the most wonderful thing until the last. I met Captain Asperton at one of Mrs. Vermont's dinner-parties, and afterwards I told him all the story about Mrs. Flexon and the envelope, and it is just as I thought. He *did* write to you, from Mrs. Flexon's house too, and he entrusted the letter to her to be sent to you; and instead of that she must have opened it and kept it, the wicked woman! I was sure some day we should find out all about it, but I never expected to come across Captain Asperton in that way."

Annette did brighten up now, though not so much as I had expected. I could not tell her *how* glad I was. I could only speak of the whole affair as just a matter of business, not anything touching, as I knew it did touch, two human lives that ought to have been one. Mrs. Flexon had been very deceitful, and now her deceit was found out. That was all I could express any satisfaction about. And, indeed, Annette herself did not let me see that it stirred her more deeply. With all her weakness of body there is wonderful power of self-control about her. Never, except that one morning in our cabin, has she dropped that veil of reserve which is so strange in one of her affectionate nature. And until she gives me leave, I cannot, even by a look, tell her that I know anything.

"But," I continued, after she had asked me a few general questions about Captain Asperton, how he was looking, and what he was doing, and what brought him to Cheltenham—questions which any friend might ask of any other friend—" I hope by-and-by you will see him yourself, and then, of course, he can clear it all up much better than he could with me. He has to go to somebody's wedding in Edinburgh the end of this month, or the beginning of the next, and he says he can easily make out Abbotsby on his way. We took very kindly to each other, and I said I should be very glad to see him for a day or two, if he cared to stay with me; so he is coming, and then, perhaps, we shall hear what Mrs. Flexon says about it, for when I came away he was waiting for an answer to a note in which he had asked for an interview with her upon a matter of business. I do wish I could

be there. I should like for once to see Mrs. Flexon
driven into a corner. What do you think about it all,
Annette?"

Annette flung her arms round me and kissed me
many times.

" I think you are a dear, good, delightful old creature,
almost the best friend I ever had, and I wish I could
ever do half as much for you as you have done for me.
But I *am* so tired. Please let me be alone now, and we
will talk about it again to-morrow. Everything seems
so strange just now.'

Her instinct was best. I came away, for I knew she
needed no company of mine that night.

# CHAPTER XL.

E have had no more conversation about it since, except in the most general way. Whatever else, as friends, Annette and I may lack, we certainly do not lack that respect for each other which prevents us from prying into matters not belonging to us.

But Mr. Justin came in a day or two afterwards, to say how much good my return appeared to have done to his wife. She was so much brighter and more cheerful, indeed, sometimes quite like a different creature, and never seemed to find the time long when she was left to herself.

"Which, you know," he added, "is very convenient just now, because I must go on with my paper for the *Review*. If one does not take up a popular subject when it is fresh in the minds of the people, it is no use taking it up at all. The public now are wide awake about sanitation and all that sort of thing. In a few months' time it will have passed over, and I question whether an article upon it would get admission into any of the good serials. So, you see, I am very anxious to finish it."

"Like the gentleman," I said, "who rushed from the

8

shop with the new bonnet for his wife, lest it should be old-fashioned before he got it home."

"Well, yes, something like it. But, you know, we must take things as we find them. The fashions of the public interest change like all other fashions, and what we have to do is to present a supply of the article whilst the demand lasts. It is a great nuisance to have manuscripts lying useless in one's desk, simply because the subjects of which they treat have passed out of the public mind."

"Exactly," I replied.

"And Annette does not understand that sort of thing, you see. She has a sort of notion of taking up a subject and keeping it in soak for a year or two, reading a bit about it now and then, and thinking it over at leisure, and so giving myself plenty of time between to chat with her and drive out together and so on."

"Well, would you like her not to think so? Would you like her to be able to do entirely without you?" I asked.

"Not entirely, of course. I like a woman to be dependent on me. Only, you see, in such times as ours, if a man wants to do anything, to make any sort of career for himself, he must give himself to it. It is no use doing things by halves. The same with my interest in public affairs in the town. It is no use dabbling ; you must go right in for them, and Annette can't see that, either."

"Well, I don't wonder at it. She has no special pursuits to give her life an interest apart from your own, and she has not health enough to be always going about

and amusing herself. Indeed, I think she is far from
strong now. I thought her looking quite altered when I
came home."

"Did you, though ? I am sure I had not noticed it
myself. She has been just a little bit whiny the last
few weeks, so much so that I never worry her now about
having people to dinner. I always see them at my Club,
which is a great relief to her, you know, poor little thing!
But in another month or six weeks I shall get this writing
off my mind, and then I really will take her away for
change. We will have a trip to Paris or something of
that sort, and you must go with us ; or I don't know
whether it wouldn't be better for you two to go somewhere by yourselves, she does think such a great deal
about being with you."

How easily Mr. Justin arranges things ! I listened
and said nothing, and he continued :

"You know it has made all the difference in the
world to her, your coming back. She is really not like
the same girl. You can talk about old times together,
and you have known the same people in India, and she
feels at home with you, as, of course, she cannot feel
with any one who calls upon her here. Annette is
wonderfully slow in making new friends. She might
have a delightful circle in Abbotsby, if she only cared
for it, and several of the county people would be quite
glad to notice her. It would be a great advantage to
me, too, if she were a little fonder of society. A man
who wants to do good in public affairs and give himself
to them at all, is so hampered if—well, you know what
I mean."

Yes, of course I knew what he meant. I dropped the subject of Annette's health, because I saw he was too full of other interests then to give it proper consideration. I begin to think she will never have now what she really needs to set her right again, unless, as I said before, she is attacked by one of those illnesses which come so opportunely in story-books. Then her husband's tenderness, which is all there still, only buried under this load of "public interests," would come to the top again, and things would go on better. But I must hold my peace.

21*st*.

I have had a letter this morning from Captain Asperton, to say that, if convenient, he will come to me on the 25th, to stay one night. The wedding is taking place rather earlier than was expected, and so much the better, for I am sure his visit will do Annette good, come what may. She has been so much brighter since she had it to look forward to.

Keren and Stump are quite in a small fever about it. Keren is especially exercised about the waiting at table. She thinks, and rightly, too, that Stump, spite of her many excellencies, will never make a brilliant figure in that department, and she suggests our having a smart young housemaid or professed waiter for the occasion.

Poor Keren! Captain Asperton's mind will be quite otherwise employed than in taking note of Stump's deficiencies, or her own. And I say that I have no wish to be seen by my guests otherwise than as I always am. The essence of hospitality, as I understand it, is in making a guest like one of yourselves, letting him see the home as it really is, letting him be welcomed into your ordinary life, not into one polished up and put into requisition for the occasion. Keren assents, but is making herself a new muslin cap to wait in, nevertheless.

Annette received the news of his coming very quietly; as she receives everything now. Gregory is quite right in saying that she has been much more cheerful lately. Sometimes of an evening he remarks that she gets quite a colour, brighter even than that she used to have on board the *Nawab* towards the close of the voyage. Poor Gregory! Those public engagements blind him to a great deal which might otherwise make him anxious. A colour that only comes at night, as Annette's comes now, and leaves her next morning so pale and wan, is not the sort of colour to be very happy about. I will wait until Captain Asperton's visit is over, and then, whether the Sanitation article is finished or not, I will tell him plainly that his wife needs the best medical advice in Abbotsby

I expect he ought to have taken her away before the winter set in, to the Isle of Wight, or Hastings, or one of those sheltered places, so that the change from India might have been less trying. Only he was so bent on cementing his acquaintance with some of the literary people who were staying in the neighbourhood just then, that it quite escaped his memory. I remember now that when they were first married he had quite made up his mind to take her away in November. He said it would be simple madness to let her stay in Abbotsby after the damp and east wind set in. He was a wise man then. But we shall see.

# CHAPTER XLI.

HE important visit is over. Captain Asperton left this afternoon, and I must say I am somewhat glad of the quiet, both of mind and body, which returns with his departure.

Keren, in her new muslin cap and the print she wore at Annette's wedding, did wonders. She really seemed to have renewed her youth for the occasion, and Stump was profoundly impressed with the honour put upon her, in being permitted to minister to the necessities of one of "them there fighting gentlemen."

But the poor girl was sorely disappointed when the "fighting gentleman" made his appearance in the pepper-and-salt of an ordinary civilian, with a wide-awake hat, and travelling-rug, and little black bag, like any other man. I believe she fully expected he would swoop down upon us in all the glories of scarlet and gold, with a cocked hat on his head, a sword by his side, spurs on his heels, and a row of medals on the left breast of his coat, like Keren's picture of the Duke of Wellington which hangs over the kitchen mantelshelf. And that he would bring a band of music with him, too, or at any rate be announced by flourish of trumpets.

I saw her round face beaming with the most intense excitement behind the banisters, as the cab drove up.

Then there was a sudden dive into the kitchen, followed
by mysterious whispers, and Keren's appearance on the
scene of action ; and an hour later, when the hero of
the afternoon had driven to see Mrs. Justin, Stump
unbosomed herself to me in the parlour.

"Law ! ma'am, he don't look a bit different to the
ruck of the quality.   Keren and me was floundered ever
so.  We didn't know they went about like that, not but
what it stands to reason as it must be a deal con-
venienter than having their swords and all the rest, as
I'm sure I was fair beat to think how he would frame at
dinner-time, with such a lot of things dangling round
about him, and me handing him the plates, as I should
be sure to get caught in 'em."

And Stump disappeared to assist in the preparation
of the little supper I had ordered for ten o'clock.

It was a very quiet little supper, Captain Asperton
not seeming inclined to talk, and I knowing too well the
delight of being left to one's own thought to attempt to
infringe upon that privilege in his case.   What little
he did say was chiefly about Annette's feeble health,
which is now so patent, even to her husband, that the
best consulting physician in Abbotsby has been sent for.

Next morning we breakfasted with the Justins.
Gregory was in one of his brightest, most genial moods.
He showed Captain Asperton all the interesting old bits
of carving in the house, and told him the histories
connected with them ; brought out his store of line
engravings and copies of etchings by Albert Dürer, the
curiosities collected in India, old Mr. Justin's coins and
medals, took him into the library to see a fine old set of

plates of the Abbey, and really did everything he could
to make the visit a pleasant one.

After breakfast he ordered the carriage, and proposed
that whilst he went to the Club to meet one or two public
men with whom he had an engagement on town business,
we should drive to the library and Abbey and Guild
courts, and see whatever was worth seeing in the place.

How pleasant it was, and how easy and courteous we
were with each other, none of us bringing up the past by
a single word, though I dare say it was in all of our
thoughts! Annette, muffled in furs and sealskin, looked
better than I have seen her for many a day. I suppose
it was a little bit rash for her to go driving out in an
open carriage, but when she laughed at my suggesting
such a thing, how could I press it, especially as her
husband, who of course ought to know better than
myself, said it would do her a world of good?

So much she enjoyed it that, when we had seen the
beauties of the little town, nothing would satisfy her but
a drive into the country, to Headingby Moor, a bit of
wild uncultivated land about three miles out, with a patch
of wood on some high ground in the middle of it, from an
opening in which there was a fine view north over the
valley, with Abbotsby Abbey towers in the foreground.

So we started in the little pony-carriage, Captain
Asperton driving, Annette in front, whilst I sat behind,
a position which suited me best, because I could be
quiet, and think my own thoughts.

For just seven-and-twenty years ago, on such a
sunny February day as this, whilst the snowdrops were
peeping up above the last year's leaves, and little purple-

black buds were beginning to show upon the elm-trees
that fringe the common, Gilbert Ross and I had gone
along that same road, and climbed that bit of steep, and
sitting on the mossy trunk of the tree whose fall had
opened out the view into the valley beneath, had talked
over life as we fondly hoped to make it for ourselves.
That was our first walk after we were regularly engaged
to each other. We could talk of our love then, and how
it had grown, and how we had little by little become all
in all to each other, until nothing could ever part us
any more.

And nothing *can* part us. He has been mine as truly,
all these years, as though we had walked side by side
through the duties which have come to me in them. It is
not death which parts those who truly love each other.

Annette would climb the little hill, too, though we
both of us tried hard to keep her from doing it—she
said it was so long since she had had a great wide outlook over anything, and she felt that for once in her
life she had strength enough to do whatever she wished.
I suppose it was the excitement which kept her up.
Certainly there was a wonderful spring and freshness
about her. She seemed to have got now just what she
had been needing for months, something which gave the
mind power to regain its mastery over the body. I
could scarcely have known her for the same Annette
whom I had found so weary and listless when I came
home from Cheltenham.

So we climbed the little winding path through the
copse, stopping now and then to rest, or pluck a snowdrop or cluster of moss, until we reached the opening

where Gilbert and I had once sat on the fallen tree. There was a bit of the root left yet, lichened and ivy-grown, and a straggling branch or two which year after year put forth its stint of leaves to show what once had been.

What strange thoughts those two must have had as they rested there, those two in whose lives the sin of another had wrought so great mischief. Robbed of their best inheritance they both were, yet they must go on to the end, hiding with due smiles and courtesy a past which was full of bitterness.

Again, as on the deck of the *Nawab* that night, I thanked God for my own loneliness, for a past so sweet that it had taught me to believe in all goodness for its sake, a past wrought for me not by man's hand, but the Divine. Yet is not every past so wrought?

I do not know. I cannot tell. One's thoughts get into such a tangle when they turn to things like these. Some people might pity me, even as I pity Annette and Captain Asperton, whose life seems so spoiled now. It may be that for them, below the bitter, there is a sweetness I know not of. It may be the tree of their hope has fallen, only to give them a fairer outlook into the things which shall be hereafter. Taking life patiently, as we may always take anything which our own guilt has not darkened for us, they may win through very pain and loss to nobleness; and some day, otherwhere if not here, be able to say that everything was well.

I think a little of this was written in Annette's face as I watched her there. Certainly it told no longer of weariness or discontent. Whatever this visit may have revealed concerning the past, I believe it is already beginning to give her the rest which comes of knowing the truth.

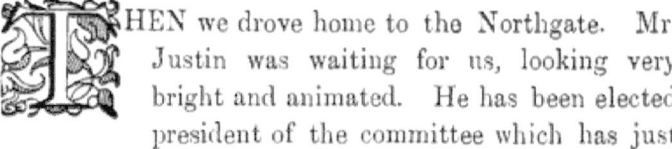

# CHAPTER XLII

HEN we drove home to the Northgate. Mr. Justin was waiting for us, looking very bright and animated. He has been elected president of the committee which has just been formed to make arrangements for the visit to Abbotsby of the British Association next autumn. This will bring him into contact with no end of great people, both literary and scientific, though I dare say it will take him more frequently to the Club, where all the preliminary meetings are to be held. This sort of thing suits Mr. Justin wonderfully. He does so delight in a definite purpose, round which he can gather all his energies ; and the more he has to do, the more bright and contented he seems. What a true development of the little Gregory of old, who was always finding out something, building, planning, contriving, laying down the law to us older but less brilliant ones, assuming so naturally and pleasantly the position of command amongst us. The popular Recorder of Abbotsby is just our versatile little playmate seen through a magnifying glass.

He lifted Annette carefully down from the carriage, and as he watched her cross the broad entrance hall with such new vigour and elasticity in her step, he said to me:

" I wish we hadn't sent for that stupid old frump of

a physician to come to-morrow. Why, the child is as strong as a little Hebe. You see all that she wanted was just something to take her out of herself. I must have some nice pleasant people to come and stay with her now and then, and you will see she will be as bright as a new sixpence."

" But, perhaps, you know, when the excitement has passed off," I suggested.

"Oh ! nonsense ; it isn't excitement. It just is that she has had something wholesome to think about. She would be like that always if only she would not shut herself up so. When I get through a little of this business, I shall take her out myself every day, and see that she gets plenty of amusement."

I told him that would be an excellent plan, but I did not tell him what I feared, that the business would never be sufficiently got through for him to put his good resolutions into practice.

We stayed for luncheon, and then Captain Asperton came home with me, to get his things together in readiness for starting by the afternoon train to Edinburgh. I told him I should be glad to see him on his way back, but he thinks of going by the through line to London, and then travelling on the Continent for a while. Perhaps that is better. His visit does not seem to have done him so much good as it has done Annette. He looks grave, dispirited, ill at ease. And yet I cannot help thinking that it must be a great relief to him to know that he has been deceived by an enemy, and not a friend. Whatever comes, he should be happier to know that the woman he loved was true.

He said nothing to me about what had passed between himself and Annette, and I did not care to begin the subject. From the added brightness of her manner, I feel sure that the meeting has been, in the truest sense of the word, successful, though it may have left on his mind a certain tinge of bitterness. Perhaps he thinks the misunderstanding has not spoiled her life as it has spoiled his. He may think that a clever, brilliant, scholarly husband, a beautiful home, and a good position, have compensated Annette for what she lost through Mrs. Flexon's deceit. And Annette, as a wife, cannot now tell him if he is mistaken in that. If he truly loved her, and thinks that she is happy now, he ought to be content. I suppose that is the essence of real love, to be able to rejoice in what appears the good of its object. But one must be so exceptionally good to realise that height of unselfishness.

I did feel that I had a right to ask him about the interview with Mrs. Flexon.

It never came to pass. First she pleaded ill-health, then press of engagements, then she found it necessary to leave Cheltenham for a few days, to complete some little business arrangements ; and when Captain Asperton left, she had not yet returned. She is a clever woman. I don't think Captain Asperton will be able to cope with her. And, of course, when she is Mrs. Byte, our pugnacious little doctor will not allow her to be annoyed by anything relating to such a remote past. He will say that ample explanations have already been given.

We parted, feeling that we had taken each other for

friends.   As he shook hands with me, he just said, very
quietly :

"Thank you, Miss Brown, for all that you have done
for me."

No more reference to the past, whatever it might
have been, than that.   But I don't care for men who
have such an unlimited power of expressing themselves.
The gratitude which lurks behind silence, is often the
most sincere of all.

"I can't say I matter him much," remarked Keren,
who generally likes to give me her opinion about any
one who comes to the house.   "He's over quiet for my
liking.   I should say, ma'am, he isn't half such good
company as Mr. Justin, and takes his vittles as if he
hadn't a bit of interest in 'em.   I never see a man as
grilled partridges was so thrown away upon, and the
bread sauce not so much as looked at, for all I'd put the
best ingredients in.   Mr. Justin isn't in that way, ma'am.
He knows as well as anybody when things is properly set
down before him, and that's the sort of gentleman I like
to do for."

Not finding me disposed for conversation, Keren
withdrew.   She has a fine perception of when to speak
and when to refrain.   But I heard her say to Stump, as
she returned to the kitchen :

"If I'd known him for one of them as has eyes for
nothing, I'd never have had my wedding print got up—
no, that I wouldn't, nor made yon muslin cap neither."

# CHAPTER XLIII.

O it is over. I find myself repeating again and again Whittier's melancholy lines :

> Of all the sad words of tongue or pen,
> The saddest are these—it might have been.
> Ah, well, for us all some bright hope lies
> Deeply buried from mortal eyes ;
> Yet from its grave, hereafter, may
> Some angel roll the stone away.

No, I think that will not be. The stone is set and sealed now, and no hand but that of death can roll it away. Annette and Captain Asperton have met, but only met as those who stand on opposite sides of a deep, swiftly running stream, across which they can never clasp hands, only look into each other's eyes, say farewell, and pass on.

It is so utterly useless, yet I cannot help picturing to myself how differently everything might have turned out, if, amongst all the steamers that were leaving Bombay during the week of our embarkation, Gregory Justin had not happened to fix upon the *Nawab* to come home in.

Other things would have fallen out just the same. Annette and I would have become friends, for he

had nothing to do with that.    Mrs. Vermont's chilling
letter received at Port Saïd would have left us entirely
to each other.    We should have come here together.
I should have gone to Cheltenham to visit Cousin
Delia, met Captain Asperton, invited him here, and
then all would have been well.    No swiftly running,
deep stream between them then ; no need only to look
into each other's faces and pass on, divided for ever.

This is how one reasons, though it is so infinitely
foolish.    I could almost be vexed with Mr. Justin
for coming by that particular ship, as though the
introduction to Annette, and all that came of it, had
been any more in his thoughts than in mine.    I feel
towards him at times as if he had deliberately cheated
Annette out of something precious and good, which,
but for his interference, might have come into her life.
And yet all the time, no doubt, he thinks he has lifted
her into happiness and position which, without him,
she could never have achieved.    Wife of the Recorder
of Abbotsby, companion to selfish, rich Mrs. Marsham
—what very opposite poles in the social scale do these
two statements represent !    Gregory knows that.    He
does not know all the rest.

And what sometimes makes me feel impatient is
that he might have been just as happy with any one
out of fifty other pretty, ladylike, intelligent girls, as he
is with Annette.    Mr. Justin is not a man who wants a
wife to do much more for him than look elegant, preside
gracefully at his table, give him a very general sort of
companionship, and look up to him as her superior
in every respect.    He has no depths in his nature

which need a woman's sympathy to fathom them, no
visitations of self-reproach and remorse, born of bygone
misdeeds and shortcomings, which the touch of a sweet,
pure soul might heal. All his life lies broadly in the
light of discretion, self-respect, useful common sense,
touched with cleverness and ambition. He has had
no terrible falls, from which, bruised, bemired, and
humbled, he arose to tread the upward path again. He
is satisfied with himself. I doubt if that is the best
sort of satisfaction.

Then the subjects in which he requires sympathy
are not those which a woman generally knows much
about. His mind turns to science, facts, experiments.
There is nothing philosophical or speculative about him.
A woman with chemistry, mechanics, sanitary knowledge, etc., at her finger ends, might supply his needs
in some respects, but the chances are that she would
signally fail in other departments more necessary to
him ; and so, what sympathy he wants in his scientific
and public life he must get from men. If Annette were
fifty times cleverer, I doubt if she would be one bit
more suited to him.

No, lacking brilliance, spirit, ambition, power to
lead in society, Annette lacks almost everything that
Gregory would like in his wife, and the finer, more
delicate touches of her character are not necessary to
him. She brings out no latent beauty in him which,
but for her influence, might have remained undis-
covered, like the pictures in those landscape pebbles,
before the hand of the lapidary is set to work upon
them. And I do not think, either, he develops the finest,

T

best traits in her nature. They have no special affinity for each other. He has given her a very pretty home, and in his own way is very fond of her, so that I suppose it is what people would call a comfortable marriage. Comfortable marriages are very excellent, but, old woman as I am, I have enough romance left in me to aspire after something more than mere bread and cheese comfort in the people I care for.

This afternoon Mr. Justin has been in to tell me the result of the physician's visit. He says she must go away at once to one of the sheltered places on the south coast, and remain for two or three months, until we are quite free from the east winds, which certainly do blow very rudely over our little town of Abbotsby.

According to Mr. Justin's account, there is no cause for alarm. System run down, constitution feeble, change from the Indian climate trying, mild but dry air necessary, plenty of nourishing food, amusement, cheerful conversation, not to be left alone too much, and so on, and so on, as one has heard it so many times. The very things that people ought to find out for themselves, and will do, too, when

> To hear with eyes is part of love's fine wit.

Then Dr. Wensley fences the case with a few general observations about everything depending upon care and attention—that if due precautions are observed, he has no doubt Mrs. Justin will soon be herself again ; but if she disregards the injunctions laid upon her as to diet, exercise, etc., there is no telling what may be the results. So that in any case he may be able to say triumphantly : " I told you so."

Mr. Justin came to ask if I would go with Annette to Hastings, and stay with her for the whole time. He will see us comfortably settled in lodgings, but he cannot be away from Abbotsby more than a fortnight just now, when so many things are needing his attention, and he has been put on the committee for this forthcoming scientific gathering. Besides, fancy Gregory Justin mooning about on the sea-shore with nothing to do, no public affairs to take an interest in, and no politicians or literary people of his own standing to talk to.

I promised to think over it, and go in to-night to tell Annette what conclusion I had come to. I have been arranging with Keren how it can be managed. Hilary must come into the house to keep her company. There is nothing worth stealing, for Gregory takes charge of my little store of plate and valuables, so they need not be afraid of thieves. Annette suggests that Stump should go with us, so that the training, whose results I am already so proud of, need not suffer. Stump will be invaluable to any one who is not very strong ; she is so patient and watchful, and has any amount of health for sitting up, running errands, and the thousand and one things which lodging-house servants are never ready to do. Besides, she will give such a domestic look to the whole arrangement, and keep us in such beautiful order, too ; for wherever Stump is, there will never be a speck of dust found. That child's abilities are not vast, but whatever she finds to do, she does it with her might. The introductory episode of pumping the cistern to overflowing was a true index to Stump's cha-racter. only that now intelligence is added to willingness.

T 2

What a sudden upsetting of all one's plans, this going to Hastings for three months! And I was going to do so much in my little garden, planting, sowing, trimming up, besides giving Stump prizes for the best mustard and cress, radishes, lettuce, and other early spring vegetables, which she could raise in her bit of ground under Hilary's window. But when I am once able to convince myself that a thing is necessary—and I am quite sure this visit to Hastings *is* necessary for Annette—I set to work to look at everything on the bright side of it. It is astonishing how pleasant even an upset becomes, when the disagreeable part is resolutely kept out of the field of view. This sounds very much like saying that superiority is very easy when one has no superiors; but there is truth in it. I could dwell on the miseries of leaving home until I got quite into low spirits about it; yet home would have to be left all the same, or a worse misery would come to me in the haunting sense of duty unperformed. So then the fact being accepted, why not get the sweet out of it, instead of the bitter?

I only hope, after Mr. Justin has left us, he will not get so absorbed in municipal and public interests, as to be quite independent of his little wife. This separation will make a change in one direction or the other. He will find either that he can or cannot do without her. I almost hope Phillips will not manage the housekeeping very well. Annette's ways are so dainty, and the little dinners she arranges for him are so perfect, that I fancy he will soon perceive the difference when an uneducated woman takes the establishment in hand. And though that is a low ground for a man to appraise his wife upon, still it is better than none at all. Keren was quite right when she said Mr. Justin knew as well as anybody if his meals were put before him properly. Where Annette learned it all I cannot imagine, for she has had no experience. She must have spent many and many an hour, unknown to any of us, in studying the copy of Mrs. Beeton which I gave her when she was married; and she certainly has an enviable talent of making those under her do their duty, however she may fail of exerting a sufficient influence upon Gregory, whose attainments are on a higher level than her own.

Stump will be coming in immediately for her evening lesson, and then I will go over to the Northgate house and tell Annette that I have arranged to go with her. Stump gets into simple division to-morrow, the proud result of seven months' training. If it had not been for this flight to Hastings, I should have tried to give her, in a mild sort of way, some insight into the mysteries of book-keeping; for if my plan of prizes for the early spring vegetables had proved a success, she was to have had most of the kitchen-garden under her own control, and I should have paid her for its produce, teaching her to keep a proper account of sales effected and moneys spent and received, in a regular little day-book. Stump has a good head for practical things. When she comes to woman's estate, she will be just the sort of person to have a shop like that which Hilary used to keep with her mother, and she will have this advantage, that, unlike Hilary, there is a vein of shrewdness in her composition which will, I think, prevent her from ever

falling into the clutches of a man who will only marry
her for the sake of having his idleness supplemented by
her industry.　Who knows but in twenty years' time
my little Stump may be at the head of a thriving
establishment in the tea-cake and penny-pie line, able
to minister to the gastronomic tastes of the rising race,
as Hilary once ministered to mine ; and may be saved
by her vigorous practicality from the long, long storm
and tempest out of which Bennet's death delivered his
patient old wife ?

# CHAPTER XLIV

 HAD a long talk with Annette last night about the Hastings project, and then about Captain Asperton's visit.

What a quite new cheerfulness there is in her face and manner now ! Not the mild resignation of one who accepts the inevitable, but the brightness and trust of one from whom a fretting burden has been removed. Whatever it may be for Captain Asperton, I feel certain that for Annette his visit has cleared away a cloud under which she has been wearying ever since the day that he left Moorkee without a word of farewell or explanation to her.

After Mr. Justin had left us to go to his books and papers in the study, she began to tell me about their evening together. There was the purity of a noble, honest, and stainless soul in every word that she spoke, now for the first time allowing me to see behind the veil of reserve into a life which seemed outwardly so successful, and yet had so much bitterness poured into it.

" Captain Asperton and I used to care for each other very much," she said, " though we had never said anything about it in the regular sort of way. And he meant, before he left Moorkee and went into camp for the cold weather, to have told me all about it. Only you know

Mrs. Flexon got intimate with him, as she used to try to
do with all the gentlemen in the station, and as he trusted
everybody then, it never entered his mind that she could
be wicked and double-faced, especially as she was always
speaking so patiently about her faded hopes, and how all
the light of her life had gone out with the death of her
beloved Herbert."

"And still more especially," I added, "as she had
such lovely gray-green eyes, and braids of soft brown
hair, and such an appealing way of clasping her hands.
Annette, she must be punished. I shall never rest now
until she gets exactly what she deserves."

"We shall all get that sooner or later," said Annette,
"so don't worry yourself about it. Well, it seems she
got Captain Asperton to believe that she was very much
interested in his welfare, and she could not bear to think
that he was wasting his affections upon a heartless girl
who only accepted them by way of amusement; for she
told him I was really engaged all the time to old Mr.
Moberley—that very old man, you remember, who used
to ride about in the grand carriage with a little dog
beside him, and such a large gold chain hanging over his
white waistcoat. It was easy for her to make him believe
this, because papa was very fond of having Mr. Moberley
come to our house; and besides, he says that numbers
of people at Moorkee were talking about it, though I
never knew anything at all."

"Of course you did not, poor child! Mrs. Flexon
was only putting it about for her own purposes, and the
last thing in the world she wanted was for you to hear
anything about it."

"Well, I suppose that was it. I never thought before that people could be so wicked. When she had got him to believe that it was all true, she advised him to write to me and reproach me with having deceived him so ; and then she said, if she had not been right in her information, I should reply and clear it all up. He wrote the letter at her own house, and she promised to send it to me herself when papa was away, as she said if it fell into his hands he might be angry about it, because, you know, he never cared very much about Captain Asperton. He wanted me to marry some one rich."

"And of course you never got the letter. She opened it and read it and said nothing more about it. Oh ! Annette, how *could* a man like Captain Asperton ever be blinded by her in that way ? "

"I don't know. Perhaps one can always be blinded by something one has never had experience of before. Captain Asperton had only been amongst men, and I think men never deceive one another in that mean, sneaking way, and about such things, too. They have bigger interests to fill their minds. When he had no answer from me, he supposed that what Mrs. Flexon had told him was true, and he was so vexed about it that he left the station at once. There was furlough due to him, enough for him to go home if he liked."

"Which was not at all what Mrs. Flexon intended him to do."

"No, not at all, I suppose, if what the people said about her afterwards was true. But, you know, a very little while after he went away, papa died so suddenly, and everything seemed like a miserable dream to me,

and all the time was taken up in arranging and packing
and leaving the parsonage, and I could not think about
anything that had happened until I was settled at
Bombay, with the lady who let me stay with her whilst
I was waiting for letters from Aunt Vermont. She knew
nothing about my life at Moorkee ; she was only sorry
for me about papa. People talk about trouble, was not
*that* trouble, Miss Brown ? And then for Aunt Vermont
to show so plainly that she did not want me at home,
and for me to have to be companion to Mrs. Marsham.
Sometimes now I think about it, and I wonder I did not
die. If people could die when they liked, with no dreadful thought of what was to come after, I think very few
of us would live out half our days."

That was a state of mind I could not comprehend at
all, having been blessed through life with a remarkably
cheerful disposition, by way of set off, probably, against
personal disadvantages. But I could understand now a
little of the sorrow which had eaten away the roundness
from Annette's cheeks, and brought that wistful look to
her eyes. It was as I thought. That letter *had* made a
great difference to both their lives.

" Ever since then," she continued, " until now, I have
had a bitter feeling about Captain Asperton, because I
thought he had been only amusing himself with me, whilst
I had given him a great deal more than that. How could
I tell that he had been true to me all the time, or that it
had cost him anything to go away from Moorkee ? I
think it was hearing nothing about him, and believing,
as I did, that he was so fickle, that made me accept
Gregory so soon. It was pleasant to know that he, at

any rate, was not just amusing himself with me. And there was such a rest in feeling that I belonged to some one who would always take care of me. Can't you understand that feeling?"

I could for her, though not for myself; and I told her so.

"Because, you know," she said, "I have had a sort of vague idea that you did not respect me quite so much after I became engaged to Gregory. You might almost have known something about my life, from the way you used to look at me. And yet it could not be that, for I never told any one until now. *Did* you think in that way, Miss Brown?"

"My darling, I can't exactly tell you what I thought. I might perhaps be afraid that you had not given yourself time enough to know what you really felt. But, however that may be, I honour you fifty thousand times over for the way you are behaving now. It would have made some women very bitter and spiteful to know all that you have learned in the last two or three days; but it only seems to have brought you a great content."

"Yes, indeed;" and Annette's new smile came over her face again. "Why should I not be content to know that the man I loved first of all is honourable and true? I have heard some people say that if you do not marry the man you care for, the next best thing is to find that he is not worth marrying. That does seem to me such a curious way of looking at it. As if it could ever be *better* for you to love a man who was not worth what you gave him! I shall be proud all my life now to know that Francis Asperton was what I believed him to be. And though perhaps I shall never see him again, it will still be better. Nothing can alter that. He *is* good and true. That is enough."

Had all this been lying hidden underneath Annette's reserve, or was it that she had suddenly sprung up into a new life? How far she seemed to have distanced her former self! What perfect common sense she was bringing to bear upon what I thought might only have saddened her life! Annette has the make of a noble woman in her even yet. It is she, I think, who will win to heights where her husband cannot follow her. And what she went on to say showed me that she was not just being sustained for the time by a vague, romantic idea of self-sacrifice, which would by-and-by burn itself out.

"I told him, when we had had a long, long talk about it, and he had got over the first burst of his indignation against Mrs. Flexon, that he must not think either of himself or me, as having to live entirely spoilt lives. I suppose we can never be just as happy as we might have been if she had not deceived us; but we may be a great deal better for the discipline it has put into our lives. One has to learn that being happy is not everything. It is only the sin we have done ourselves, or that some one we love as ourselves has done, that can really crush our lives. I cannot tell you the great peace which has come to me since I know that Captain Asperton is not what I have been picturing him to myself all this time. I almost think it is worth the pain and separation to have found that out."

"You little philosopher," I said, folding her in my arms, "who taught you all this wisdom?"

"I don't know, I'm sure. It has come to me since I gave over being bitter and discontented. I am not the same Annette any more. Something better is waiting for me. I know it is. I only feel vexed now to think how often I must have spoiled Gregory's life by wanting him to spend all his time and thought over me, instead of doing the work which he ought to do in the world."

"My dear," I replied, sententiously, for I was not going to let Annette take quite all that blame to herself, "it is not Mr. Justin's business to give himself entirely to the world's work. A very old-fashioned book that we are accustomed to take as the rule and guide of our lives, says that when a man married a wife he was to stay by her side for a whole year, and even if war came in the land he was not to be expected to fight, but just stop at home and comfort the girl he had taken to himself away from her own friends and people. And if that does not imply that a man's home duties are more important than those he owes to anything outside, I don't know what words imply at all. No, my dear, I hope your husband's literary and municipal reputation will never be built up at the expense of the home virtues."

Annette only laughed.

"I don't think it will now, for I feel as if I had such a lot of cheerfulness in me that I can make things ever so much happier for him. I don't wonder he went off to his study when I was always moping and looking like a martyr. He has been very patient."

I uttered an inward protest. Annette must not become too unselfish. Unselfishness is a splendid virtue, almost as splendid as the humility which enables you to

sit contentedly at the bottom of a ship's table, but it
often fosters a contrary spirit in those who are too much
warmed and comforted by it. One gets to look at the
givers-up as born to that sort of thing ; nay, don't we
sometimes come to consider ourselves as doing such a
good work in the world, by affording them a means for
the exercise of the noble virtue, that we think our occupation of being served rather a lofty one, after all ?
There ought to be a blind figure of Justice to hold the
scales in every family. And I felt still more inclined to
protest as Annette continued :

"I suppose it is rather strange, but finding out that
Captain Asperton is what I always wanted him to be, has
given me so much more trust in my own husband. You
know, I began to have a sort of idea that men only cared
for themselves, and the name they could make in the
world, and I thought Gregory was only like all the rest
of them. But now I know that we can't judge everything. Gregory is a great deal better than I gave him
credit for, just as Captain Asperton is. Why shouldn't
I trust when I can't understand ? "

I could not answer. That sort of trust is very well
when exercised from the earthly towards the heavenly.
When exercised towards those of like passions with ourselves, the results are dubious. But why disturb the
faith which was dawning in Annette's mind ?

Like a wise woman I let it alone, more especially as
Gregory himself came in just then, looking as bright and
pleasant as possible, with a bulky packet of manuscript,
folded and sealed, in his hand. Annette turned upon
him a look of wifely pride and content, which I think
must have been eminently gratifying to him.

"Well, pet," he said, as he kissed the pretty lips, "how have you been getting on without me?"

"Very well indeed," she said, mischievously. "I have had Miss Brown."

"The meeting proposes a vote of thanks to Miss Brown," he replied, making me a low bow. "Carried unanimously. And really," he continued, more seriously, "I don't know what you have been doing to my little wife, for she has been as bright as a sunbeam ever since you came home from Cheltenham. I expect, when you two get settled at Hastings, Annette will be so happy that she will never want to take up housekeeping again —eh, madame?"

"Certainly not," I replied for her, "if you are going to be always writing on sanitation and ventilation, and other things, contrary to the law of Moses, which enacted that for the first year of his married life a man should not go out to battle, or have any charges of business put upon him. When I get into Parliament, I shall propose that that statute be entered as part of the code of the realm."

"You are bringing dissension into the camp, Miss Brown. Annette would never have thought anything about it, if you had not put it into her mind. Confess, pet—would you?"

"Yes, I should," said Annette, as saucily as could be, but with a little blush, nevertheless. "I have been thinking about it a great deal. But I have given over that sort of thing now, and you shall do just as you like for the future."

"If you look as sweet as you are looking just now, I shall like to spend all my time with you then. Will

that content you ?   You see, you are not going to have
all the goodness on your side.  But I know," and Gregory
came and placed himself on the arm of her chair, and
began to play with her pretty braids of hair—"I know I
have spent a great deal of time over this stupid paper.
It cost me ever so much more trouble than I expected,
and I am beginning to wonder whether the game is worth
the candle.   Next time you see this word, ventilation, I
hope it will be on the title-page of the ——— *Review*."

"And so do I," said Annette, "for I am heartily
tired of seeing it on your study table.   You don't mean
to write at Hastings, do you ? "

"No, my pet, only take care of you.   And I hope
you will reward my care by growing as plump and rosy
as Captain Asperton said you used to be at Moorkee."

Phillips came in then to say that Keren was waiting
to go home with me.  I cannot say I was sorry for something to change the conversation.   Though the time will
come, I know now full well, when Annette, in the
strength and goodness of her life, will be able to tell her
husband everything.

So I came away.   Annette's glance followed me for
awhile, but not with the wistful, longing look of the old
days, which seemed half to reproach me for leaving her
to her loneliness.  Before I was out of the room, she had
turned it back upon her husband, full of peace and
content.

Surely there are good years in store for them, and I
will not complain if, in the joy which these bring, they
learn to do very well without dear old Miss Brown.

# CHAPTER XLV.

ORE than a year ago.

When I was a child, I had a habit which I have not quite lost yet. I learned it, probably, from some story which took a strong hold upon my imagination. When the mood came over me, I used to take a little blank book, write in it as vivid a picture as I could of my thoughts, feelings, and fancies just then. Also of my troubles or fears, if I had any, and of the exact state of things as they existed in our home at the time. Then I wrapped the book up, sealed it, and made a faithful promise to myself that I would not open it again until the lapse of twelve months.

By-and-by what a vague, indefinite sense of awe I had when I looked upon that little sealed packet, tucked away under books, dolls' clothes, and keepsakes in the drawer, which during those childish years was all that I had for my very own. How sometimes, for weeks and even months, press of all-absorbing pleasures and occupations would drive the book quite out of my thoughts, until one of those periodic diets of setting to rights, which used to be so delightful to us, occurred, and revealed the forgotten treasure, bringing with it

U

such fruitless speculations as to what had been written therein. For, to the transient memory of childhood, four or six months seem such a long way off, quite far enough for a flowery screen of new hopes and interests to grow up and hide the past; yet not far enough for the solemn awe to be forgotten which attended the folding up of the record, and the making of the vow not to open it until the appointed time.

As the day approached, generally a birthday, for at such times I was more prone to these circumspective vagaries, what a curious excitement came over me, growing in intensity until the very morning of the day when with trembling hands I might break the seal and let the little prisoned memory flutter forth. Ah! how infinitely far back it seemed, with the lights and shadows of a child's year gathering round it! So far back that sometimes I could by no effort recall it to life. It was to me a hieroglyph, of which I had lost the key.

Many a time since then I have done the same thing, partly because it brought my childhood back to me, partly because that one link, kept bright and fresh, drew along with it others, until the past grew clear again and I saw as in a mirror things which had long passed from me.

But I had no such purpose when, just thirteen months ago, I locked up this little book, its last page telling of Annette's fresh dawning content. I had written that page in the quiet evening time, after Stump had finished her Bible chapter, and whilst she and Keren were having a diet of conversation in the kitchen. At such times it is an amusement to me to fall back upon my diary. When I begin, I go on and on, the life of the present crowding upon me, or sweet thoughts of the past, days of my childhood here in this old home, days when the faces of my father and mother were not a memory, and when I have sat by this fireside, speaking to Gilbert Ross as now I can only remember him.

Then Stump comes in, her heavy step resounding along the passage, and she brings the covers for the things, thus reminding me that it is time to go to bed; and when the "things" have been duly pinafored, Keren in her turn comes to rake out the cinders in the grate. Keren will never let a live coal remain below when the household is wrapped in slumber above. She knows her place better than that, she says, "and the papers as full as they are of them nasty fires, as Christian people may be burned alive in their beds, if somebody doesn't have a care."

And the old woman looks at me with such an air of superiority as she says that word "somebody." She knows well enough who the somebody is, none other than herself, to whom the orderly course of things in this cottage is due, faithful old soul!

I suppose the day had ended thus, after I put away this little book more than a year ago. Ah, me! Through what blinding mist of tears I read the last page, which, when I wrote it, gave me only content, because I thought it told of pleasant days to come for those I loved.

And are they not pleasant, for her at least, on whom no shadow can fall any more now?

For Annette is dead.

Opening this book again, with so wide a chasm between then and now, everything comes to me very freshly. I trace my steps backward and backward along the stream of memory, until I come to that little bend which is overhung by willows and marked by a grave. In my childish days I should have buried a snowdrop for Annette Lislethorpe. Now I remember her, and am glad that she is at rest.

I recall so vividly that night when we had our last talk together—how she said she felt as if something better was waiting for her. So it was—something better indeed than we could think. And as I said good-bye to her, there was such a smile of hope and brightness on her face.

Next morning I had to go over to Pengbrook, where my solicitor lives, to see him about some business arrangements. He had been summoned suddenly away, would not return until the next day. and as I was not able to make another visit just then, in consequence of this going to Hastings, his wife very kindly asked me to stay all night and transact my business on his return. Next day a heavy snowstorm had blocked up the roads, so that I was weatherbound, and the end of it was that I did not reach home until the morning of the third day after I had started.

Keren received me with a sorrowful face. She said Mr. Justin had been many times to inquire for me. Mrs. Justin had been seized with violent inflammation of the lungs, and when the last message was sent, an hour or two before my arrival, the doctor had almost given up hope for her.

So that was the end of her drive in the frosty February air. How mad we had all been to let her go ' But she looked so bright, and had enjoyed it so thoroughly, and when one's friends are put, as the phrase goes. "under medical care," one does not feel at liberty to lay down rules for them. We might all of us have said what we liked. She would have gone just the same, she felt strong enough for anything then.

I went at once to the Northgate house. Keren's report was only too true. There was a strange hush and stillness about the place. The street in front of the house had been littered with bark, so that the carriage wheels as they passed had a muffled sound of death. Gregory, looking worn and anxious. but evidently determined not to let himself believe that his wife was in danger, came to meet me. He tried to convince himself that it was only Dr. Wensley's way of putting things.

" He is such an alarmist, you know," he said. " Did you not tell me yourself that Mr. Carbery's son said he was an alarmist ? He will frighten people out of their senses. in order that, when the patient does recover, it may seem like a more wonderful instance of his own -kill. It is impossible for Annette to be really so ill. Until yesterday she kept wanting to talk and ask me all sorts of questions, but she is quieter now. Dr. Wensley said she was not to be disturbed on any account, but I think it would do her good if you were to go in and see her. She has been asking after you many times. He said this morning he should come again about noon."

I thought I had better wait until I had his permission to go into that room from which such a strangely quiet influence seemed to have spread over all the house. At noon he came, stayed a long time, had a long interview with Mr. Justin in the study, then came to look for his hat in the drawing-room, where I was waiting. A quiet, precise, studiedly cheerful man, with an impenetrable face such as doctors generally acquire in the course of a long experience.

"Do you think I might see Mrs. Justin?" I asked.

"Yes," he said, with a keen look at me, to judge, I suppose, whether I was a near relative, and could bear the news breaking suddenly. "Yes. It will make no difference now."

And with that he went quietly away.

I suppose Gregory knew too, for there was a strange, cramped, self-possession in his face as he came to take me into his wife's room.

How very quietly she lay there, so weak, I think, that there was no room for suffering, either of body or mind. Poor child! As I looked at her and thought of the doctor's so lately removed injunction of perfect silence, it seemed to me that quite other than silence had been needed by her for many a month past. Her life had depended upon the love and companionship which had been thoughtlessly withheld. Annette was dying of overmuch silence.

Yet she seemed entirely content. When, from time to time, as with an effort, she opened her eyes, there was neither hunger, unrest, nor fear in their expression, only peace. I wonder if she knew that she was dying. It might be, perhaps, that weakness of body prevented her from realising anything, even her nearness

to that dim otherwhere from which most of us shrink
with infinite distrust. I think, too, she did not need
our whispered words of comfort, when, as that fateful
day drew to its close, we felt that her short little space of
life was closing too. A love more tender than ours was
caring for her. At nightfall she died, leaving us full of
wonder and questioning.

I hope I shall never again see such agony of self-reproach on any human face as I saw on Gregory Justin's
when he knew that his wife was dead. Why must repentance ever come to us when it is too late ?

And yet he had been, as the world would say, very
kind to her. He had given her all that could make life
pleasant, a beautiful home, dress, furniture, the best of
food and drink, a certain amount of affection, for he was
really very fond of her, especially when she was prettily
dressed ; and in all their short married life he had probably never said an unkind word to her. Nay, until he
stood by her death-bed, the chances are that he had
thought of himself as rather a model husband, especially
to a wife who had brought him nothing.

But now ; but now ; how vain seemed everything
else, set against the one thing withheld ! Into what
terrible reproof had those patient, wistful looks turned,
which many a time she had bent upon him when he was
going away from her to his own, as it seemed, perfectly
legitimate and even praiseworthy pursuits. How little
was everything he had done for her, compared with the
enforced loneliness which had eaten out her life ! And
she had borne it so quietly. And she was bearing it so
quietly now, lying there in her white grave-clothes ; poor

Annette ! the last in the world to give any one a
moment's pain, still less to pierce her husband's heart
with poisoned arrows of remorse.

I suppose that was the very sting of it. *So* quiet.
*So* unconscious. Not a word of reproach from the lips
he would have kissed oftener had he known the time was
so short. If she could but have put out that stiff little
hand and choked him ; could but have poured into his
ear a woman's bitter reproaches for the hours she had
spent so utterly alone in the beautiful home he had
made for himself and her. But to be so quiet, that was
the cruellest thing of all. Oh ! if the dead could only
have arisen and reproached, even though no defence
could have been given or pardon uttered, how Gregory
Justin would have blessed the bitterest words from those
peaceful and for ever folded lips. But it was too late.

# CHAPTER XLVI

ANNETTE was buried in the churchyard of St. Maurice at Headingly, not far from the foot of the little knoll where we sat that February morning. Headingly is the mother parish to which the upper part of the Northgate and outlying district originally belonged, and Mr. Justin's people for generations back are buried there. So are mine.

People soon forget—at least, the bitterness of death passes. Gregory is himself again, with a man's will for the world's work. After the funeral he sent his plate to the Bank, warehoused all his beautiful furniture, and went to travel on the Continent for three months. When he came back, one could not see, except by the deepening of those two lines between his eyebrows, that a great grief had visited him.

Since then he has been more of a public man than ever. His house, with all its costly belongings put back again, only Annette excepted, is a gathering place for the cultured society of Abbotsby and the neighbourhood. The most elegant dinners, when he requires them, are sent across from the "Star and Garter." What a pity that solution of the difficulty did not suggest itself to poor Annette! Her husband soon found it out when the ordering of the establishment devolved upon himself; but men are naturally more self-helpful than women.

His papers now form a prominent feature in the contents of the ——*Review*. He deals very forcibly with most subjects of general social interest. At the Scientific Association meeting last year, the preparation for which cost Annette so many solitary evenings, he won much honour. Indeed, his contribution to the Public Health department, a description of a new method of ventilating public buildings, was considered one of the best papers of the whole session, and was reported at length in the leading London journals.

For my part, I think the best method of ventilating public buildings is for people to keep away from them. They would then be supplied with air enough and to spare, and possibly the people would be no worse. But this is only private theory, and it does not apply to churches, which being, by the advanced thinkers of the present day, so little needed, can scarcely any longer be denominated public buildings.

Mr. Justin entertained the more prominent members of the Association at a most perfect little dinner, quite private, of course, in consequence of his recent bereavement, but still everything that could be desired under the circumstances. As several lady members were present, I acted as hostess for him, being arrayed in that low black body, well smothered in plenty of net, of whose too stylish appearance I was uncomfortably conscious when Mrs. Vermont came to introduce Captain Asperton to me at the Cheltenham party. I had my thoughts connected with that now so far-off evening, but, like a wise woman, I kept them to myself.

Since then Gregory's career has been one of marked success. Every one says he will be member for us before long. If so, I am quite sure of this, that Abbotsby will never have need to be ashamed of her representative.

Things go on quietly, as usual, in my old-fashioned little household. Neither Stump nor myself have ever had cause to regret the day when she was "took in here." She is now beginning to develop in an upward direction, as regards her person, so that some of these days we may hope to see her a fairly grown woman, instead of the comical little figure, something between a roly-poly pudding and a quartern loaf, which she now presents. Intellectually, too, she is taking root downward and casting forth branches upward; and though she masters ideas slowly, she makes them blossom out into a useful life when once she has got hold of them. And at the foundation of her character there is an unspoilable simplicity which is fifty times better than intellect—at least, for Stump's purposes.

Hilary is blossoming in her old age. The dear old woman apologised to me the other day for living so long.

"I reckon, ma'am, if you'd ha' known how I should ha' perked up, you wouldn't maybe ha' tooken me on so kindly; but for as sure as I'm a living woman this instant, ma'am, I was that wore out and worretted, what with the scraping up the rent, and them stairs every time I went to the Board, and scarce ever a bit of butcher's meat, while I didn't think I'd a twelvemonth before me—no, that I didn't. But, ma'am, I'm not the woman to wear out a welcome, not me, and I know there's a many as has a better right to the favour."

I told poor Hilary she might make herself quite comfortable on that matter. The little lean-to room was to be hers so long as she wanted a roof over her head, and when she wanted it no longer, Keren should have it, still keeping a sort of supervision over Stump, who by that time, I hoped, would be able to take a senior place in the house. When I have to choose Stump's successor, I shall look out for a maiden of different build, both physical and intellectual, one that will take more kindly to the external proprieties of life, and develop something different from what may be called exclusively kitchen-garden produce. Not that I undervalue my worthy little Stump, but there are diversities of gifts.

Cousin Delia has been to stay with me. It was in the summer-time, when my garden was looking its brightest, the borders under the trees which my father planted just one sweet smile of roses, lavender, and clove pink. And then Hilary, in white apron and whiter cap, sitting at the door of her little room, backed up with ivy and woodbine, made, as my cousin remarked, quite a picturesque addition. Indeed, I think Delia looked upon the dear old woman more as a " picturesque addition " than anything else.

She was so amused with Stump and Keren, and sorrowed with me on the impossibility of anything like " entertaining " with two such helps. And when I told her that I did not conjugate the social verb, to enter-

tain, in either its active or passive mood, she sorrowed
with me more than ever. But I didn't mind it, neither
was I much distressed by her evident pity for my primitive ways, which interpose such a barrier between me
and all that my cousin thinks worth living for. When I
told her that I was very happy with the past for my
companion, and the quiet little duties of the present for
my daily food, she "spake no word, only sighed," and
said, after a pause, that she supposed there was no
curing me.

No, Cousin Delia, I hope not. I trust that my
malady, such as it is, will stay with me, even unto death.

She told me that Mrs. Flexon was married to Dr.
Byte about a couple of months after I visited Cheltenham, and lives now in St. John's Wood, where he has a
very good practice.

"Brougham, and all that sort of thing, you know,
my dear, and quite a stylish little circle of society, they
say. She was a woman who would always come to the
top somehow, and I hear that her husband dotes upon
her. Mrs. Spring, that pleasant little old lady with the
gray curls, you remember, says they are very happy,
though India has certainly made a great difference in
her complexion—at least, I suppose it is the coming
back to the pinching air of England that has done it,
after the damp heat, you know. But still she has a pretty
fascinating sort of way that will always make a man fond
of her."

"Until he finds out that she intercepts his letters,"
I suggested.

"Oh, and even that does not go so far as the pretty

ways. But, my dear Hester, don't bear malice. Let
bygones be bygones. You know one day we shall all be
judged at a higher tribunal."

With which excellent moral reflection my cousin
Delia changed the subject.

Captain Asperton, too, has been to see me since
Annette's death. We went together to her grave in
Headingly Churchyard. Gregory has erected a beautiful
monument over it, from a design of his own : a slender
column, broken midway, the capital and broken part of
the shaft lying at its base, with a chaplet of lilies upon
it. Sweetly pretty, say most people, especially the
younger ones ; almost worth dying for, to lie under
marble like that.

I suppose none now but Captain Asperton and myself
know why the fair column of Annette's life was broken,
nor who laid the hand of the spoiler upon it.

Leaving him to think his own thoughts there, I went
to the simpler grave of my father and mother, and Aunt
Miriam, and Gilbert Ross, who, having neither kith nor
kin of his own to claim him, lies buried with them. It
looks so very plain by Annette's—just a headstone,
with the birth and death dates of those who lie beneath,
and of Mark in India, and this legend graven round the
names :

They are all gone into a world of light.

No need for any tears over that grave. How kind
and restful is death, compared with some other evils
which visit us in this world ! I read the names of those
who are dear to me, and I thank God that their lives,
though blessed with very little of what people generally

call success, were free from the bitter pains of human
deceit.   And if, when I am dead, others can say of me,
as I have said of my own departed :

Gone into a world of light,

it will all be well.

Captain Asperton made another attempt to see Mrs.
Flexon after her marriage, and was successful.   She
made an elegant apology to him for any unpleasant
consequences which had resulted from the detention of
his letter.   She explained so prettily that after having
advised him to write it, and taken charge of it herself to
give to Annette, she had seen reason to change her mind
as to the prudence of the course, and had decided at last
that her best plan would be to destroy the letter and let
the whole affair drop.   She was exceedingly sorry.   She
would not for the world have injured either of them,
and he must accept her assurance that, if pain had been
caused, it was the farthest possible thing from her intention.   In fact, she should have told him herself that
the letter had not been sent, but he left the station so
unexpectedly, and she had so many things upon her
hands just then that really——

I suppose her round, white eyelids and clasped hands
did the rest, for that was the end of it.

So Annette lies under her broken marble column,
and Francis Asperton goes his way, a solitary man, with
not much faith in this world or the next ; whilst the
charmer who spoiled the story of life for both of them,
takes her fill of prosperity in St. John's Wood, with a
"brougham and all that sort of thing, you know."

But as Stump said the other Sunday night, when confiding to me her own private opinions about the fate which overtook the "little ones" in that matter of Korah, Dathan, and Abiram :

"Law ! ma'am, but there's a vast o' things in this here world as us unedicaten folk can't square up, nohow."

Even so, Stump.

THE END.

LONDON : SPENCER BLACKETT, ST. BRIDE STREET, E.C.